"I recommend it to readers who like their good and evil well defined but human enough to entertain, and all who have longed to cheer for nature and the bonds of community in the struggle against an alienating and avaricious lust for progress that is really all about amassing power. The sensory stalks of the 3-gendered Kyn, interspersed histories of the gods, many races of unhumans, charming illustrations of the characters throughout the book, unexpected connections between characters, handy glossary and many other details and touches contribute to the story's richness and originality."

Lynda Williams, SF Author of *"The Courtesan Prince"*

"There is action and adventure aplenty in this epic tale of conflict between Humans and other-worldly Kyn, but there is something deeper as well. Like the magic that imbues his imagined world of spirit-trees and talking beasts, a true sense of wonder and enchantment wells up through Daniel Heath Justice's words. This is a realm that fantasy fans can immerse themselves in, and return to again and again: a realm that feels at once fresh and new, yet old as the oldest myth."

Alison Baird, Author of *"The Hidden World"*

The Lawless
A DANGEROUS AND FIERCE DOMAIN OF MEN AND MONSTERS
THE VARSENAITH WILDS
To THE AXIAL POLE
Sarvannadad
BOUNTIFUL LANDS BEYOND THE REACHWARDEN'S AUTHORITY
RAMAVAR
The Ever-Land of the Un-Human Tribes
SAVAGE TERRITORIES
THE FENBREAK
THE ORM RIVER
THE REAVING COAST CLIFFS
The Riven Sea
EROMAR CITY
Eroman
THE GREAT DREYD-LAW PROVINCE
THE SERPENTINE COAST
Green Karathia
THE EASTERN STORM-WATERS
THE BEAR'S CLAWS
CHIMIAK
THE OLD WINDLE ROAD
WIDLEY'S PIKE
THE GOLDEN FIELDS
To CHALIMOR, THE JEWEL OF THE REACH
SHARD FORD
KATELINE CROSSING
THE HALF-MOON HILLS
Dûrûk
A BLASTED, UNINHABITED LAND
The Great Kultul Sea
THE GREAT GROVE
Béashaad
THE CENTRE OF CIVILISATION IN THE REACH OF MEN
BATH-IVANIDUR
THE GREAT WAY ROAD
2006

WYRWOOD

The Way of Thorn & Thunder

Book Two

Daniel Heath Justice

Kegedonce Press
Cape Croker Reserve
R.R. 5 Wiarton, Ontario
Canada N0H 2T0

Wyrwood

First edition

Book design: Rhonda Iadinardi

Cover & inside images: Steve Sanderson

Published by Kegedonce Press
Cape Croker Reserve, R. R. 5 Wiarton, ON Canada N0H 2T0
www.kegedonce.com

Editor: Kateri Akiwenzie-Damm

Library and Archives Canada Cataloguing in Publication

Justice, Daniel Heath, 1975-
Wyrwood / Daniel Heath Justice.

Contents: v. 1. The way of thorn and thunder.

ISBN 0-9731396-7-6

I. Akiwenzie-Damm, Kateri, 1965- II. Title.

III. Series: Way of thorn and thunder; bk. 2

PS8619.U84W95 2006 C813'.6 C2006-905539-4

Kegedonce Press gratefully acknowledges the support of the Canada Council for the Arts and the Ontario Arts Council

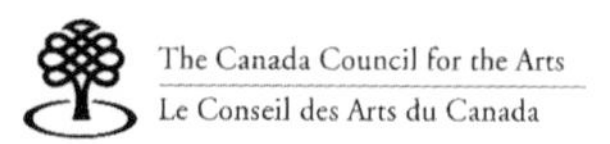

Distributed by Lit-Distco
100 Armstrong Avenue
Georgetown, Ontario Canada L7G 5S4
Tel: 1.800.591.6250 Fax: 1.800.591.6251
Email: orders@litdistco.ca

Member of Cancopy

Printed in Canada

Acknowledgements

There are so many people to thank for all the support, loving kindness, and enthusiasm they've shown me over the past few years as these books have come together; please forgive any oversights or omissions. A few folks in particular deserve special note.

The incredible and incomparable Kateri Akiwenzie-Damm and Renee Abram at Kegedonce Press have helped make my dream a reality—words can't express my gratitude to them for believing in me and my vision. Steve Sanderson's great illustrations have given dynamic life to the characters. Michelle St. John and Richard Van Camp have been amazing advocates, and I'm so honoured to have gotten to know them better over the last couple of years. My book launch for *Kynship* was an incredible event, thanks in large part to Jonathan Hamilton-Diabo, Jennifer Wesley, Jackie Esquimaux-Hamlin, Shannon Simpson, and Sally Macchiusi of First Nations House, and Janet Romero, Ruthann Lee, and Anjula Gogia at the Toronto Women's Bookstore. Photographers Keesic and Michael D. White did a great job with their respective author photos. The Ontario Arts Council provided a Writer's Reserve Grant that proved essential in giving me the time and resources to develop this book.

Special thanks also to Jeremy Patrick, Sophie Mayer, Sara Salih, Bob McGill, S. F. Said, Qwo-Li Driskill, Lydia Allain, Jill Carter, Kelly McFadden, Jorge Vallejos, and Mariko Tamaki for their friendship and encouragement. To Mom and Dad go my deepest love and gratitude.

And a particular note of appreciation goes to Kent Dunn, who reminded me that a heart heals best when it's loved. Thanks, sweet man.

DEDICATION

This book is gratefully dedicated to Sky Youngblood, Stephen Radney-MacFarland, and Jeff Simpson, who've travelled with Denarra the longest.

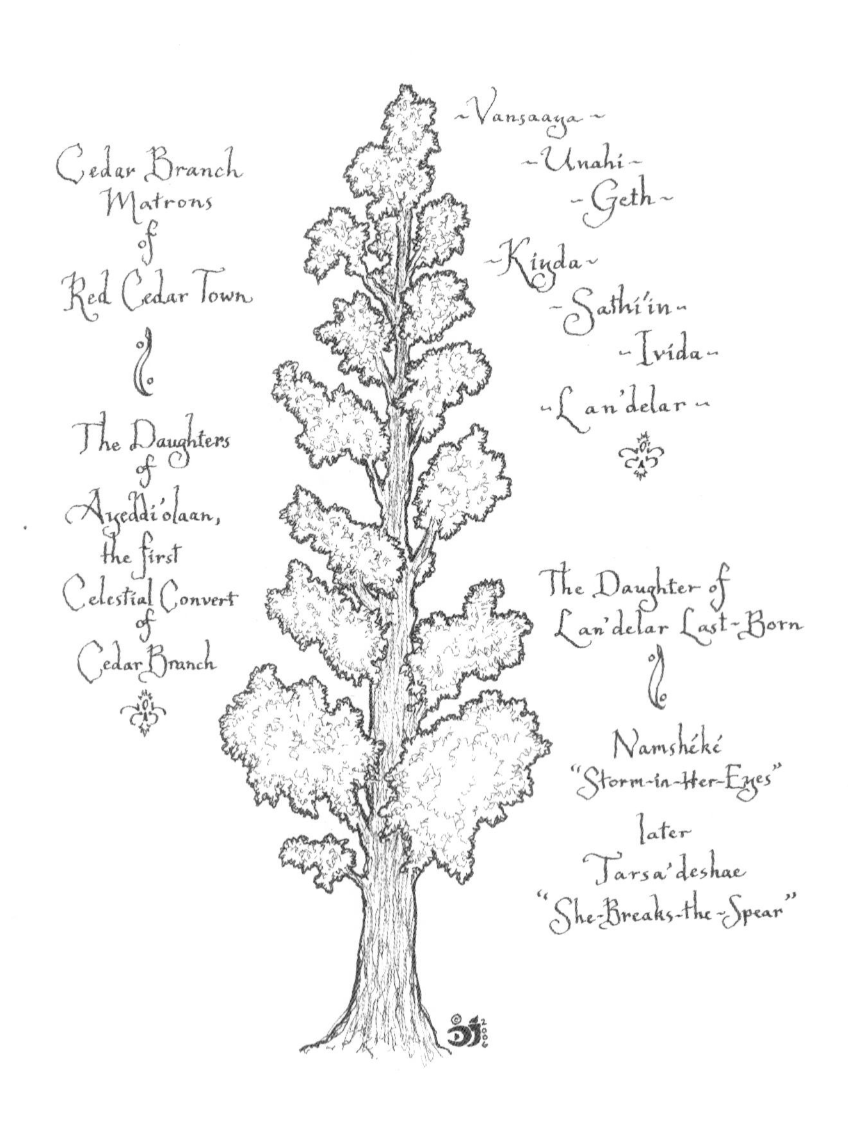
Cedar Branch
Matrons
of
Red Cedar Town
The Daughters
of
Ayeddi'olaan,
the first
Celestial Convert
of
Cedar Branch
~Vansaaya~
~Unahi~
~Geth~
~Kinda~
~Sathi'in~
~Ivida~
~Lan'delar~
The Daughter of
Lan'delar Last-Born
Namshéké
"Storm-in-Her-Eyes"
later
Tarsa'deshae
"She-Breaks-the-Spear"

CYCLE THREE
IN REMEMBRANCE OF TREES

This is a story of the Eld Days, long before the Melding, long before these troubled times.

It is a teaching.

The Wielders were not the first among the Kyn to comprehend the voices of the Wyr. If not for the Makers, those voices would have remained unintelligible, for it was the Makers who first revealed the spirit-ways of the Wyr, and who first harnessed its transformative powers for the benefit of the Folk. The Makers stood tall and proud among the Kyn, and they were honoured above all others, save for Zhaia, the True Tree and mother of the Kyn, and her mossy-haired husband, Drohodu. The seven nations of the Folk knew and gave respect to other powerful spirit-beings-Avialle, the gentle river mother; Shobbok, the ice-hearted Winter Witch; Jenna, Granny Turtle of the Tetawi, and her adopted nephew, the mischievous squirrel-spirit, Kitichi; Sky-fire and Thunder, the powerful Storm-Born Twins; among others-but for many of the Kyn, it was the Makers who were first in mind when needs arose, when danger threatened, when desire crested.

The Makers were powerful medicine-people and spirit-workers, at once beautiful and terrifying to behold. Flesh and fear held no mysteries to the Makers, for they were the greatest of their kind. They could change their form at will and whim, and none knew if they had a true shape or were simply meant to be ever-changing, untouched by the ravages of the elements, unburdened by fragile flesh. When they did take embodied form, they were the fairest of the Kyn, with dozens of tendril-like braids that fell to their knees, with feathers, stones, bird bones, twigs, and other detritus woven into their the thick hair. Their multicoloured skin was covered with bright sigils and signs of unknown origin, as though the very words of Creation were etched onto their bodies for the wonderment of the world. They were armed with Wyr-shaped staves and cudgels, and wore tunics of crafted tree-bark, leaves, grasses, and flowers as armour. None could best the Makers in combat, nor endurance, nor passion. Never many, the Makers would sometimes gather in remote places to share their knowledge with one another, then bring those understandings to the towns of People, their generosity untouched by pride or avarice.

It was they who learned the healing powers of the wyrwood trees, who rode the winds and waters, who first comprehended the nature of stone, flame, and whirlwind. They gave living voice to the Wyr, and showed their kith how to open their spirits to the hidden depths of the Eld Green. In so doing, the Makers unveiled the very heart of the Eld Green and its many peoples, and gave the Kyn knowledge of their primal connection to the verdant world that flourished, untamed and bountiful, around them. Born of wyrwood and sky-fire, moss and rain, the Kyn came to know themselves as true inheritors of the Eld Green's lifeblood, and this understanding made them stronger than they had ever been.

And as the Kyn grew stronger, their need of the Makers grew less, though their gratitude remained strong. Yet the Makers, once humble teachers and wisdom-bearers, came to fear the growing strength of the People, and remembered the days when they walked alone in the high places of the Eld Green. Now, after generations of sharing the Makers' powers, others came to know and wield the delights of the deeper Wyr-ways, and the greater medicine-makers grew jealous of the time when others trembled in fear, awe, and hunger in their presence. They saw only through the veil of memory, seeing loss for themselves instead of gain for their people, unwilling or, perhaps, unable to see what wonders had been achieved through the wise use of their once-unselfish gifts. That other Kyn might aspire to speak in the language of Creation was unimaginable to the Makers, and they began to hoard their knowledge, parsing it out in small fragments, and only to those who lowered themselves before the Makers in submission and, ultimately, in debasement.

Watching in increasing despair, the ever-patient Zhaia and Drohodu warned their proud children that this path would bring nothing but pain and destruction to everyone. Once housed in the spirit, pride and resentment could never be sated; the first-born were turning against their own, and no family can flourish when its members feed upon each other. A common fire burned in the heart of all the Kyn: when one spark faltered, it diminished the strength of all. It was wisdom that the Makers themselves had taught to their kith, yet in their resentment they had forgotten this lesson, and they grew prouder, crueller, and ever more selfish.

The Makers soon called themselves masters of their younger kindred; fear and pain grew twisted where once blossomed honour and pleasure. They turned away from their own teachings and the deeper ways of the wyr. They would be the first and greatest, or nothing. They even began to quarrel and fight among themselves, for their parents' warnings had indeed come to pass: envy had burrowed into the heart of every Maker, and they all ceased to see themselves as part of the Eld Green and its elemental ways. They could no longer see the tender ties that bound them to the green, growing world and its peoples.

No one remembers how the War began; that story is lost to the ages before the Melding. All we know is that, once begun, the ravages of War consumed the great Makers, and their wisdom withered like the drought-shrunken vine. Hot blood flooded the land; the mountains and oceans writhed in pain; the People fled yet died anyway. Each Maker saw the world as enemy or possession. There was no love, no joy, no balance. The green lands turned brown; great rivers shrank to dust-choked trickles; the parched trees cried out first in thirst and then agony as hungry flames consumed them. All was desperation, terror, and pain.

Yet the teachings endured, and the teachings that the Makers had abandoned were what, in the end, saved their younger kindred. The lesser medicine-keepers of the Kyn called to Zhaia and Drohodu, and they opened their minds and hearts to the Deep Green. The wyr of the world responded. On a blistering summer night when the air sat still and heavy, the Wielders gave themselves fully to the Wyr, surrendering themselves to whatever balance was necessary. And the land rose up against the Makers. Too late the great ones realized how far from wisdom they had fallen~too late, because they had long ago forgotten the songs that had calmed the spirits of earth, sky-fire, whirlwind, and rain. The Eld Green rose against the Makers, who fell screaming into jagged, dark places of cold stone, or were tossed, torn and wailing, into the burning heart of the raging storm. They tried to remember the songs, but their voices were broken and cracked, and their once-lovely forms had become corrupted by the harvest of selfishness that they had sown so carefully, so heedlessly.

By the morning, when the amber glow of the sister suns filtered through the first soft rains of the new era, the Makers were no more. They had returned to the land that had given them birth, and only their memory remained. It was the first dawn of the days of the Wielders, who, even now, keep the teachings of their predecessors, and learn with each Awakening of the terrible lesson of the Makers' rise and fall. The memory makes them mindful of their duty to serve the People, not rule them. It was a lesson well-learned.

Yet they know too well that their people have remembered this story, too, for it was the memory of the Makers that the proud Shields used to incite the Purging, when so many of the Kyn turned against the Wielders and their Wyr-rooted ways. And thus continues the legacy of the Makers, and thus endures the threat of blind, prideful power.

This is a teaching, and a remembrance.

CHAPTER 1
FLIGHT AND FURY

Another burst of jagged white sky-fire exploded in the air, followed within the space of a breath by a blast of thunder so loud that it rocked the Stormbringer and its battered passengers. The freezing rain smashed against them with blistering force, and nothing seemed to keep its chill from clawing into their muscles and bones. The galleon twisted around in the air again as another spear of lightning flashed across the deck to fill the air with a bitter, metallic tang.

Tarsa was bent nearly double, holding her head between her knees, trying to find a *wyr*-fed place of calm from the terror and motion sickness that jumbled her thoughts. She and Tobhi were firmly tethered to a stout oaken mast; they wouldn't be lost overboard in the upheaval of the storm, but the constant spinning and slamming of the ship had bruised them badly, and the constant drenching of cold rain did nothing to help their discomfort.

She'd long since given up any attempt at maintaining her poise; she simply sat curled in a tight ball in the failing hope that this nightmare would finally come to an end. The iron-ward had kept the poisoning at bay but not the nausea, and the Wielder had retched until her stomach ached and her eyes burned from the strain. Her sensory stalks were firmly wrapped; had they not been, the sickness would have been even more incapacitating. Tarsa, Tobhi, and the other diplomats had earlier tried to enter the Stormbringer's inner hold, but the intensity of being surrounded by so much of the toxic metal was too much even for their protective talismans, so all the non-Ubbetuk aboard found makeshift seats on the upper deck, where the chill open air gave some small bit of relief.

Tarsa almost regretted that decision now. Her senses had gone wild when the galleon entered the perpetual black storm that lay on the northwestern edge of the Everland. It was past these brutal clouds, where lightning and thunder ruled supreme, that the lands of the Folk ended and the world of

Men began. This was an elemental borderland unlike any other in the Melded world, and Tarsa's growing awareness of the *wyr* seemed to make her more vulnerable than the others to the flood of sensations and atmospheric upheavals.

For his part, though drenched by icy rain, bruised by the chaotic movement of the airship, and more than a little sick himself, Tobhi found the journey fascinating. While not much of an inventor himself, Tobhi had always liked strange and unusual things—he was a lore-keeper, after all, with a particular love of weird tales and stories—and this was by far one of the most unusual experiences of his life. The rumours of Ubbetuk airships were creative, but they fell far short of the brutal, visceral reality of sky-fire, ice, and wind. He spent most of his time watching the bulging gas-sacks and whirring machinery on deck, or catching occasional glimpses through the lightning and darkness of the silver-skinned storm drakes who flashed through the clouds past the ship, their massive fanged mouths open in roars of defiance against the puny land-walkers who dared take to the skies in their iron-wrapped abomination. This ethereal world was so unlike the heavy earthiness of the great forests below, and though his heart lurched from time to time as the galleon jolted away from another arc of lightning, Tobhi felt as much exhilaration as fear.

They'd left Sheynadwiin in the early afternoon and traveled through the night before reaching the storm. Now, hours later, the wind grew louder, more intense, becoming a desperate wail of anguish and grief. Clothing was no barrier to the bruising rains that now pummelled their flesh. They couldn't breathe, could barely think, as the air itself seemed to push down against them, relentlessly forcing them against the deck, smashing their bodies into the wood, the breath from their lungs, the very heat from their flesh. Their heads bowed, they clung tightly to one another, and this connection was soon the only reality either could focus on. The wind and rain and ice and thunder and suffocating pressure grew fiercer, more brutal, and still they held on, groaning in mingled pain and defiance.

And then, without warning, it was over. As though a door slammed shut behind them, the Stormbringer slipped from the rain-choked darkness of the storm and into bright sunlight. The air at this frigid height was little warmer now than it had been before, but the thin light of a single sun and blue sky were welcome to those who had been buffeted around for hours in the stinging rain. Some of the Ubbetuk, casting suspicious glances at their passengers, whispered amongst themselves about the surprising violence of the storm on this particular journey; it was almost as if the dark clouds had been targeting the galleon for their full force of rage and anger. Yet now, as the wall of roiling gloom receded in the distance, it became a shadowed memory in the brilliant light of a new day. All on the deck lifted their squinting eyes to the sky, and more than a few shed grateful tears.

But Tarsa was not among them. Her face was hollow with something greater than pain.

"What is it?" Tobhi asked, wiping his eyes with the back of his hand, as the she-Kyn unwrapped her sensory stalks and pulled her hair away to let them move, unhindered, in the sunlight.

Her voice was ragged. "I didn't know this would happen. It's so much worse than I could have imagined."

"What are ye talkin' 'bout?" His eyes were fixed on the serpentine stalks, two on each temple. They nearly always danced and curled with a rhythm all their own, as though each had a quickening heartbeat pulsing within. But now the tendrils hung limply down the sides of Tarsa's head.

"The *wyr*, Tobhi. It's almost unreachable here...I can barely feel it. What are we going to do? I can't be a Wielder without the *wyr*."

The cloud galleon landed on the banks of Lake Ithiak and unloaded the diplomats and baggage. They joined a courteous green-capped Ubbetuk driver named Gweggi, a large, four-wheeled coach, and four strange brown ponies, each identical with a flat-trimmed mane and bobbed tail. Before they had departed the great Kyn city of Sheynadwiin, the Ubbetuk Chancellor, Blackwick, had explained that landing a ship of this size in Eromar City itself during these tense times would be a sure sign of invasion, so the wiser course was to land in a thinly-populated location and move swiftly across the ground using the carriage in the ship's hold. The Humans might still be suspicious upon their arrival, but at least this option had the trappings of diplomatic normalcy. It was small comfort.

Less than an hour after surrendering its cargo, the Dragon was airborne again, and its passengers were left to travel the rest of the journey alone.

And they were now truly alone, for here, unprotected by the *wyr*-powers of the Everland and its familiar skies, they would come face to face with the Man who threatened all they treasured: Dreydmaster Lojar Vald, the militant prefect and Authority of the state of Eromar, who lay claim to the bounty of the Everland for no other reason than his own ambition and greed. The leaders of the seven greatest nations of the Folk had gathered as the Sevenfold Council in Sheynadwiin to debate Vald's treaty terms, but this mission to Gorthac Hall, Vald's home in Eromar City, was a private plan conceived by Garyn Mendiir and Molli Rose, the respective speakers of the Kyn and Tetawi at the Council. Their purpose for Vald was two-fold: the four other Kyn merchants and minor diplomats would try to again plead the Everland's case to the Dreydmaster, while, doing the true work of the mission, Tobhi and Tarsa would search for the last survivors of the previous political contingent, in the hope that they might have some information that could prove useful in the ongoing resistance. It was a desperate and delicate plan, but these were desperate times, and the decision of the Sevenfold Council to be delivered in six days would not likely please the Dreydmaster. The sooner they could return to the Sevenfold Council with this information, the more hope they had to resist Vald's inevitable wrath.

The young warrior-Wielder had managed to connive her way into the group, following Tobhi, her friend and adopted Tetawa brother, much to the anger of her Wielder aunt, Unahi, and others, who wanted a Greenwalker traditionalist with more experience to be part of this important mission. Yet Tarsa had prevailed in the end, convincing the lovely, green-haired she-Kyn mercenary Jitani to give up her place on the airship. Even after the terrors and bruises of the sky-borne journey, Tarsa was certain that she'd made the right decision, though she wasn't prepared for the fear rising in her thoughts about the *wyr's* distance from her thoughts and feelings.

Tarsa stood apart from the others and looked out over the lake. She held Unahi's wyrwood staff firmly in her hand; it gave her some small measure of comfort. It wasn't enough that she felt so exposed and vulnerable outside of the deeper channels of the wyr that she'd so recently come to know; she was a Wielder, true, but she was also a Redthorn warrior, and she now observed the world around her with a warrior's unflinching eye. Uncertainty and fear were no enemies here, but only if she maintained control of herself and her feelings. Clear-minded response to the land and its ways, more than emotional reaction, was needed now.

Stark, rocky hills stretched out far into the distance. There were no trees, although the Wielder could see the remains of an ancient forest in the charred and jagged tree trunks scattered throughout the hills. Those fragments poked out through scrubby thorn bushes growing wild and unchecked in the shallows of the hills, which were themselves broken only by the grey expanse of Lake Ithiak. Linked to Eromar City by the river Orm, Ithiak was a lengthy stretch of silt and ash-choked water that stank of dead fish and sulphur. Orange foam clung greasily where the waters lapped sickly against the shore. Though they stood in broad daylight, the water was dark and impenetrable.

This wasn't just a dead world–it was a poisoned place, murdered and left to rot. The Wielder, though a stranger to this land, could still feel the deep, burning ache that radiated off the waves, the soil, the bloated bodies of fish so noxious that not even insects sought sustenance. And everywhere lingered the stench of iron-wrought blood and death.

As Tarsa took her first view of the Human world, she began to realize how much she would need both her warrior's wits and whatever Wielder's strength she could muster in this strange and devastated domain. And in spite of her earlier bravado, the fear returned, stronger now, weighing her down like a snow-crusted blanket. *My coming here was a mistake*, she thought to herself as she re-wrapped her sensory stalks against the pervasive corruption. *I'm a danger to Tobhi and the others. I should never have come.*

She heard Tobhi call to her. He waved from beside the coach, pointing at the ponies and slapping his floppy brown hat gleefully against his knee. "They's mechanical contraptions, too, just like the Dragon!" he yelled. "They en't real ponies at all! No wonder we didn't hear no commotion durin' the storm. I was wonderin' 'bout that." The Tetawa returned his attention to Gweggi and began plying him with questions.

She couldn't share in Tobhi's excitement. *Lifeless ponies in a dying land–what kind of nightmare have we entered?* Taking a deep breath, she held it for a few moments as her thoughts cleared, and returned with a heavy spirit to the coach. The younger two diplomats stood talking softly to one another beside the coach door but stopped when Tarsa drew near. The dark-haired he-Kyn bore an ill-disguised sneer on his face, but the listless she-Kyn beside him merely looked bored.

"There isn't any more room in the coach, so you'll have to ride in the front with the Goblin and the Brownie," the he-Kyn said blandly as Tarsa approached, ignoring the Wielder's bristling response to the slurs.

Just as the Wielder began to retort, the coach door opened and another he-Kyn diplomat waved Tarsa forward. "Nonsense, Hak'aad–there's plenty of room for all here. The Wielder is a member of our company as well. Please, forgive him. He is quite young." Hak'aad glowered at his elder's comments, but he lowered his eyes and stepped aside.

Tarsa motioned to Tobhi, who shook his head. "Thankee, but I'd rather sit up here with Gweggi and find out more 'bout them ponies." The Wielder nodded and entered the coach, followed closely by Hak'aad and the young she-Kyn. The door closed. A strange, metallic ping clicked across the length of the vehicle, and the coach slid forward with a smooth, measured movement, flowing like a flat-bottomed canoe on ice.

The interior of the coach was spare yet comfortable, with cushioned benches along each wall and curtained windows that could be opened for fresh air. It was well-lit by two green everlights on either end, but these could be veiled by hinged shutters. There was little decoration, as gaudy excess was shunned by the Ubbetuk, but such modesty was suited to the structure.

The he-Kyn who had intervened on her behalf introduced himself to Tarsa as Reiil Cethwir of Ash Branch. He was fluent in the Upper Rinj dialect of Mannish, the most common tongue of Eromar, and had frequently traveled through the lands of Men on trade runs. One other trader joined Reiil on this journey, the young she-Kyn Athweid, as well as two career diplomats: Imweshi, an unpleasant, thin-lipped she-Kyn who pointedly ignored the young Wielder, and her son Hak'aad, whose attention had again returned to the young and blushing Athweid.

The smooth rhythm of the coach lulled everyone out of conversation and into a steady, drowsy silence, their thoughts their own as they moved ever closer to Eromar City. Tarsa fell asleep for a short time, waking with a start to find everyone but Reiil leaning against the cushions, slipping in and out of sleep. In the distance she could hear Tobhi's voice in enthusiastic conversation with the Ubbetuk driver.

The old trader looked at her and smiled. "You should try to get a little more sleep, Wielder. It was a rough journey."

Tarsa wearily returned his smile. "Don't remind me~my stomach has only just started to settle. But I can't sleep right now. Everything is so strange here; I want to stay awake and get my thoughts around this place."

"I understand," Reiil nodded. "It's always difficult when you first leave the Everland. I imagine it's even worse for someone like you, who's still connected so much to the Old Ways of the land." He shrugged. "That was never much of a concern for me or my family. We turned from the Tree to the Pillar of the Stars a long, long time ago. It has never much troubled me much to leave the Everland."

"All the more reason to give it up," a hard voice responded. Old Imweshi was awake now, and her cold eyes were fixed hard on Reiil. She glanced sidelong at Tarsa before shifting to the trade tongue, unaware that Tarsa was able to understand nearly everything she said. "The only way to be a part of the world is to look to the future, not to the past. And the future belongs to Men."

Tarsa wanted to respond, but she held back as Reiil interjected, "I hope not, because Men have little use for us, Celestial or Greenwalker alike." He looked at the Wielder. "Don't you ever wonder what we might have become, Imweshi, if we'd have known the Old Ways better, certain of our place in the world rather than being tossed around on the ever-changing wind, never sure if we're worthy enough to even be an afterthought in the world of Men?"

Imweshi's lip curled scornfully. "You speak blasphemy, Reiil, and you speak foolishness. Where you see strength I see stubbornness, and a dying past that should be hastened to its grave. Look at her. Look at those witch-marks on her skin. This isn't something to praise, Reiil: she's a barbarian and a conjuror~at best misguided, at worst perverse. She clearly put some witchery on Garyn to convince him to send her on this mission. She wasn't meant to be here." She shook her head. "No, you'll not find any longing in me to be of her kind. She sickens and fails when beyond her trees; her kind could never appreciate the sky-born grandeur given to us. Ours is the way of freedom and redemption, not hers. No, never hers." Her root-brown eyes narrowed at the Wielder. "Far better to die among enlightened Men than to live among the debased and lost."

Reiil turned his face to the window and pulled the curtain aside to stare silently at the passing landscape, a lingering longing in his eyes. A thousand different arguments flew to Tarsa's lips, but she said nothing, sinking instead into her own thoughts.

After a long time in silence, she gently touched the old he-Kyn's shoulder and spoke in the trade tongue. "It's never too late to return home, Reiil. I was raised in a Celestial home, but the Eld Green endured. You don't have to be poisoned and made bruised and bitter by shame. You don't have to listen to those who hate themselves and want to become like our persecutors. You can choose despair, or you can choose an honourable life with your People." Imweshi's face went white with rage. She moved slightly toward the Wielder, but Tarsa turned calmly toward the old she-Kyn and slid her hand to Jitani's gift knife on her belt. Not a word was spoken between them, just brown eyes locked on blue. At last Imweshi slid back against the cushions, her hatred of the Wielder crackling like fire in the air. Hak'aad and Athweid remained asleep and curled against one another in the cushioned corner. Reiil nodded at Tarsa before returning his gaze to the window.

Tarsa slid to the opposite curtain and pulled it aside to see a bit of what lay beyond. They'd long since left Lake Ithiak behind, but the main road to Eromar City followed the Orm River, and its blasted banks gave mute testimony to the nation's history. The waters of the Orm, like those of the lake into which it sluggishly flowed, were choked with sediment and bright with strange liquids that drained from the jumbled grey stone and brick structures squatting at its sides. These massive buildings stretched high into the air, all harsh lines and sharp angles, with few windows but many dark chimneys that belched out clouds of dripping black smoke. Even sophisticated Ubbetuk coach-craft couldn't keep the acrid stench from creeping into the carriage and nearly choking its passengers. Hak'aad and Athweid coughed themselves awake.

A wrongness pervaded the harsh stone structures; they were festering wounds, infected to the very core with a seeping miasma that stretched into the soil and sky. Yet Tarsa's shock at seeing these caustic towers and fumes was nothing compared to the sight of the creatures who lived in and among them. This was the true horror. Worn brittle with hunger and want, poisoned for years by the massive foundries and mills, the Humans lived now as they had since the first wars of conquest that the Dreyd and their followers used to solidify their hold on the province and extend it to the lands beyond. The children were ragged and covered with open sores, their bruised and pinched features sullen, nothing like the playful Kyn younglings who ran with abandon through their mountain homes. Old before their time, Women gathered in groups of four or five, heads covered by dull brown or black caps, and crouched with long, rough skirts trailing in the frigid river waters to slap shreds of cloth against oil-slick rocks. The upper banks of the river were covered with bearded Men of various ages, but each bore the heavy weight of poverty on his wasted countenance. They sat together and stared hungrily after the carriage.

"Why do they look at us that way?" Tarsa asked, her voice tight. A knot of bile rose up in her throat.

Reiil sighed and let his curtain drop. "Why shouldn't they? This is the only life they know. They live and die by the will of their masters in the mills and the mines, discarded when they aren't of any more use. And ever in the shadows is the will of Eromar, demanding more iron, more weapons, more labour, always driving the people further and further. But they do it, always with the hope that their Dreyd-blessed next life will be better than this one."

"That is not the only reason," Imweshi growled, but her sharp features had softened to something resembling pity. "They blame us for their misery."

"Us? But we've done nothing to them?"

Imweshi stared out the window. "No? Look at them, conjuror. The masters of Eromar have told them for decades that their poverty, their suffering, their pain and degradation are all a result of those greedy, selfish, and brutish creatures lurking in the green and fertile Everland. They are told that we worship evil spirits, that we engage in debauchery and bloodshed, that we kidnap, violate, and butcher Humans of all ages, that life means nothing to us beyond the gratification of our animal pleasures. As evidence of our witchery, we have tainted their lands, sent evil winds to curse the crops, poison their cattle, kill children still in the womb, and bring down the strong. It has to be our fault–after all, hasn't all this happened since the Melding a thousand years ago? And we have used those dark arts to make our own land rich beyond measure, with gold and other precious metals deep in our mountains, just waiting to be found by those with unbending determination."

"But those are lies!"

Imweshi turned with a frigid smile. "Of course they are! But who cares? Does it matter to *them*?" She gestured toward the window. "Who are they going to believe? Us? We well-fed, clean, healthy, wealthy, coach-riding Kyn? Perhaps you with all your savage finery can convince them that the mechanical beasts that draw this carriage are something other than dark sorcery. What will you say to them, my truth-telling Wielder? Will your truth feed them, clothe them, give them warm homes? What would they rather hear: that Lojar Vald and his kind have driven them halfway into their graves out of greed and selfish ambition, that the promises of another life are mere manipulations to ensure their subservience in this one, or that a small group of backward barbarians are the only thing between them and their salvation? If you stood in their stead, whom would you believe?"

The carriage crested a hill and left the foundries and the empty-eyed Humans behind. Tarsa slid a hand to the window and let the curtain fall.

CHAPTER 2

THE HOUNDS UNLEASHED

Eromar City was built on an unlikely location: a high, wind-smoothed butte that stretched in a wide arc over a steep canyon, through which flowed the wildest stretch of the Orm River. "The City on the Water" had once been the seat of learning in the North, the northernmost outpost of the early Reach, a city of stark beauty and people who were dignified and free. Yet it changed when the old gods of Men were overthrown and the rule of the ambitious, once-Human Dreyd took their place. One massive edifice now dominated the city from the central apex of the butte. The structure--Gorthac Hall~was a mass of gables and shadowed nooks, named by Vald to honour an obscure but influential legal sage who advocated the rule of Dreyd-law over the secular philosophies popular throughout the rest of the Reach. The city itself was built between six descending stone and timber walls that led to the foot of the butte, each wall marking the social stratification within the city, with the boxy, narrow buildings becoming progressively shabbier, the streets narrower and more dangerous, as they moved closer to the city's edge. The smelting foundries and mills squatted at the lower levels of the city, as did the most impoverished of the people who found shelter anywhere they could among the ash-choked factories. Mountains of crushed tailings and burnt-out cinders stretched from the city's walls for miles in the distance, and great gushing sprays of acidic liquid bubbled from the mills through grey lead pipes into the river below.

The carriage sped along at an easy pace through the ruined structures that flanked the road toward the city. In spite of the surrounding dilapidated and crumbling buildings, old trestles, and stone columns, the road itself was remarkably smooth and clear. The mechanical ponies needed little care, as they had been ingeniously crafted to wind themselves by their forward movement. Angular and sleek, the ponies were a lesser marvel of Ubbetuk design: hundreds of individual sheets of darkened metal joined cunningly to one another so as to resemble the wrinkling of flesh; the wheels, springs, weights, and toothed gears within were fully protected from the elements by the careful Ubbetuk artistry. Gweggi's primary duty was to lead them in the right direction and to watch for any irregularities on the path ahead. The ponies took care of the rest. It was an easy task.

Tobhi had stopped talking, choosing instead to wrap himself in a blanket and settle into the steady movement of the carriage for some much-needed sleep. The driver's bench wasn't particularly comfortable, but the Tetawa had slept in much more awkward locations than this one, so it took little time for him to be snoring softly, his well-worn hat pulled down over his eyes to keep out the dimming sunshine.

Though he was much too polite to say it out loud, Gweggi was thankful that the chatty Tetawa was asleep. Ubbetuk were generally reserved among strangers, and the constant questions from the long-haired scribe had nearly driven the Ubbetuk to uncharacteristic agitation. He hadn't been pleased with this assignment–he was, after all, the private driver of Lady Shudwagga, one of the white-capped Consulting Council of the Swarm. Yet the request had been made by the Chancellor himself, so Gweggi accepted the duty without complaint. It was a short enough drive, and in a land that he was quite familiar with; he'd driven Lady Shudwagga and even the Chancellor himself down this very road not so long before on trade-related meetings, and the route was predictable enough to allow him to relax and continue work on the short booklet of philosophical poetry he'd been writing over the past few years.

So it was that Gweggi was mumbling through a complicated rhyme scheme about the moral virtues and difficult delights of faithful service when the crowd of Men stepped from behind the crumbling walls of an old smelting mill to block the road ahead. The Ubbetuk looked up and pulled steadily on a lever beside his seat. Slowly, gently, the clockwork ponies came to a halt. The fiery smokestacks of the foundries in the city beyond burned bright in the deepening gloom, casting a reddish pall across the sky.

Gweggi could make out at least twenty Men slipping out of the darkness, and the scuffling sound of boots on rocks behind the carriage made his heart beat suddenly faster. He reached over and touched Tobhi's arm. "We're not alone, friend Tetawa," the Ubbetuk whispered evenly.

Tobhi's ears twitched at the warning in Gweggi's voice. He slowly lifted his hat brim and scanned the approaching Men. His hand slipped to the thong that held the hatchet to his back, but he remained curled in the blanket like a watchful badger. "I was beginnin' to think we wasn't gonna have much excitement on this trip."

Although the golden-haired Seeker was young, he wasn't stupid; he and his hunting hounds had trapped Merrimyn in the ravine rather easily, relying on the exhausted Binder's own terror to do most of the work. Like coyotes driving a stray sheep to exhaustion, the dogs loped on each side and kept Merrimyn moving in the desired direction, forcing him down the creek bed, staying just far enough away to further undermine his already much-strained reason. Now that he saw the high cliffs of the gully above him, the Binder cursed his panic and lack of good sense, but it didn't change anything–he was still in worse danger than he'd been since fleeing Eromar City. The snaring-tome pulsed painfully in his arm, as if emphasizing his precarious situation. If he didn't think of something quickly, he'd be on his way back to Vald's prison; unless, of course, this hot-headed Seeker had orders otherwise. A fugitive could be killed with impunity here; as far as Merrimyn knew, he was still in Eromar and still under the authority of the Dreydmaster. The merchant train he'd seen earlier in the morning was too far away to help him now.

The narrow ravine opened up, and the creek emptied into a wide, cold pond that stretched across the base of the cliffs. He was trapped; the only exit stood at the other end of the pond, and he couldn't swim. He might try wading, but the pond looked deep and murky, and he didn't relish his chances in strange waters. Harsh howls from back up the creek ended all hesitation, and he plunged forward, splashing awkwardly into the pond. Whatever his chances might be here, they were better than he'd have with the Seeker's kill-trained hounds.

The escape from Eromar City had been easier than Merrimyn expected, and that, he now realized, had eased him into a dangerous overconfidence. After leaving his Unhuman rescuer at Gorthac Hall, he'd slipped through the stables and out one of the granary chutes, grabbing a saddle-blanket and a sack of biscuits and bruised apples on his way. He'd wound his way down to the gates, where he joined the late-morning rush of labourers heading to the smelting mills beyond the city walls. From there he'd simply slipped off the road and followed the foul-smelling Orm River south. Although occasionally harassed by thugs and children on the road, his timely revelation of the snaring-tome and chains invariably sent his assailants backing away, too frightened even to mutter against him.

Such moments of self-preservation were no doubt a glaring trail that took the Seeker no real effort to follow. Merrimyn didn't know he was being hunted until just a few days past, when the hounds rushed out of the darkness and woke him from a deep sleep in the small, mossy hollow he'd camped in. It was a simple strategy, but effective. The dogs kept him from sleeping or resting; each time he tried to slow down, they moved in closer with teeth bared. These Dreyd-raised creatures had no fear of the snaring-tome, so he'd stumbled ever onward, increasingly more exhausted, until at last their master was ready to move in.

And that time was now. Merrimyn gasped and coughed in the pond, the water up to his chin. His eyes were wide with fear, but he still struggled on in the brown water, unwilling to turn back.

«Enough running, you whimpering coward~it's time to go.» The Seeker knelt by the edge of the water with his sword unsheathed. He wasn't much older than the Binder, although his travel-leathers testified to a much more worldly existence. His pale hair and sparse moustache stood out starkly against sun-bronzed skin. He smiled, clearly quite pleased with himself and his successful catch.

«I…can't….» Merrimyn cried. «I can't swim back!» He struggled against the muddy water, sinking under the waves for a moment, then his head surfaced again. «Help me…please!»

The Seeker shook his head in disgust and whistled to his dogs, but they stopped at the edge of the water and whined, unwilling to move forward. He sighed. «I don't know why you're worth all this trouble, long-neck. You'd better not get my hair wet.»

He slid into the pond and recoiled slightly as the frigid water flowed over the tops of his boots. Seeing Merrimyn's terrified eyes focused firmly on him, the Seeker shrugged off the discomfort with a laugh and swaggered his way through the water. But when he reached the flailing Binder, his arrogant features clouded with confusion. The water was only up to his waist. So why was the Binder drowning?

Merrimyn exploded out of the pond with a guttural howl and threw his snaring-tome chain around the Seeker's neck. Before the stunned Man had a chance to react, Merrimyn whipped open the strange purple book and pushed the pages hard against the Seeker's face. The hunter shrieked and splashed backward as acrid smoke billowed out of the book, but the Binder pulled the chain tighter, his eyes wild, trapping the Man in the tome's deathless hunger. There was a sizzling, popping hiss. The Seeker's hands fluttered desperately against the book's binding, like the wings of a wounded bird, but the struggle was brief, and his body quickly went limp and dropped heavily into the water. Merrimyn didn't need to look to know that the Seeker's face had been eaten away by the snaring-tome.

A raw, vital rush of strength pulsed from the cursed book into the Binder's veins, and he groaned with fear-filled pleasure. He wasn't a cruel Man at heart; this life had been chosen for him by a tyrannical, Dreyd-fearing father, and his own soul recoiled every time he opened those pages to force eternal imprisonment on another living creature. This self-loathing was why he'd failed Vald, and why he now fled Eromar City. Still, he couldn't deny that there was a tantalizing ecstasy in Binding; it gave him pleasure and vigour like nothing else. Binders were forbidden from physical gratification with other bodies, as their links with the snaring-tomes required unyielding chastity to keep them from the madness that came with the excess of sensation, but he thought that these moments of light-headed delight must be something akin to the sensual joys experienced by the rest of Humanity.

The sudden cold realization of the dead Man floating in the water brought Merrimyn's thoughts back to the present. Whatever other Humans experienced, at least their pleasures didn't require the snuffing out of another living spirit. Their connective ecstasy was something he would never know; he would always be untouched, alone. He struggled out of the water and the dogs fled, whining and yelping as they ran back up the creek bed. The Binder wanted to cry, to rage against the unending horrors of this life, but he was too soul-sick and weary. It was his fate to bring death to the world around him; only in self-imposed exile could he hope to struggle against it.

He thought back to the traders' wagons on the road a few miles back from the upper end of the gully. They were heading south. Perhaps he could find a respite among strangers, at least until he was far from Eromar. Then he'd find his way in the world–alone, but a danger to none. Tears stinging his eyes, Merrimyn staggered back up the ravine and away from the faceless body that sank slowly into the cold, dark water.

"We've stopped," young Athweid said.

Reiil pulled himself up and rubbed his eyes. He smiled at Tarsa. "I didn't know if I'd be able to fall asleep. I'm glad the journey is over; it will be nice to get out and stretch for a while." He reached for the door handle.

Tarsa's sensory stalks twitched slightly in their wrappings, and she bolted upright. "I don't think we should–"

The door opened. Torchlight flashed in the darkness beyond, and Reiil jerked backward, eyes wide, his bright blood spraying like hot red rain from the iron-tipped crossbow bolt that tore through his throat.

"*Bandits!*" Tobhi's shout echoed shrilly in the twilight.

Athweid screamed out and grabbed Hak'aad, who squirmed away from Reiil's thrashing form. Tarsa pulled the gurgling trader toward her, desperately trying to stop the flow of blood, but she dove to the carriage floor herself as the roar of a musket blasted through the air and shattered the windows. Imweshi and the others dropped beside her.

"We've got to help him!" Imweshi screamed, wrapping her hands around the steaming wound. Tarsa nodded, but her mind was on what was happening outside the carriage. She'd felt Reiil's spirit escape in the brief moment she held him; there could be no help for this sad, lost elder. Now she had to make sure the rest of them stayed alive. She crouched low and tried to listen beyond the weeping cries of the three Kyn beside her. Though a Wielder, her first training was in the arts of war and defence. She was a Redthorn still.

The carriage suddenly lurched forward, throwing everyone askew. Then it was moving again, flailing wildly back and forth, plunging down the road. Stripping off her leaf and feather cloak of office, Tarsa kicked the door open. She slid to the side to see what was beyond before swinging onto the outer side of the carriage.

So much was happening that it was difficult to see what was going on. The Ubbetuk was dead or wounded; she could see his thin, green-capped shape slumped down and lodged tightly between the seat and baggage rack behind it. Tobhi was bent double and viciously fighting off two Men who were balanced precariously on the seat above him. Another Man clung to one of the mechanical ponies with one arm while readying a large crossbow with the other. She turned to see several more Men on horseback galloping toward them from behind. And in the distance ahead rose the fiery shadow of Eromar City.

"Hold on!" Tarsa shouted to the Kyn in the carriage and pulled herself up to the roof, where she saw another Man kneeling unsteadily with a long knife in his hand. He lunged toward her, but the knife slashed empty air as the Redthorn warrior ducked back to the side of the carriage, tensed, and flew upward again, her momentum carrying her fully to the roof. Her fist shot out and snapped hard into the Man's throat. He jerked backward, tumbled off the carriage, and fell screaming down into the road.

A sudden jolt shook the coach again, and Tarsa stumbled down, cracking her knee on one of the luggage chests lashed to the roof. Gritting her teeth, the Redthorn warrior pulled herself forward. One of the Men fighting Tobhi had moved to the edge of the roof. He was too busy trying to maintain his footing to notice the she-Kyn who slid behind him, or the wyrwood knife that flashed over his back for the briefest moment to slice cleanly across his throat.

Saying a silent prayer of thanks to Jitani for the blade, and ignoring the Man's death agonies that pulsed through the wrappings of her stalks, Tarsa kicked his twitching body off the coach as Tobhi smashed his head into the other attacker's chin, opening enough room between them to drive his hatchet into the Man's belly. The Man screamed, and then Tarsa's booted foot struck into his mouth, knocking him into the air. His cries were lost in the heavy crunch of his body smashing into a jagged rock wall.

The carriage rolled on.

Tobhi nodded in gratitude but had little time to relax, as a crossbow bolt splintered the wood beside his hand. The Man on one of the front gearwork ponies had secured his position and readied another bolt. Tarsa reached down, jerked the bolt out of the seat next to Tobhi, and threw it at the archer. It flashed past the Man and skittered harmlessly into the dirt. He turned his crossbow on the she-Kyn with a leer. The smile vanished, though, as Tarsa launched herself through the air with knife in hand and landed, too heavily, on the pony beside the Man's. Something snapped in her side, and a red haze of pain swept across her vision. Gasping for air through broken ribs, Tarsa pulled herself up on the unyielding pony, and jerked the knife at the Man beside her. He dodged and readied his crossbow again, but slipped a bit on the mechanical creature as Tobhi yanked on the braking lever.

Attack!

"No!" Tarsa hissed, barely able to speak. She pointed her knife behind them. Tobhi turned to see the horsemen gaining ground. He spun back, released the braking lever, and pushed hard with all his strength on the propulsion lever. The ponies shot forward again, sending the carriage snapping back and forth from the sudden shift in momentum. The Tetawa fell to the floorboard with a grunting curse.

Tarsa lost her grip and slipped between the ponies; the Man clung helplessly to his rushing mechanical mount, his crossbow now lost on the road behind them. The she-Kyn kicked her legs out and she hung there, suspended with her feet on one machine and her back tensed against the other. Sliding her knife into its scabbard, she crept upward, inching her feet and back upward at the same time, until she was free of the gap and could push herself backward toward the pony she had landed on. She nearly fainted from the searing agony in her side, but she made it to the top, where she sat breathing heavily and trying to focus her thoughts. The Man ignored her; he just clutched the pony with white knuckles and shaking hands.

Tobhi picked himself up and looked backward. The riders were lost in the thick dust; he wasn't sure if they were still following or not. He heard a metallic crack from one of the rear gear-work ponies and saw a billowing cloud of black smoke rise from its underbelly.

Tarsa could barely breathe; her broken ribs burned with every jolting movement. Looking up, she saw the log palisade of the city gate yawning open toward them. She turned back to see the Man watching her, and a cold chill crept across her skin as her gaze drifted toward his chest, where the crest of the House of Vald was emblazoned on his vest. He was waiting for the gate, too, waiting to call down the guards upon them.

Their attackers all wore these jerkins. She understood. The diplomats were never meant to reach Gorthac Hall.

Heedless of the pain in her side and stalks, Tarsa flung herself at the Man with a shrill battle trill, her unsheathed knife now slashing through the air like cougars' claws as she landed on him and clamped her legs tightly around the pony's belly to trap him, face-down, beneath her. The Man thrashed, struggling to free himself while maintaining his grip, but it was useless~he couldn't stop the ferocious storm of blade and fist. Blood sprayed into the air, and his screams rose to a thin, screeching wail that went suddenly silent as the coach bore down on the gate.

From the shadows of the gate house, guardsmen rushed out to see a handsome Ubbetuk carriage, pulled by four brown ponies shrouded in smoke, rushing toward the great wooden gates with the sound of clanging thunder. The Men barely had time to duck out of the way before the ponies and carriage smashed into the gates with a deafening roar. Springs, shards of metal, and fragments of wood rained down on the wreckage through thick black clouds.

The Men stepped from cover to examine the strange scene, stopping in fear and amazement as a small shape emerged from the smoke, followed closely by three bent, coughing figures. The strangers moved away from the debris and stood together, faces grim, staring at the smoke in expectation.

A great rolling plume billowed forward and parted to reveal another shape stumble from the wreckage, her head held proudly, honey-brown hair flowing behind her on an unseen wind. Her bright eyes burned in the torchlight, and her tattooed face was grim. She carried something under her right arm; the other curled protectively against her side.

Tarsa walked up to the wide-eyed guards and raised the head of the crossbowman in the air. Her voice icy, she growled with obvious distaste in the Mannish tongue, «Tell Dreydmaster Vald that his guests have arrived.» She tossed the brigand's head to the ground at the guardsmen's feet.

CHAPTER 3

GORTHAC HALL

Tarsa hissed as Tobhi pulled the linen strip tighter beneath her breasts to keep her broken ribs from moving. The Tetawa waited with lips pursed and brows furrowed while the Wielder took a few shallow breaths and tried to push her thoughts past the pain. At length she nodded, and Tobhi carefully continued wrapping until the bandage was secure. Tarsa sighed heavily and nodded in thanks, sliding the thick wyrweave blouse back over her chest, securing it again with her wide chanting-sash. This was followed by her leaf and feather cloak, which was singed and blackened in places from the fiery crash of the carriage. Her eyes were heavy with pain and exhaustion, but rage burned there too, and it was that fire which gave her strength now.

Their present accommodations were hardly welcoming. The militiamen at the outer walls had led the group to a squat stone building, where they would wait until summoned by the Dreydmaster. So Tobhi and Tarsa sat, together with Imweshi, Hak'aad, and Athweid and most of their recovered gear, on rough wooden benches in a smoky, low-ceilinged meeting room that stank of Man-sweat and blood. Four long tables, each pitted and gouged with the wear of time and rough use, stretched down the length of the room. The muted crackle from the fireplace at the northern end of the narrow chamber gave no comfort; if anything, its furtive light gave a decidedly ominous mood to the shifting shadows. The shrouded bodies of Gweggi and Reiil lying on a table at the other end of the room chased away the few remaining flickers of warmth.

Tobhi walked to the table nearest the fireplace, drew out his badger-etched leaf pouch, and sat down. He withdrew the lore-leaves from the pouch and unwrapped them from their protective red cloth, checking each individual leaf for signs of damage or wear. Though all eighty-six were unharmed, they felt different now, heavier and less responsive. The Tetawa focused his thoughts and lifted a couple into the air, but they dropped to the table and snapped apart.

"What does it mean?" Tarsa asked, slipping carefully onto the bench beside him.

The Leafspeaker folded the broken leaves together and sighed. "Just what yer own dampened Wieldin' means. We en't much in touch with the *wyr* no more, so we gotta be careful. We en't got these gifts to rely on now."

"Can you read them at all?"

"Sure," Tobhi nodded. "But I can't be certain what I read is truthful, 'cause my thoughts is all muddled up with all this smoke and foulness. My thoughts en't as sharp here as they was in the clear air back home. But I can still do it. Do ye want me to try?"

Tarsa considered, but finally shook her head. "No, not yet. I don't even know what I'd ask you, anyway. Let's think about this for a while. We've got enough to try and figure out right now." She looked at the three Kyn diplomats who huddled together at the far end of the room. Lowering her voice, she said, "Those Men who attacked us weren't just roving thugs. They wore the badge of Eromar."

"Yeah, I saw 'em. You think Vald sent 'em after us?" Tobhi returned the leaves to their pouch.

"Why not?"

"It just don't make no sense. Why would Vald risk goin' after us on the open road, where we might be able to get away? Wouldn't it be more sensible to just wait 'til we was up at Gorthac Hall, where nobody would see what was goin' on, and throttle us in our sleep or somethin'? We was probably a whole lot safer on the road than we'll be in his house."

The Wielder smiled grimly. "Yes, but don't forget one important thing, Tobhi: *he'll* be much less safe once we arrive at Gorthac Hall, and he knows it."

The night was deep upon them when the door to the meeting house swung open and a group of armed Men entered. The three Celestial Kyn had remained at a distance from Tarsa and Tobhi since first arriving in the room, but now they skittered to the Folk warriors with faces pale and eyes wide. Tobhi puffed calmly on a thin-stemmed pipe and remained on the bench. Tarsa stood to face the newcomers, her hands crossed over the amber top of the wyrwood staff in front of her.

These Men wore long, stark black coats that reached to their knees, matching in grim tone their wide-brimmed grey hats. Most of the Men had thick beards or muttonchops, and all wore heavy leather boots and thick, brass-buttoned leather vests that rose nearly to their chins. Most bore wide-bladed daggers, thin clubs, or crossbows in their hands, although Tarsa noticed short flintlocks strapped over the shoulders of two of the Men. The three-tined star of the House of Vald was embroidered on each Man's vest.

For a moment the two groups regarded each other warily, until the Men's ranks opened to reveal another figure, a green-eyed he-Kyn with black hair and golden skin who stepped forward and held his open hand to his chest in greeting. With a sidelong glance to the Men around him, the he-Kyn said in Mannish, «Welcome, my kindred. Dreydmaster Vald sends his greetings, tempered by heartfelt condolences for your loss. The Dreydmaster has asked me to escort you safely to your chambers at Gorthac Hall, with the further request that we break fast with him in the morning. There is much for us all to discuss.»

Imweshi's sour features softened into a smile. «Please tell the illustrious Prime of Eromar that we would be honoured to join him at his leisure, and that we send our most sincere thanks for his hospitality.»

Tarsa turned toward the elder she-Kyn and opened her mouth to speak, her eyes narrowing dangerously, but Tobhi turned toward her and, while knocking the ashes from his pipe, shook his head slightly. The Men shifted uneasily at the sight of the angry tattooed she-Kyn, but Tarsa took a quivering breath and stepped back beside the Tetawa.

Imweshi turned to give Tarsa a cold smirk, and walked across the room to join the dark-haired he-Kyn, whose own eyes lingered for just a moment on the Wielder before he took the elder she-Kyn's arm and led her out of the room. Athweid and Hak'aad followed them.

«What about our other companions?» Tarsa pointed to the covered bodies on the table beside the door. The language of Men was cold ash in her mouth. She rolled the words over her tongue, and they came away empty.

A Man who seemed to be the eldest in the group frowned and shook his head. «We're here to take you to the Dreydmaster. Nobody said anything about carrying corpses. Leave them here and come with us.»

Tarsa laughed bitterly. «No, I don't think we'll leave them. I've seen too well how your kind treat the dead.» She slipped the staff into the back of her waist-sash before bending down to lift Reiil's body over her shoulder. Tobhi did the same with Gweggi, who was lighter than the Tetawa had anticipated. He could see Tarsa's pain as Reiil's body weighed down on her broken ribs and made each breath like a fresh wound in her chest. But the Wielder stood proudly, her muscles and jaw tight, and glared at the Men, who looked uncertainly at one another.

With a heavy sigh, the leader pointed toward the door. «Just go--and don't expect any help from us.» He stepped out of the meeting house. Taking a deep, measured breath, Tarsa followed, Reiil's body held gently in her arms.

The group-fifteen Men, five Kyn, and a lone Tetawa-moved from the guardhouse toward the brick-cobbled street that stretched up the butte toward Gorthac Hall. The streets were crowded with dull, soot-smeared Humans, but they gave Vald's militiamen a wide berth, thus providing the Folk free passage through the streets. Tobhi gagged at the heavy stench in the air; it clutched at the back of his throat, the thick, sour weight drifting in part from roughly-chiselled open sewage ditches on each side of the street that snaked down the side of the butte toward the river. Rats and worse slid across their feet and between their legs as they walked. Athweid was soon sobbing in terror, but Hak'aad was no comfort, for he was beside his mother fighting down his own fear. Acidic smoke rolled through the alleys and buildings from the foundry stacks above to join the stink of sewage and the bitter, ever-present tang of iron. The thick air held an eerie, greenish-yellow hue, sometimes so heavy that it choked off the sputtering light from the coal oil street lamps lining the streets. The newcomers soon found themselves fighting for breath from the foul air, and even those who had lived here for some time found the stench to be almost overwhelming. But they continued on.

The journey was worst for Tarsa, whose proud endurance was crumbling with every step. The toxic air burned her lungs; each cough was a spike of burning agony in her side, and Reiil's body weighed heavier on her shoulders. By the time they reached the third palisade, Tarsa could barely move. Although most of the smoke and fetid air crouched behind them over the lower levels of Eromar City, every new breath tore through her like a knife. She was ill again, and her stalks, although bound and eased somewhat by the iron-ward, were almost overwhelmed by the pain of this place.

Step, step, step. Breath. Step, step, step. Breath. Breath. Step, step. Breath. She had a pattern now, yet it was breaking down. She would never make it to Gorthac Hall. But how could she leave kind Reiil behind in this place of poison and misery?

She stumbled, and as she fell she knew that she wouldn't be able to stand again. But then a hand was under her arm, pulling her back to her feet. The binding on her chest tore slightly, and Tarsa groaned from the searing pain. It was a strange voice in a familiar language. "Be strong, Wielder. We don't have much farther to go. Let me help you."

Tarsa's mind cleared a bit, and she turned to see the green-eyed he-Kyn beside her, his polished black leathers shining in the Men's dull torchlight ahead of them.

"I don't need…your help," she growled. Though she tried to pull her arm away from him, he held her firmly.

"Then let me help Reiil, for he was long known to me, and I always thought him a friend." Tarsa noticed for the first time that the he-Kyn's golden face was itself dark with exhaustion and sorrow.

Her strength wavered, and she nodded. The he-Kyn slid Reill's body from her and staggered under the weight as he shifted the body to his own shoulder. He said nothing, but he looked at the Wielder with surprised admiration. Tarsa slid the staff from her sash and leaned heavily on it as they walked together up the dark street.

Gorthac Hall was no less imposing from closer observation than from afar. Built of heavy granite and stout timbers torn from the now-vanished Folk forests of northern Eromar, the Hall stood on the top of the butte, where the Dreydmaster could survey his world without obstruction. Known throughout the province as the "Hall of a Thousand Gables," Gorthac Hall was a rambling building of sharp angles, jutting gables, hooded eaves, stout doors hidden in shadowed recesses, narrow balconies and wide, darkened walls. Its clay-shingled central tower stretched eighty feet into the air, reaching like a piercing spear into the night sky. A broad wooden balcony at the top of the tower, lit by iron braziers on bars that stretched outward from the roof above, was Vald's favourite observation point. None found comfort when the Dreydmaster strode the balcony.

Secrets were comfortable in Gorthac Hall, and things crawled among the shadows without fear of daylight. The will of its makers had penetrated the Fey wood with every iron nail, the stone with every mason's chisel mark. Many rooms in the rambling estate had never been seen by living eyes, and others were known to the Dreydmaster alone. Indeed, strange corners and chambers appeared on occasion, although the ring of builder's hammers had been unheard for nearly thirty years. A steady stream of servants came and went, or arrived and were never seen again, lost in the wandering, oak-paneled walls. With every passing year, the Hall rooted itself deeper, clutching the wind-blistered butte with a determination beyond reckoning.

Tarsa was nearly delirious with pain and sensory exhaustion when the group arrived at the great iron-banded oaken gates of Gorthac Hall. Their duty done, the militiamen returned to their quarters in the city. The green-eyed he-Kyn asked the Hall Steward to find a suitable place for the dead Kyn and Ubbetuk to be kept until proper funeral services could be arranged, then led the survivors to their quarters in the western wing. The Steward joined them shortly after.

All the Kyn were housed in the same hallway, a cold, drafty series of rooms with narrow windows that looked to the jagged northern highlands. Hak'aad had a room to himself, while his mother and Athweid shared a small chamber with a single bed. All of the bed linens were rough and musty, but they were clean.

When they reached the room designated for Tarsa, Tobhi said, «If ye don't mind, I think I'll just bed down here with her. There's plenty of room.»

The Steward blanched. «That's impossible.»

«Why?»

«I'm afraid I cannot allow it. It's improper.»

Tarsa, clutching at the door frame, whispered hoarsely, «I would very much like…for him to be here. He's trained in medicinals, and he…»

The Steward waved his hand dismissively. «We have a fine alchaemical doctor here. You will be well cared for, I assure you. I will send for him.»

He turned to lead them down the hallway, but stopped when Tarsa lunged forward and caught him by the throat, her eyes blazing. «I'll have nothing to do with your witchery!»

Gasping, the Steward clutched at the she-Kyn's hand, and though she was weakened by her injuries and stood a full head shorter than the Man, he couldn't break free of her grasp. The green-eyed he-Kyn stepped forward and pulled her hand away, gently but firmly.

«She is ill, Steward, and is in need of particular skills found only in the Everland. This Brownie,» he glanced at Tobhi, using the Man-land name for the Tetawi, «is here to care for her. There can hardly be anything 'improper' in that, can there?»

The Steward frantically shook his wispy-haired head, eyes bulging, lips trembling. Tarsa pushed the Man against the wall and staggered into the room. Tobhi bowed to both the Man and the he-Kyn. He followed Tarsa and shut the door behind them.

«I will speak to the Dreydmaster about this outrage, you can be assured, Ambassador,» the Steward coughed, smoothing the wrinkles from his silken jacket.

The he-Kyn spun around. He drove the Steward to the wall again and held something cold and sharp against the Man's bristly neck. His green eyes burned with barely-contained frenzy. «Are you threatening me, you gibbering imbecile? If you are, I'll cut out your tongue and feed it to you in slivers. Do not forget, alone of my people I have survived. Don't imagine that you'll be able to succeed where better Men have failed.»

The Man's mouth gaped and quivered, and the sharp tang of hot urine filled the hallway. The he-Kyn looked down at the floor beneath the Steward and smiled with grim satisfaction. «Get out of here, stink-skin, and don't return unless it's to clean up this mess. I won't be so gentle with you again.»

He stepped back, and the Steward stumbled away. The he-Kyn stood watching the darkened hallway long after the Man had fled. At last, a voice in the Everland trade tongue broke his reverie. "Ye en't the drag-tailed dog I took ye for."

The Tetawa stepped into the hallway and pulled the door closed behind him. His hat and satchels were in the room, but he held his lit pipe out to the he-Kyn, who took it and drew deeply. "It's been so long since I've heard a familiar word, or shared a pipe. I am Daladir Tre'Shein, Ash Branch brother of Sheynadwiin. *Tsodoka.*"

"Name's Tobhi. It's a pleasure." They leaned against the hallway wall for a while, passing the pipe between them. The cleansing scent of fresh tobacco lifted the gloom somewhat. When the bowl was finished, Tobhi tapped it against his boot, knocking the ashes to the ground. "Where's the other diplomats? We en't heard nothin' about 'em since we got here."

The he-Kyn gave Tobhi a haunted look. "There are no others here. Of the fourteen who came here last spring, and of the five who survived through the winter, I'm the only one who remains."

"Nashaabi!" the Tetawa cursed. "The only one?"

"Until now, yes."

"Well, it'll be easier than we was guessin', although it's grim news, to be sure."

The he-Kyn looked at Tobhi quizzically. "What do you mean?"

"C'mon in. We better talk out of the hallway." Tobhi led the he-Kyn into the room and slid the door bolt firmly behind them.

The he-Kyn looked around. A smoking oil lamp glimmered softly on the windowsill, casting its gentle light across the small room. His eyes were drawn immediately to the bed, where Tarsa lay asleep, her dark, tangled hair floating across the thick coverlet, one tattooed arm resting on top of the blankets.

"How is she?" he asked, his voice barely above a whisper.

"She'll be better after a bit of sleep, I think. It's been a long trip for us all, but 'specially her."

The he-Kyn smiled. "I think you could use some rest, too, Tobhi."

"Yeah," Tobhi yawned. "Ye won't hear no complaint from me there. But that'll have to wait a bit, I think." He smiled warmly. "Daladir, we're here to take ye home."

Relief and fear flooded the he-Kyn's face. "It's over, then?"

"Not yet." Tobhi re-filled his pipe bowl. "But the Sevenfold Council en't takin' too kindly to Vald's terms. When they do make their decision, it en't likely that ye'd want to be anywhere near here. So we're here to make sure you en't."

They sat in silence as the ambassador reflected on the news.

"It won't be easy," he said at last, his eyes returning to Tarsa's sleeping form. "The Dreydmaster is no fool, and your sudden arrival, especially with a Wielder, puts us in terrible danger. You won't know it for some time, however~Vald is nothing if not the measure of rigid courtesy. He'll toy with us, like a sated cat, until he tires of the game. And then he'll strike with a predator's ruthlessness, as he's done so many times before."

Exhaustion pulled at the he-Kyn's words, and though he looked largely hale and strong, there was a furtiveness about him, a dread that lurked behind his green eyes, the certainty of oblivion crawling slowly toward them. Tobhi suppressed a shudder. *What happened in this awful place to fill him with so much worry?*

"I must go~I've been here too long. She made an unnecessary enemy in the Steward this evening, and I didn't help matters afterward." Daladir stood suddenly and walked to the door. "Be wary, Tobhi, friend of the blue-eyed Wielder. You're in the dog-pit now, and the hounds grow hungry." He glanced back to Tarsa's sleeping form before slipping into the darkness.

Tobhi lowered the lamp wick, took off his overgarments, and slid under the covers beside the wounded Wielder, curling close to keep her warm in the deepening chill. He slipped easily to sleep, but those haunted green eyes lingered long in his thoughts, and his dreams brought no comfort.

CHAPTER 4

THE DREYDMASTER'S WELCOME

«Welcome to my table, honoured guests.» Dreydmaster Vald stood at his seat and bowed to the visitors as they entered the sooty dining hall. The wide room was stark and bare of decoration, except for a long table of burnished cherry wood that stretched nearly from the door to Vald's massive seat. A large fire blazed in the Man-high hearth behind the Dreydmaster. The dull light of morning crept into the room through uneven panes of thick glass set every few feet in the panelled walls. Though weak, the sunlight was welcome, as it brought more warmth to their flesh than did the leering fireplace that belched out smoke and hissing embers.

Daladir led the group to the seats nearest the Dreydmaster who, except for a few faithful retainers, was otherwise alone in the room. Tarsa's gaze never left the Man. He was nothing like she'd expected. He had no striking features other than the thick brows that bristled over his hawk-like nose, no particular aura of malice. A tallish Man, neither fat nor skinny, handsome nor ugly, Vald was indistinguishable from the hundred other Men she had seen in the past few days, except for his fine grey garments, neatly trimmed peppered muttonchops, and his broad, ink-stained fingers that were free of callus and wear. She had expected a monster, but instead she'd met a surprisingly ordinary Man.

Daladir bowed low. «Dreydmaster Vald, Sanctified Voice of the Province of Eromar within the Reach of Men, I wish to introduce you to my recently-arrived companions, who have traveled at great risk and urgency from the Everland to speak with you at your leisure and grace. I believe you have met one of them before, when she was last assigned to this post.»

Tarsa and Tobhi exchanged quick glances.

«Yes, I recognize the Lady Imweshi,» Vald said, his voice as smooth and cold as river stone. «It is a pleasure to welcome a Celestial matron of such wisdom to my home once again. Please introduce me to your companions; I am quite curious about them.»

The elder she-Kyn flushed slightly. «This is my youngest son, Hak'aad, and with him is Athweid, daughter of my cousin's wife. They have accompanied me to learn better the wisdom of Men, so that they might one day bring that wisdom to the service of our people.»

Vald smiled slightly, and he nodded to the younger Kyn. Then his eyes turned to the tattooed Wielder who wore her singed leaf and feather cloak of office over her travel-worn leathers. «And who else have you brought on this visit?»

Imweshi began to speak, but Tarsa's hand slashed through the air, silencing her. «I am Tarsa'deshae, the Spear-breaker.» Her voice rose clear and strong in the room. «I was born to the matrons of Cedar Branch in Red Cedar Town, daughter of Lan'delar Last-Born, niece of the Wielder Unahi Sam'sheyda, grand-daughter of Ayeddi'olaan. My people know me as a Redthorn warrior and Wielder of the Deep Green. Imweshi's words are her own; she does not speak for me.»

The room went silent. All held their breaths as the Dreydmaster and the Wielder coolly regarded one another. Tobhi's sharp ears caught the sound of boot nails on stone in the hallway, and though he knew the gesture was futile, he slid his hand toward the tiny sheath on his belt. Vald was indeed no fool; while his hall spoke of welcome, he left nothing to chance. Tobhi hadn't wanted to leave his hatchet in the room, and now he wished that he had more than a little wyrwood dagger between his flesh and Vald's militiamen.

Vald bowed, breaking the tension. «Welcome then, Tarsa'deshae of Cedar Branch, to the world of Men. It has been many years since a bearer of the Old Ways of your people has come willingly to Eromar. Perhaps this is a sign of a new spirit of cooperation between our nations.»

Tarsa nodded but remained silent.

Daladir introduced Tobhi, whom Vald ignored, and the Dreydmaster motioned to the main door of the hall. The air crackled with unseen energies, and the door swung open to reveal a small, pale Woman in a dull saffron dress and white head cap, followed by two thin, dark-eyed girls in green. The militiamen remained in the hallway.

«My wife, Betthia, and daughters Sheda and Methieul.» Vald clapped his hands. «My son, Sadish, will be unable to join us today, as he is touring the foundry district. We will eat, now.» Betthia and her daughters bowed their heads and slipped like shadows through the door behind the Dreydmaster, to emerge moments later with thick platters of greasy meats and gravies, long loaves of heavy-grained breads, and bowls of thin oat porridge. Vald didn't share their food; he had his own plate of meat and bread, delicately spiced. The Women kept their eyes averted from their guests. When young Methieul brought the porridge to Tarsa, the young Woman trembled visibly.

Vald watched as the plates were piled high, all but that of the Wielder. «Does our food displease you, Wielder?» he asked gently.

She shook her head. «The breads and vegetables are more than adequate for me, Dreydmaster.»

«But my wife prepared the suckling roast in your honour.»

«I thank you, Dreydmaster, but I cannot eat animal flesh. It is not the way of my people, even though some may have forgotten this.» She looked at Hak'aad and Daladir, who both held meat forks in hand.

The master of Gorthac Hall leaned forward, and his voice took on a hard edge. «It is discourteous to refuse food given by your host.»

Tarsa smiled, but it didn't reach her shining eyes. «A courteous host wouldn't prepare food that his guests couldn't eat.»

Imweshi dropped her knife, her face pale, and Daladir coughed on a bite of food. Tobhi listened to the conversation without much interest and continued to eat his roast, as this Kyn tradition was not shared by the Tetawi. The meat was overcooked and had a slightly bitter aftertaste, but it was a welcome change from the nuts and dried fruit in his satchel. The bread tasted fine, especially when dipped in the greasy gravy that sloshed at the edge of his plate.

The Dreydmaster suddenly broke into a smooth laugh. «Too true,

Wielder, too true. Very well~you will be served those foods that best suit your delicate constitution. I trust you do not object too strenuously to your companions' eating habits?»

«What they eat is none of my concern.»

Vald clapped his hands. «Good. All is settled, then.» He turned back to Imweshi. «I understand that you lost companions yesterday during the attack by ruffians. My condolences to you all.»

Tarsa glared at the Man, but Imweshi pointedly ignored her. «Yes. A Goblin, and one of our own, Reiil Cethwir, whose uncle Damodhed once served beside you in the Battle of Downed Timber on the borderland of the Everland and Eromar.»

«Kyn and Men fought together?» Athweid asked, incredulous.

«Yes,» the Dreydmaster replied. «We need not always be enemies. When I was much younger, brigands swept down from The Lawless to the north, threatening both the lands of Men and of the Folk. It took us a few months, but we managed to stop them before they reached Lake Ithiak. In fact, it was Damodhed who saved my life during that battle. I had been struck from behind and knocked to the ground. Just as an enemy was preparing to run me through with his spear, Damodhed took off his head with a well-placed blow from his war club. I am sorry to hear that his kinsman has died in such unfortunate circumstances.»

«It was more than unfortunate,» Tarsa growled. «We were ambushed.»

«Yes, so much hatred, so much unnecessary pain.» Vald shook his head sadly. He smiled at Athweid. «And yet there is always hope. Misunderstandings arise, and people suffer because of them. But there are always opportunities for brave individuals to take control of their own destinies and take a new path, a wiser path that can break down these age-old prejudices and bring us all closer together, to give all people the hope of a good future, not just the remnants of a fading past.» The young she-Kyn smiled at his words and turned to Hak'aad, who returned her smile and clasped her hand under the table.

Tarsa looked toward the windows. «If I may ask, what is the future you're offering us, Dreydmaster?»

Vald turned to her and smiled, as though indulging a petulant youngling. «Why, progress, my dear Spear-breaker. What could be more important?»

«Progress? By whose measure? I'm not sure I understand what that word means here. Iron machines belching yellow smoke, hungry people and poisoned waters. It seems to be a gift my people could do quite well without.»

Hak'aad let out a strangled gasp, and Athweid held her hand to her mouth. For the briefest moment Tarsa saw the Dreydmaster's face contort into something else, an ill-concealed and ravenous thing that pulsed behind the Man's courteous demeanour. Then it vanished. Vald sighed heavily and turned to Athweid with wounded eyes. «This is what I speak of. The Wielder, not understanding the power of industry, its ability to strip away shiftlessness and weakness, instead chooses to attack it, to surrender to her lower urges, to give way to fear. But gentle lady, do not be angry with her. Pity her. Her time is at an end, and she knows it. You and your solid friend there are the future, for you understand that the ways of Men are not bad in themselves. They can help you live virtuous lives beyond the wilderness. Why slink around like whipped dogs when you can fly with the eagles?»

Vald stood and wiped his mouth with a napkin. «The world is changing, my friends, and you must change with it or be washed away by the flood. None of us can stop this storm~it is inevitable. Now you must decide, will you build a boat that will carry you to safety, or will you stand and let the waters wash over you.» He held his hand out to Athweid and motioned for the others. «Come. Let me show you what this future can bring. We have created a world unlike anything imagined by your ancestors, or ours, for that matter. Let me show you what Men can offer to the Folk.» Hak'aad and Imweshi followed, leaving Tobhi, Tarsa, and Daladir alone in the dining hall.

"What are you doing?!" Daladir hissed when the door creaked shut. "Are you trying to get us killed? Do you have any idea what Vald can do?"

Tarsa walked over to the window and looked out. "Of course I do. Look for yourself. He's killing his own people, poisoning their bodies as well as their minds. When was the last time a tree grew in this land? The hills ache from deep roots left to rot. The Everland sent medicinals to help plague victims in Eromar years ago. Did you notice that he never mentioned this gesture of kindness? He cares nothing for healing. The only stories he tells are of metal, war, and bloodshed. What would you have us do, just sit around and wait for him to kill us and our people, like you've done since you've been here?" Her eyes flashed with building rage.

"You don't know anything about me, about what I've had to do to survive here! And you don't know a damned thing about Lojar Vald. I do. I know what he's capable of, and I've seen him do things that you can't imagine. You think you can just walk into this monster's lair, spit in his face, and walk away? This isn't your back-country village, Wielder, and things aren't so easy here. I've had to watch as my friends, as much my family as my Branch-kith, died one by one at Vald's whim. They died, Wielder, in order for Vald to break me down, bit by bit, to tear me into pieces, all for the simple joy of watching me crumble. Why he chose me, I don't know. I could have just as easily died in the darkness with a knotted bed sheet around my neck, just one more of many 'accidents.' But I survived it. And then you ride in, the great brave Redthorn warrior, and you're going to stand up to the Dreydmaster of Eromar? You're an arrogant fool, and a danger to all of us. You don't know anything about this." He stormed out of the room.

Tobhi stood up and walked to Tarsa's side. "Don't ye worry 'bout him," he said. "He's just scared, that's all."

"Yes, he's scared. But he's right about one thing." Tarsa walked to the window. "I don't know anything about this world or these people. This place is built on lies and pain and cruelty, all twisted up and tangled like a briar thicket. I don't understand this place, Tobhi." The cloak was heavier than ever with the weight of sudden doubt. "Maybe I *should* have stayed back in Sheynadwiin. Why should I think I know any better than Imweshi, or Hak'aad, or even Vald?"

"Because, Tarsa, ye know what's goin' on *beneath* them lies and pain and cruelty. I watched ye as his wife and daughters came slinkin' through with our food, and you saw what the others didn't want to see. These Women is sufferin' terribly; they fear this Man like nothin' else in the world. That their great fear should come from the one Man who should love 'em the most is a sad, sad thing. Imweshi and her kind don't see none of that, and Daladir is grievin', too caught up in his own hurt. There's a lot more to the world than what's on the surface, and in this place it's what's under the skin that's most important. He can't deceive ye, not unless ye let him break ye down."

Tarsa placed a hand on the Tetawa's shoulder and squeezed gratefully. "Besides," Tobhi whispered as they moved toward the door and their room beyond, "I don't trust nobody who serves a meal with more grease than gravy. There's a sure sign that somethin's wrong. If nothin' else, Tarsa, trust yer stomach."

When the big people were all finally out of the room, the rats sped out, rushing around to capture stray bits of food. As no one came out to take the dishes, the brown creatures clambered up the chairs and onto the table, where they fell hungrily upon the chunks of roast and the few crumbs of bread that remained. The sound of the kitchen door swinging open sent the rats scurrying back to their hiding places, back into the safe shadows in the walls.

And it was there, a few hours later, that they died, their claws scrabbling at the fouled floor, their bodies contorted into grotesque shapes, squealing through foam-flecked mouths as the poison ate through their blistered bellies and made its way to their blood. The poison didn't work so quickly in larger bodies, but in small forms it was swift. The end result, however, was always the same.

None survived.

CHAPTER 5

THE DARKNESS BEFORE DAWN

"I'm sorry to have brought ye such unhappy news, Wielder."

Unahi sat in silence at the table of the small, two-storied roundhouse she shared with the she-Gvaerg, Biggiabba. The kind, hulking Wielder was gone this night; the only time she could meet with her people was in moonlit darkness, when the sister suns' deadly rays offered no danger to the he-Gvaergs who'd travelled down from the far north mountains to join the discussions of the Sevenfold Council. Sunlight harmed only he-Gvaergs, turning their living flesh to frozen stone, and only great wrappings of wyrweave prevented that terrible fate for those who had no choice but to travel under the suns' watchful gaze. As wyrweave was an increasingly precious trade good, due to the recent disruptions of the trading network, the most practical option for the stone-born Folk was to gather beneath the softer light of the midnight stars.

On the nights when Biggiabba was away, Unahi generally retired to her pallet early for much-needed rest, as her days were becoming increasingly busy with the ever-larger numbers of refugees from around the Everland. More invading Humans meant more displacement, danger, and death for the Folk, and the great peace city of Sheynadwiin was still one of the last safe places for them to flee. Kyn, Tetawi, Gvaerg, Beast, even an occasional Ubbetuk and allied Human, along with all manner of unusual and rare Folk-creature, now called Sheynadwiin their temporary home. There was food and water enough, for now, but space was dwindling, and tempers were fraying with each passing day. There had already been a few outbreaks of violence and illness, which the Wielders and some of the Shields had managed to keep from growing out of control. All the medicine workers who remained in the city, Greenwalker and Celestial alike, were overwhelmed with the needs of their respective peoples. They were already exhausted, and everyone knew that it was only going to get worse as the days went on. Much, much worse.

An early rest would have been very welcome, but it wasn't going to happen tonight. Her guest had brought unexpected news that had deeply shaken the bent old she-Kyn, and she sat in stricken silence for a long time. At last, she licked her lips and said, "Tell me again, please. What happened?"

Molli Rose, the principal speaker of the Tetawi delegation at the Council, sighed deeply. "We don't know too much, but some of the survivors arrived earlier tonight. I was already in the refugee grounds and heard 'em talkin' to one of the Shields who's helpin' organize things down there. It was raiders, that's for certain. The attack was well planned. They had caging wagons ready for those they could catch."

"And for those they couldn't?"

Molli Rose hesitated for a moment. The Tetawa was well known in the Council for her frank speech and forthright manner, but she knew that such a style wasn't ideal for all occasions. This conversation required particular care, even if it was hard to know how to possibly share such horrible news in a gentle way. Molli Rose admired honesty and courage, and for this reason was quite fond of the old Wielder, who considered issues deeply and spoke her own mind with conviction. It was this warm regard that had made the Tetawa decide to bring the news to Unahi directly rather than entrust it to someone else.

She pulled her brown shawl tighter around her shoulders. The room was cold, but Molli Rose couldn't tell if it was from the strange weather that had recently affected the Everland or Unahi's grief. "Most of the grown he-Kyn were killed on the spot. A few zhe-Kyn may have escaped, we en't sure, but at least one was mauled to death by the Men's war-hounds. As for the survivin' she-Kyn and cubs, they were rounded up and put into the cages. They're likely on the way to Eromar, like those from other burnt-out towns and settlements."

It wasn't a new story. Slavers and bandits were growing bolder and crueller with every passing day. Hundreds of Folk had been kidnapped and taken to slave markets throughout Eromar, and thousands of Beasts had been killed already. It wasn't an exceptional story, but this attack was on Red Cedar Town, the youngling home of both Unahi and her niece, the Redthorn Wielder, Tarsa'deshae. And there was no word of the fate of Tarsa's aunts, Unahi's four surviving sisters.

"I'll keep askin' around down there, to see if anybody knows anythin' else. I'll let ye know as soon as I learn more." She softly patted Unahi's wrinkled grey-green hand and stood to leave.

The Wielder didn't look up. "*Tsodoka*, Molli Rose. I appreciate you coming here yourself to let me know."

"My prayers are with ye and yer family, Unahi. I'll be back tomorrow to tell ye what I hear."

Unahi sat at the table for a long time after the Tetawa had gone. She couldn't quite absorb the news. It was almost impossible to imagine that the town was destroyed. Even though she'd been exiled for years from Red Cedar Town, which had long ago rejected the Deep Green that Unahi had dedicated her life to preserving, it had never occurred to her that the town wouldn't always be there. That place was immovably rooted in her mind and memory. She'd visited only a few months earlier, on the traumatic occasion of Tarsa's own Awakening into the Old Ways, and though the town had changed in significant ways from her youngling days, it was still her home more than any other place in the world. To hear that Red Cedar Town was now gone was too much to fathom.

And her sisters. Two of the six had died years before, including Tarsa's mother, Lan'delar, and were buried in the red soil of their ancestors amidst the now smouldering ruins of the town. Unahi's relationship with most of the others was strained beyond repair, but they were still kith, still her flesh and blood, and she still loved them. Sweet, fragile Geth. Dignified Vansaaya, haughty Sathi'in, petulant Ivida. What had happened to them on that terrible day? Did they still live? If not, did they die quickly? If they weren't yet dead, what were their lives like now? Though few spoke openly of it, everyone knew what horrors awaited she-Folk at the mercy of Men, and the very thought brought a choking sob from the Wielder's trembling lips. To think that the she-Kyn she'd grown up with, played alongside, loved and fought and wept with would know brutalized lives in Eromar....

Eromar. She dropped her face into her hands, her heart too heavy for tears. It wasn't just her sisters who faced the threat of that dangerous land. Tarsa was there now, too, and likely in as much danger as the others, if not more, as she was in the bleak beating heart of Eromar itself: Gorthac Hall, the home of Lojar Vald. The elder Wielder had tried to keep Tarsa from going, but the young warrior was every bit as stubborn as her aunt, and was more resourceful than Unahi had anticipated. In the end, and against Unahi's wishes, Tarsa had arranged to join the group sent to rescue the surviving Kyn diplomats from Eromar City, and the old she-Kyn had watched, fearful for her niece and furious with herself, as the Ubbetuk airship disappeared into the storm-choked skies.

Yet, unlike the situation with her sisters, Unahi wasn't entirely helpless with Tarsa. She reached into a pocket of her skirt and pulled out a jagged chunk of red-veined amber. As a parting gift, Unahi had given her old wyrwood walking stick to the headstrong warrior. The staff was capped by a piece of amber that matched the one in her hand; each was etched with the slash-and-circle mark that all Wielders shared. The two resinous shards were linked across the vast distance between the Everland and Eromar, both by origin and by special Wielded art, and it was this link that would help Unahi track Tarsa's journey through her niece's dreams. A partial picture, admittedly, and a treacherous one—the dream-world was inevitably erratic and difficult to decipher, even in ideal conditions—but it was the old Wielder's only way of being of help. She was powerless in so many other ways; she needed to know that she could be of service to the one she-Kyn in her family that she'd promised to protect. With the news about Red Cedar Town, it still gave her hope, no matter how thin.

Unahi quickly gathered the materials she needed from double-woven cane baskets and brightly painted clay vessels scattered throughout the room. She took a few cinders from the fireplace, placed them in a large blackened abalone shell, and covered them with a handful of tobacco leaves, some cedar sprigs, and a few blue-green berries. Cupping her hand over the shell, she blew on the dried plants until they began to smoke, then whispered a prayer as she wafted the smoke across her sensory stalks, forehead, face, and body, taking care to leave no flesh or clothing untouched by the sweet-smelling vapour. When satisfied, she rummaged through another basket for a small black root, dried and foul-smelling, which she immediately popped into her mouth and swallowed, ignoring the bitter taste and sudden light-headedness.

Returning to her seat, she brought the piece of amber to her forehead and closed her eyes. Her eyes grew heavy, and her head began to spin. The chill in the room faded, replaced by a dry, heavy heat. The fingers on Unahi's free hand ran across the medicine songs beaded onto her chanting sash, and as the words formed on her lips and her sensory stalks began to pulse in unison, she let her spirit drift free into the dream-world, where a blue-green light in the misty darkness drew her forward.

Tarsa stood in the cavern again, but it was a chill, empty darkness. She was naked, and alone. No water flowed from the cavern's depths or hung in the air around her, no rich blue light sent her skin tingling. Even the waterfall was now gone. The deep pool was dry and cracked, and she could see down almost to its sandy centre. The wind whipped mournfully across the old pool's weather-worn walls.

Dust swirled listlessly around her. She could almost taste iron in the air, just the slightest bitter tang that clutched with dry claws at the back of her throat. She looked around—it couldn't possibly be the same place. But the same slender vines and leaves were etched into the walls, and though the water was gone, the trough in the floor that led into the darkness was achingly familiar.

"Why am I here?" the young Wielder asked aloud, but silence was the only response. She looked back, just once, at the empty pool, then turned

and walked back into the cavern toward the Eternity Tree.

Her bare feet scraped painfully on jagged pieces of rock torn out of the wall. The only light was the dim, blue-green glow of her tattoos, but it was enough to guide her way. It was a short journey. The brown-legged creature in the mask was gone, but the standing stones remained, the sole reminders of her first journey through this place, a shroud of deep, impenetrable gloom crouching around her.

Tarsa felt something in her hand. It was a small bundle of red cloth, wrapped delicately with a white thread. She knelt on the ground and unfolded the cloth to reveal dozens of leaves, each marked with a different image. Yet as she reached out to touch the leaves, they crumbled into ashes, which were carried into the darkness by a sudden gust of icy wind. Tarsa cried out and tried to grab them, but the wind pulled them out of reach, and then she lost her balance and, flailing wildly, plunged headfirst into that unending darkness. A familiar voice called out to her~Unahi?~and then all she could hear over her screams was the mocking wind as she fell downward, downward, down….

She shot awake, her heart throbbing painfully in her chest. The bedroom was stiflingly hot. Her skin dripped with sweat. She put her head in her hands and tried to calm herself. "Just a dream," she whispered, but the words gave no comfort. Her stomach burned. For five nights she'd slept beneath the roof of Gorthac Hall, and each evening brought terrible nightmares and a rising, indistinct fear. Vald had been the model of restrained hospitality, joining them for dinner each evening, spending time in vigorous conversation with Imweshi and the others, paying little attention to Tarsa and Tobhi. Even Daladir avoided her, the spark in his eyes becoming more remote with each passing day. This evening the Dreydmaster had seemed almost giddy, and this disturbed the Wielder far more than his earlier condescension.

Her stomach clenched suddenly. Something was wrong. She remembered Vald's pleasant smile as she ate her bland dinner of boiled carrots and potatoes and drank a bit of the salty wine. Another jagged pain shot through her belly at the memory. The wine had been strange, but she was unused to alcohol, and the dizziness seemed normal.

A thin, muffled whimper caught her attention, and she turned to see Tobhi's small, sweat-drenched form twisting beside her, a pinkish-white froth on his bloody lips, his eyes rolled back and hands clutching at the air.

"Tobhi!" Tarsa whispered, but he couldn't hear her: his body was contorted nearly beyond recognition. A wordless gurgle slid from his throat. The Wielder pulled herself on top of the Tetawa to keep him still, but the convulsions were too strong, and her own pain was too great to hold him down. His legs flew out, catching Tarsa in the chest. She fell onto the plank floor, and blinding pain exploded in her side from the earlier injury.

It took a long time before she could crawl back to the bed and pull herself up. Her breath came now in shallow gulps, but she reached down and grabbed a blanket from the floor that Tobhi had thrown off in his unconscious flailings. She threw it over him as his spasms became more violent and desperate. There was a streak of blood on the headboard where his head had smashed against the wood.

Tarsa pulled the blanket tight around him, desperately hoping that this measure of restraint would keep him still. She didn't know what to do. For an instant she almost called for the Steward and his doctor, but Tobhi would be dead before they arrived, if they answered the call at all.

She touched his bloody forehead, but pulled back as the iron-ward around her neck went ice-cold. Tarsa snarled in fear and frustration—the iron-ward protected her from that poisonous metal, but it did so by dampening her own link to the thinned *wyr* of this land. The amulet turned cold again in warning as she reached out. Tobhi's body twisted violently beneath her, nearly lifting her off the bed again. A thin, bubbling shriek tore through the Tetawa's throat.

There was no other choice. Choking back tears, the Wielder pulled the iron-ward from around her neck.

Tarsa fell across the Tetawa, gasping in renewed pain and shock. She felt like Gorthac Hall itself had collapsed on her. The presence of every piece of iron in the room burned into her flesh and mind. Wood-nails, hinges, knobs and bedposts–they all flared to caustic life when the amulet left her flesh. Her sensory stalks twisted in pain, like earthworms held to a flame. She turned her head and retched until tears streamed down her face and her body trembled from pain and exhaustion.

But she couldn't allow herself to surrender, not while their lives ebbed with each heartbeat. She was getting weaker, too. Driving the pain to a hidden corner of her mind, Tarsa took a deep, quivering breath and pulled the convulsing Tetawa against her, chest on chest, heart to heart, their pain-filled bodies linked by the touch of tender flesh.

The *wyr* was weak in this toxic land, but it still endured, and it flowed slowly between them. Tarsa took Tobhi's pain, and her consciousness eased through him, following those burning blood currents to find the deadly imbalance raging there.

It didn't take long. Her heart chilled as she suddenly touched the poison of weltspore in his blood, a bitter yellow fungus that lost its distinctive taste when mixed with something stronger, like the juices of cooked meat…or heady wine. As a youngling, she'd seen a playmate in the early stages of weltspore poisoning; mistaking one of the enticing yellow buds for an edible mushroom, he'd eaten an entire cap at once. It had been a swift and terrible death.

For an instant Tarsa saw Vald's piercing eyes at every gathering over the past five days, the sudden veil that dropped over his eyes as he ate his own meals. Vald's vengeance was subtle, and patient; he'd played with them the whole time, dropping only enough poison to weaken them, day by day, watching them die a bit more with each passing dawn. It was brutally fitting that he'd chosen a poison from the Everland to do the deed.

No, Tobhi, her mind spoke to his, and she shared her fading strength. *I won't let you die. I can't survive this place by myself.*

One of Unahi's teachings suddenly returned to her, unbidden but welcome. *"Until you stop fighting the bloodsong and give honour to the wyr that flows through you and through all the Eld Folk, you will always be a stranger to the Deep Green."* She could allow fear to drive her to continued self-doubt, or she could embrace it in all its beautiful, terrible power, and all the responsibility that such power demanded. She'd been a Wielder before, in name more than deed. Now, at last, she was ready to understand the full measure and danger of what Wielding truly was.

Tarsa opened her spirit wide and surrendered to the bloodsong that she'd so long held in check. The calming words beaded into the chanting sash were released, and the bloodsong was free, the flood drawing her down into its swirling depths. The *wyr* grew stronger, unhindered by the iron that surrounded them, gaining force and speed, rushing inward to cleanse the weltspore from their blood, from every tissue and fibre of their calming bodies. She trembled now with renewed strength–the poison hadn't affected her as much as it had Tobhi, but even the one goblet of wine would have been deadly in the night if the dream hadn't wakened her. Tarsa held Tobhi tightly as the *wyr* drew the poison away from their bodily depths, coming closer and closer to the surface. She retched again, felt the poison rush away from her own flesh in a gout of orange ooze, then placed her mouth over Tobhi's and pulled the weltspore out, spitting it on the ground. She repeated the process, sucking out the poison again and again until her mouth was numb and she was certain that they were both past danger.

The Wielder's body pulsed with the rush of *wyr*-fed power. It was suddenly as if all the *wyr* remaining in Eromar was flowing right through her, summoned by her need. Tobhi lay unconscious but alive. She sighed in relief, but the feeling was short lived, as she suddenly remembered that Tobhi was not the only one who ate from Vald's poison table.

She was strong again–stronger than she'd been in a long time. Grabbing her knife-belt and vest, Tarsa jumped to the floor, staggering a bit as the blood rushed to her head. The feeling passed; the bloodsong still flowed strong, and her senses were alive with the intensity of it. It was a strange moment, to be both in control of her senses and yet to feel them pulsing at the edge of her strength and conscious thoughts, yet the delicate balance endured. Unahi's patient training and calming songs had worked–Tarsa was no longer a slave to the bloodsong. She waited for her thoughts to clear a bit before leaving the room.

The hall was empty, and there were no noises in the chambers beyond. She pushed on Hak'aad's door, but something blocked her way. She shoved again, hard, and the door slid open to reveal the he-Kyn's stiffening body on the floor. In the bed, twisted into filth-stained sheets, lay poor, gentle Athweid, who had slipped into Hak'aad's room and arms deep in the night. Their bodies were mercilessly convulsed, mangled and broken until they were both almost unrecognizable.

The Wielder pulled the door shut. They were far beyond any help she could give.

Tarsa moved silently down the hallway and pushed Imweshi's door open, but the room was empty. The mystery of the elder she-Kyn's disappearance was solved, however, when Tarsa stumbled farther to find Daladir. There, crumpled at Daladir's doorstep, lay Imweshi, her hands twisted into claws of pain. Her delicate fingers were bloody and torn from trying to drag herself to the he-Kyn's door. Tarsa swallowed a sob and reached out, but she stumbled back again as Imweshi let out a wheezing hiss.

Falling to her knees, Tarsa pulled Imweshi to her own chest. As before, the *wyr* rushed to draw them together, but Tarsa felt the Celestial's proud spirit push against her.

Imweshi! Let me help you!

~No. Leave me be.~

You stubborn fool~you'll die if you don't let me help you!

~Then I will die. Better to die sanctified than to abandon the Pillar for the Tree.~

Imweshi...please. I'm here to help! Imweshi?

Imweshi....

The *wyr* drew back, and Tarsa was alone in the hallway again, Imweshi's suddenly limp body in her arms.

Tarsa lowered the elder to the stone floor and stood, shaking and weak with rage. She'd never felt such fury, not when she'd battled the Stoneskin, not even when she'd fought the grave-robbing Men. So much death and shame, and so much spirit-poison. It was worse than the weltspore; at least the weltspore had its place in the way of things. Its origins were far from the seeping lies that crept across the Melded world.

She thought back to Reiil's words in the coach as they rode toward Eromar City. He'd looked so sad. There was a longing in his eyes, a wish for a past that could have been, choices that might have been unmade.

But Reiil was dead now, as was Imweshi. Hak'aad. Athweid. Garyn had compromised on the latter three when he sent them on the mission, but he'd put his hope and faith in Reiil, Tobhi, and–though reluctantly at first–Tarsa. He'd given them his trust that they'd bring hope back to the Nation. Trust that they'd bring Daladir and the others....

Daladir! Tarsa pulled away from her reverie and threw the door open. A thin, flickering candle the only light in the cold room. The he-Kyn lay groaning in his narrow bed. Sweat streamed down his pale face; the poison was spreading through his body. He pulled himself up as Tarsa stepped into the room.

"Wielder," he whispered hoarsely, but his words were lost in a fit of coughing. He slipped back to his feather pillow as Tarsa pulled his shivering body toward her. "I don't want to die here, not like this."

"Don't struggle, Daladir. Let me help you now, as you once helped me." Their flesh touched, her mouth closed over his, and she felt him surrender. *You won't die, Daladir,* she promised as the *wyr* pulsed between them. *We're going home. Tonight.*

The boiling black clouds spread across the sky like an army with drums of thunder. The air crackled dangerously, almost as if it burned with anguished fury. Storms were not uncommon in the skies above Spindletop, but there was a dark spirit to this thunderhead, and everyone felt its presence. Wind and rain and hail stretched out ahead of the lightning, smashing like spears into the fragile land below, tearing at leaf and flower and flesh with equal ruthlessness.

Medalla joined Gishki in pulling the shutters and doors closed while their pepa, Lubik, finished bringing in an extra store of firewood before the storm prevented him from reaching the woodpile. The rest of the family was at Medalla's house, preparing that building for the storm. Quill stoked the fire again. Though it was nearing midsummer, a bone-numbing chill had crept into the world as the storm crept closer, and without the fire they would have nearly been frozen. As it was, they all wore winter robes and mittens, and they weren't warming up very much.

Gishki rubbed her hands together. "Did you ever hear of anything like this before? What a wretched night. Pepa, you sure we have enough wood?"

Old Lubik scratched his tattooed chin and nodded. He was a quiet elder, a *par fahr*, more inclined to listen than speak, like most of the older generation. Quill respected that. Indeed, she often wished that the Tetawi her age were like the elder *fahr*, especially the young he-Tetawi. She sighed and drove the green-wood stick back into the embers, stirring them around distractedly. It hardly mattered. There was only one *fahr* that Quill spent much time thinking about, and he was far, far away. There was no telling when, or if, she'd see him again. She didn't like to think about that possibility.

Quill glanced up to see Gishki and Medalla looking at her, their eyes warm with concern. The Dolltender smiled weakly.

"If you don't need me anymore, I think I'll just go check on the dolls." Old Lubik nodded, and Quill slid down to the room that she'd share this night with Gishki's young daughters. The room had one window looking out over the Edgewood with a view not so very different from that of her own little cabin nearby, which now stood empty since the recent sightings of the cannibal Skeeger. The creature had been far too interested in the Dolltender lately, and though her home was a short walk away, she felt better with her cousins in the next room rather than across the meadow.

The dolls stood side by side on makeshift shelves around the room. Their dark, shining eyes followed her in irritated resignation. Quill shrugged her shoulders.

"It's the best choice, you know. It isn't safe to be at home by ourselves tonight. We either stay here with family or we take our chances out there. I prefer to stay here, at least until things get a little calmer."

It was time to feed the dolls. The Dolltender pulled a small leather bag of tobacco and dried cedar from her apron pocket and walked to every doll, talking in a low, quiet voice to each in turn and leaving a small pile of the fragrant shavings at their feet. Though they weren't pleased about being taken from their shadowed cedar boxes in the old house, where they could dream undisturbed through the night, they seemed to be willing to accept the change without much fuss. The Dolltender had to spend a little more time talking with Green Kishka, the most stubborn of the bunch, but eventually even that old apple-head spirit gave the *firra* something resembling a smile.

Quill turned to the window as the hail grew more ferocious. The hailstones were large~each at least as big as her thumbnail. She crawled on the bed to look outside. Suddenly a flare of lightning illuminated the night, followed closely by a roar of thunder so loud that the entire moundhouse trembled. The Dolltender threw herself flat on the bed with a gasp.

In the moment between the lightning and the thunder, something pale and massive flashed into view. She'd seen it before.

The Skeeger had come for her.

Another lightning blast burned through the darkness, and then the thunder upended the night. The roof beams quivered and groaned. Quill heard the splintering of wood and screams from the other room, and Medalla, Gishki, and Lubik rushed down the hallway to her room. The front door gave way and a rush of cold wind embraced them. Lubik held a stone hatchet in his hand with the easy grace of an old warrior who'd never forgotten the ways of war. Gishki had grabbed a stick from the woodpile, and Medalla held a stout clay jar. Quill shivered behind them and watched the door.

They stood together for a long time. The cold wind whipped through the room, chilling flesh despite their winter wear. Then, outside, they heard the pigs screaming, a high-pitched, desperate sound that grew more and more hysterical. Quill covered her ears and burst into tears.

"They're being butchered alive," Medalla whispered. Lubik started down the hall, but Gishki stopped him, saying nothing. He nodded and held his daughter's hand.

As suddenly as the squealing started, it stopped. One long, groaning cry, and then it was over. But the silence that followed was almost worse than the screams.

"We can't just stay here all night," Gishki whispered at last. The thunder continued to split the night, but the silences between grew longer and longer. "Maybe the door opened on its own. After all, we were in a hurry to~"

A large shadow filled the doorway, and the Tetawi fell back in alarm. Old Lubik lunged forward, but a booted foot flew out and sent him spinning into a corner. The three *firra* grabbed one another in terror.

Lightning flashed through the window to illuminate a bearded Man standing in the room. Water dripped from his wide-brimmed hat and his wrinkled cloak. A patch covered one eye, but the other gazed at them with a frigid blue calm.

"Don't be stupid," he growled to Lubik in the trade tongue as the *par fahr* slowly regained his feet. "I want food, a fire, and shelter from the storm. Do as you're told and I won't hurt your family. Cross me, and none of you will live to see dawn." He turned to the window. "Besides, without me and my friend here, that creature out in the pen wouldn't have stopped with the pigs."

Quill's eyes strayed to the common room, where another, shorter figure crouched. In the dull firelight she could barely make out the shape of a Feral deer-kith, his arms bound behind his back. She shuddered and quailed as the Man caught her gaze. He regarded her in silence for a moment, then turned and stalked down the hall. Gishki and Medalla helped old Lubik to his feet. The Man said something, and they followed carefully.

Quill slid over to the dolls. They were more agitated than she'd ever seen them before. "You felt it too?" she whispered.

"Quill," Medalla called out, her voice trembling. "He wants us *all* in here." The Dolltender turned to the little figures on the shelves around her. "Don't worry. He'll be gone by dawn." Ignoring the fear in their wrinkled faces, Quill smoothed out her apron and headed down the hall, feeling for all the world that times were getting very bad very quickly…and only going to get worse.

Just before dawn in Sheynadwiin, when Biggiabba finally lumbered back from the Gvaerg gathering, she found Unahi sprawled unconscious on the floor, a small shard of amber glowing softly in her outstretched hand. The she-Gvaerg bent swiftly and carried her friend to a sleeping pallet, then watched over her with growing concern as Unahi thrashed in delirium for hours. River-willow tea and cold compresses seemed to help, and to Biggiabba's great relief the worst of the fever finally passed by mid-morning.

At last the old she-Kyn slowly opened her eyes. "It's begun, Biggiabba," she whispered hoarsely. "May Mother Tree save us all, it's finally begun."

CHAPTER 6

THE LAWMAKER'S DECISION

It took very little time for Tarsa to gather their gear together for the journey, but it was nearly dawn by the time Tobhi was well enough to travel. The Wielder returned her iron-ward to its place around her neck. Tobhi had had the golden globe with the nightwasp in his satchel, but Tarsa transferred it to her belt-pouch—when they were in the open air of the night, she would break it open and summon the great Ubbetuk Dragon to return them to the Everland. She would need to carry Tobhi's satchel, as he was still very weak.

Her first instinct was to hunt down and kill the Dreydmaster. After healing herself and her remaining companions as best she could, she'd called upon the medicine of her chanting sash and muted the bloodsong again. In its place rose a rage so bitter that she could almost taste it. She wanted Vald to know pain, and she wanted to be the one to inflict it. Twice she stepped to the door, the wyrwood staff in her hand, only to stop, trembling, with the knowledge that Daladir and Tobhi would never be able to escape the Eromar City without her. She would help them, but it was all she could do to restrain the call of blood vengeance.

"I hate this. I en't much use to ye now, am I?" Tobhi whispered as she helped him dress. The Tetawa leaned heavily on his hatchet, careful to avoid the sharp stone blade.

She gently pinched his nose. "Not much, little brother, but you'll be better soon enough. All you have to do is move silently and as quickly as you can; we'll be fine."

He smiled weakly. "Sure am glad ye came, Tarsa."

"Me too," she responded, her voice soft.

Daladir sat on the edge of the bed, conserving his strength for the journey ahead. "Do you really think we can escape, Wielder? Vald has more than mere Men at his service."

Tarsa's face hardened. "He'll need more than Men if he hopes to stop us. Yes, Daladir, we'll get away from this place, and we'll be home soon. Trust me."

"I do." He smiled. "I'm sorry for my earlier words."

She began to respond, but a noise in the hallway cut her words short. "Wait here," she hissed. Taking her staff firmly in hand, she snuffed out the candle and slipped to the side of the door, waiting.

A few tense moments passed in the darkness. No one moved, though they all watched the doorway and listened, senses straining, for the slightest sound.

At last, the door creaked open. The Wielder felt the toxic ooze of iron radiate through the doorway as the shining tip of a crossbow bolt shimmered in the dull lantern light from the hall. The door opened wider. The weapon moved forward.

Calling out in her warrior trill, the Redthorn Wielder fell upon the intended assassins, her thirst for vengeance finally unleashed, the wyrwood staff whirling in the narrow corridor with deadly accuracy. Her first blow shattered the crossbow and sent the Man sprawling backward. The second caught another Man in the throat, and he fell with a strange, choking squawk. The sudden ferocity of her attack caught the other three Men by surprise, and they stumbled away.

A blast of *wyr*-drawn wind tore through the corridor, snuffing out their lanterns. The darkness now belonged to the she-Kyn warrior. Her boot caught the crossbowman in the face, quickly ending his threat. Tarsa crouched low and listened, her *wyr*-heightened senses drawing in every sound, scent, and shift in the air around her. She was still for a moment. Then, like a whirlwind, she flew forward and spun her staff in a diagonal arc, catching another soldier's arm and sending his long knife flying.

"Now, Daladir! Take Tobhi and go~I'll finish them!"

The he-Kyn didn't hesitate. Pulling Tobhi onto his back, Daladir slipped out the door, stumbling down the hall and away from the chaos of the battle. He didn't let himself think about what Tarsa was facing behind them; he simply had to trust her, and hope that he and his passenger didn't encounter any of Vald's troops on the way.

It was almost too dark to see in the hallway, but with Tobhi's guidance Daladir was able to make his way toward the eastern stairs, which would lead them to the stable yards. They slid quietly along the darkened corridor for a long time~Daladir couldn't tell the distance, and Tobhi was concentrating on listening for approaching enemies.

Once they reached the stairway, the quickening dawn through the windows aided their movement, and they made good time. Daladir was once again amazed at the size of Gorthac Hall~the place seemed so much bigger on the inside than it appeared from without. It wasn't a comforting thought, especially at this particular moment, when sanctuary already seemed so very far away.

Tobhi was still weak, and the rough bouncing on the he-Kyn's back sent his head spinning, but the Leafspeaker was aware enough to trust his instincts. The darkness ahead was dangerous.

"Wait," he hissed as they neared the top of the stairs. "I hear someone comin'."

"Is it Tarsa?"

"I can't tell yet." The Tetawa listened, his ears twitching nervously. "No, I don't think it is. Mebbe it's comin' from beneath us."

"Let's hope not," Daladir whispered, continuing forward.

The sound grew louder. It was coming from down the stairs, and approaching quickly. Daladir slid Tobhi to the floor and pulled out his knife. The shuffling of boots on the rough planks of the stairs grew louder, and suddenly the Steward appeared, a short-stocked musket in his quivering hand.

The Man and the he-Kyn stood staring at one another in surprise. A leering grin twisted the Steward's pock-marked features into an expression that was far from friendly. He pointed the musket barrel at Daladir's head and pulled back the hammer.

«What was it you said, Ambassador? That you'd cut my tongue out? Do you remember? Well, I'm going to blast your Unhuman face all over the walls, and let the hounds lick up the pieces. I'll show you what happens when you don't show Men the proper respect.» His finger tensed on the rod's firing lever.

«Ye talk too much,» Tobhi growled from the floor as he drove the sharpened end of his hatchet up into the Man's paunchy belly. The Steward let out a piercing scream. Daladir's hand shot forward, shoved the barrel of the gun under the Man's chin, and pushed on the trigger. The air exploded in blood, bone, flesh, fire, and smoke. The Steward's half-faceless body teetered for a moment on the stairs before collapsing backwards, smacking wetly all the way down. Wiping the gore from his face, Daladir swept Tobhi into his arms and slipped down the stairs, barely missing the Man's twisted body in his haste.

He stopped and peered around a corner. Satisfied that they were alone for the moment, he slid into the shadows of a long, westward-leading hallway. The only stairs downward met in the centre of the wood-panelled corridor. He and Tobhi said nothing, for at that moment they reached one of the few large windows on the second floor and looked outside. Dawning twilight lit the hallway.

"The Ubbetuk galleon!" Tobhi sighed. "They've arrived already! Tarsa must've already called 'em." The giant ship was anchored to the upper parapet of Vald's tower. It was a rather bold move, but perhaps the best option. It was a different Dragon than the one they'd arrived in~grander and much larger, shaped somewhat like a massive grey wasp~but this one looked far more protective than the last.

"We've got to find Tarsa." Daladir looked around. He now recognized where they were. This hall led to a central stairwell that opened to the first floor and various back passages. If they could avoid detection, they'd soon be at the stableyards.

A knot rose up in Daladir's throat. He remembered all too well the murder of his friend Fear-Takes-the-Fire in those very yards not so long before. It was an unwelcome memory right now, and it filled him with dread.

"We'd better go, Tobhi. Maybe Tarsa's already at the galleon." Shifting the Tetawi to a more comfortable position across his shoulders, Daladir looked back to the shadows one more time before dashing down the hallway toward the waiting Dragon.

The battle was fiercer than Tarsa had anticipated, especially after she encountered another group of Men on their way to ensure that the diplomats were dead. By the time she'd chased, battled, and disarmed the last of eight militiamen, she was in an unfamiliar part of the house. Her ribs were sending sharp spasms through her chest, and the shallow cuts and darkening bruises she received during the skirmish were slowing her down, but the pain was manageable, for now. What mattered most was reaching Tobhi and Daladir and getting out of Gorthac Hall. She would break the globe with the nightwasp, summon the Dragon, and then they would be on their way. Daylight wouldn't be their ally, but the galleon was swift, and once aboard they would have little to fear from the world of Men. At least for a little while.

She rushed down the hallway, which ended in a narrow door. Listening intently for a few brief moments for any suspicious sounds, Tarsa pulled on the latch, hopeful that this was the direction her companions had travelled. The door opened easily. The Wielder slipped into the dark room beyond and pulled the door shut behind her.

A thin window in the wall was the only source of light, but it was enough to show Tarsa that dawn had nearly arrived. She had to hurry. Looking around, she noticed that this small chamber was merely an entryway to another room that lay beyond a stout wooden door in the corner. The biting stench of iron was heavy here, and it made her weak, even though she had wrapped her stalks on the run and slipped the iron-ward back around her neck after the last encounter. She closed her eyes, breathing deeply. She could feel a sharp tingle in the air; something strange was strengthening the iron here.

Still, she had to go forward. Each moment brought them that much closer to discovery.

The she-Kyn used her wyrwood staff to softly lift the iron latch on the door, but it didn't move. She hissed angrily and looked around for something to help her. There was nothing. Cutting a strip from her leathers, Tarsa wrapped it around her hand and pulled on the latch, ignoring the sharp pain that streaked through her flesh. The door was heavy, and stubborn, but it was unlocked, and after straining a bit, Tarsa was able to pull it open enough to look out.

The door led to a narrow balcony overlooking a large chamber with stark, unvarnished plank walls. A large plaque with the three-tined iron star of Eromar dominated the wall opposite Tarsa's hiding place. A series of benches stretched across the lower floor, all facing a tall raised dais where Lojar Vald stood with a large group of Men, as if in anticipation. A narrow door in one corner was closed, and their eyes lingered there. Vald wore a fur-lined mantle over his thick jacket and well-tooled breeches, and a wide-brimmed black hat with silver buckles covered his head. The Men with him were similarly dressed, although none wore a hat in the Dreydmaster's presence.

They're waiting for something. She hadn't yet been seen. Her thirst for vengeance was largely sated; now she just wanted to find her friends and escape. She was tired, and the pain was getting worse.

Tarsa started back toward the small room when the far door opened below. Her eyes grew wide, and she suddenly couldn't breathe. Blood filled her mouth as she bit down on her tongue to keep from crying out.

It had to be a trick. It couldn't be the truth.

No. Not now. Not here.

Neranda Ak'Shaar, the she-Kyn leader of the Celestial Shields in Sheynadwiin, stood in the doorway, her silver cloak flowing like liquid moonlight down her shoulders, her pale blue features cold and proud. Behind the regal Lawmaker walked an unfamiliar Kyn wearing a blue head-cloth and black jacket, along with a handful of Shields that the young Wielder recognized from the Sevenfold Council.

Vald stepped forward and took Neranda's hand in his own. «Welcome, Lady Neranda. I was confident that your people would at last accept the inevitable. I assume that you have come to announce the happy news your-self?» His voice echoed almost too loudly through the chamber.

«No, Dreydmaster.» Neranda's demeanour was icy; she was in no mood for Vald's sarcasm. «The Sevenfold Council voted against your terms. They rejected the treaty unanimously.»

The Man dropped her hand. «Is that so?»

«It is.»

Vald looked at the group of Kyn and smiled softly. His features became almost gentle. «I see. If the Sevenfold Council has rejected this most gener-ous offer, my Lady, why are you here?»

Neranda seemed to shrink slightly, as if the burdensome weight of ages had suddenly settled into her bones. «Most of the Folk are superstitious and ignorant of the wider world. They are easily influenced, especially by the long discredited conjurors who use the fear of ghosts and spirits to separate the People from their good sense. They are not capable of making a wise decision in this matter. It is thus a heavy burden that my compatriots and I must assume. We have come to make the difficult choice for all the People, even if it against their baser wishes. We have come to sign the Oath.»

Tarsa shook with rage and terror and grief. *I could stop them. I could bring this hall crashing down on them, smash their treacherous skins into the dirt, drive them to the shadows once and for all.* Her skin began to burn as the *wyr* bubbled up, fighting past the iron-ward around her throat. The songs woven through the chanting sash no longer restrained her fury; rea-son and self-protection could no longer hold back her vengeance. It might mean her death, but she would destroy all the enemies of the Everland in one quick, swift blow.

Slowly, the power swirled around her, building in strength. Tarsa watched in disbelief as Neranda and the other Kyn in the chamber below each took a pale white quill in hand and signed their names to the Oath of Western Sanctuary. When they finished, Neranda turned away and walked slowly out of the room, her head bowed. Vald rolled up the parchment and smiled.

In that moment, at long last, the wave crested. With a roar, Tarsa flew from the balcony and landed, hard, just yards away from Vald and his retainers. A guard rushed to block her, but the wyrwood staff flashed in green fire, and he fell screaming, his body consumed by unquenchable flame. She drew Jitani's gift knife as other soldiers stepped in. Smiling broadly from a safe distance, Vald tipped his hat at the howling Wielder and followed Neranda through the door.

One of the soldiers leapt toward the Wielder, bringing his sword down with practiced ease. Tarsa easily blocked the blade, twisting the knife around to catch the Man's tunic, cutting down to the flesh. He cried out and stumbled away as another soldier threw himself at Tarsa's back, catching her around the waist and bringing her to the ground. Her staff flew across the chamber. Three more Men ran in with weapons drawn, and the wounded swordsman followed closely behind. They slid to a stunned stop, however, as their companion on the ground shrieked in sudden torment. Tarsa slowly stood, and the Men saw that her flesh had changed~dozens of long, wicked spikes covered her flesh like green knives, and the soldier who'd grabbed her was pierced through in a dozen or more places. He was delirious with the pain, and his blood-slick hands tried to push against the jagged barbs that impaled him against her, but it was hopeless, and he soon quivered in his death agonies.

Tarsa arched her back, the spikes withdrew, and the Man's body fell to the ground. She lifted her hand, and a green vine flew from her outstretched palm to the staff, wrapped firmly around the carved shaft, and drew it swiftly to her. The remaining Men turned toward the door, but a wall of spiny tendrils spread across their path with terrifying speed. There would be no escape.

"The reckoning has begun," Tarsa whispered, her eyes glazed over, her gaze distant. Voices called on the wind, voices that had too long been silenced by cold iron and wilful forgetfulness. She was the spark, and they were the tinder. The voices now inhabited the Wielder; she couldn't understand their words, but she understood their rage and grief, and she became their embodied will. They would be heard now.

The Men cried out and begged for mercy, but the Wielder ignored them. Holding the wrywood staff high in the air, she spoke in a low, hollow voice, and the air of the chamber crackled. A warm wind rose up, followed by blistering rains and a crash of thunder that shook the building's foundations. The floor split apart. Great green stalks as thick as tree trunks whipped upward, breaking through the ceiling and sending a shower of tile, plaster, and shattered wood crashing down on the screaming Men below. The she-Kyn's eyes glowed bright blue as she pointed the amber-topped staff at the doorway. A rush of green flame roared outward, and the chamber exploded in blood and fury.

The room was slick with sap and mud, and smoke hung heavy in the air. A great hole gaped wide where once the door had stood. Vald's militiamen lay dead around the room, their bodies ravaged by the elemental forces that the Wielder's grief and rage had unleashed. But the carnage was a failure: Neranda and the Dreydmaster were gone, and with them the treacherous treaty. Tarsa fell screaming to her knees, driving her bloodied fists against the shattered tiles on the floor.

Something jabbed the she-Kyn in her side, breaking through the haze of pain and anger. Her pouch had been knocked open in the chaos, and small, golden shards of thin metal lay crushed where she knelt. Her heart stopped as awareness flooded back. Hands shaking, Tarsa reached into the pouch and pulled out the fragments of the nightwasp's orb, along with the summoning insect's broken silver body.

"No," she groaned. "No...."

Betrayal

The nightwasp was dead. There would be no cloud-galleon, no rescue for her or her companions. The Expulsion had begun, and they were trapped in Gorthac Hall.

CHAPTER 7
BETRAYAL

"That en't the right ship," Tobhi whispered hoarsely. He and Daladir looked up at the docked Dragon with growing despair. They had followed the stairwell to the lower levels of Gorthac Hall, rushed through the servant galley to the stable yards, and slipped from shadow to shadow, stopping at an unused stall to catch their breath and prepare for the next desperate rush. Now they crouched in mouldy, dung-strewn hay that made Tobhi's nose wrinkle, and slowly comprehended the bitter certainty of the danger they now faced.

Daladir watched the great cloud-galleon with burning green eyes. Even with his own iron-ward, a necessity of all diplomats to Human lands, he shrank from the great iron machine and the clank and whirr of the gears and great gas bellows. Although tethered to the great tower of the Hall, the Dragon hovered at just the right angle above them to obscure the ship's passengers from their view. Another smaller airship—one of the numerous Ubbetuk trading skiffs that carried goods to and from the city—lay docked at the far end of the stable-yard.

A memory fluttered at Tobhi's thoughts. There was something familiar about the larger ship, something about the great wasp's alien visage crafted onto the bow. He'd seen it before. "That wasp ship. It belongs to—" he began, but the sharp blat of horns tore through the early morning stillness and silenced him.

Darooomah. Darooomah. Darooomah.

Horns of warning.

Horns of war.

A flurry of activity caught their attention. The great gas-bladders of the cloud-galleon began to swell, jets of steam and smoke shot out from the ship's underbelly, and the gangplank sagged from the march of feet hurrying across it. The Dragon would be leaving very soon.

Darooomah. Darooomah. Darooomah.

Then, something else came into view, a flash of green skin with dark hair flying behind. Tarsa was running toward the ship, and a raging storm followed, the staccato flare of lightning shimmering through dark clouds in her wake.

Darooomah. Darooomah. Darooomah.

Tobhi and Daladir watched in fascinated horror as the wooden gangplank began to wither, like a vine left too long in the hot sun. It buckled and twisted, groaning with the pressure until it exploded against the galleon in a shower of piercing fragments. A red-capped Ubbetuk cried out and plunged from the deck, followed by a figure wrapped in fluttering white robes, its body impaled by a massive spike from the shattered gangplank.

Casting caution aside, Tobhi and Daladir rushed out to find the broken bodies lying tangled together in the ice-rimmed mud of the stable yard. Tobhi called upward, uselessly trying to catch Tarsa's attention, while Daladir stared at the dead figures on the ground. The Redcap lay with wet eyes staring sightlessly into the sky, his body twisted backward, arms akimbo. It was the other shape, however, that now commanded the he-Kyn's attention. The shimmering white silks, like moonlight moving on snow, revealed as much as did the figure's oak-leaf ears, grey skin, and two tightly bound sensory tendrils.

"What is a Shield doing here?" Daladir asked softly, but he already knew the answer. He knew even as Tarsa stood on the tower parapet and pulled the iron-ward from her throat, her anguished voice ripping through the air with pain so deep and primal that the wooden timbers throughout Gorthac Hall buckled.

"SHAKAR!" A sudden surge of *wyr* crackled around them, sucking the air from their lungs. Thunder and lightning exploded in the sky, and where once an early dawn had greeted them, now fell icy sleet and blistering hail. Daladir stumbled back to the stable, dragging Tobhi with him, and they watched the bodies of the Shield and Redcap disappear in the sudden white blast. The small cloud-skiff slid in slow helplessness to the earth, over-

whelmed by the force of the storm.

"SHAKAR!" Tarsa shouted again, and again, through the raging winds and stinging hail, as the Dragon rose higher into the air away from the tower. A jagged fork of lightning skittered across the hull of the galleon. The air was alight in fiery response, but when the glow faded the Dragon sailed away, disappearing at last into the roiling clouds.

The Wielder remained standing on the tower, unfazed by the maelstrom around her. She had given a name to her quarry.

Shakar.

Traitor.

And the horns of Gorthac Hall blared on.

Neranda stood on the deck of the cloud-galleon and watched the tower of Gorthac Hall disappear in the distance, and with it the young Wielder whose grief-ravaged voice still burned in her ears.

Shakar.

The fury of the storm abated, the clouds thinned, and the cold daylight of early morning ruled the sky as the Dragon moved eastward toward the Everland. Neranda still watched the boiling storm in the west, unwarmed by the morning sun at this frigid height.

"Do you think we're safe now?" Pradu Styke emerged from below deck to stand beside the Lawmaker, who pulled her cloak closer to her chilled flesh. Though they were allies now, it was an alliance of necessity, not choice, and she still hadn't forgiven him for his earlier attempts to bribe her vote on a trading bill in the Kyn Assembly of Law. She had called his act treachery, yet the word was ashes in her thoughts now. Styke's voice still dripped with characteristic arrogance, but he clearly trembled from more than the cold.

The Shield shook her head. "We will never be safe again, Captain Styke. As you said before we arrived last night: 'We go to sign away our lives.' They will not forgive this treachery."

"This was not betrayal, Lawmaker. We simply did what no one else had the courage to do."

Shakar.

"Yes, of course we did." Neranda turned abruptly away from the he-Kyn and walked into the ship's hold, pulling the dirty hem of her robe away from her slippered feet as she descended the stairs. The oak-paneled hallway was lit by small oil lamps in recesses along the wall. Unlike the steady Kyn everlights, the glow from these lamps flickered and danced with the movement of air on the galleon, casting shifting green shadows along the walls. The Lawmaker thought for a moment about returning to wind and fresh air on deck, but instead opened the door to her own quarters. Styke's presence sickened her. The whole affair had gone too far out of control. She felt much like the cloud-galleon, tossed and battered by a storm not of her own making.

"Perhaps a restful sleep will ease your mind." The lamp-light in the hallway grew dim, almost dark, and then flashed to life again. Blackwick, the Ubbetuk Chancellor, stood in the open doorway. "May I join you for a moment before you retire?"

Neranda smiled gratefully, and the Chancellor limped forward, leaning heavily on his wasp-headed staff. His robes were less ornate than those he'd worn at the Sevenfold Council, but the lack of adornment seemed merely to enhance his imposing presence; the white fabric shimmered with the iridescence of woven diamonds. The she-Kyn and Ubbetuk nodded at one another before slipping into the plush chairs that sat bolted to the floor.

"The return journey will be a bit more leisurely than the first." The Chancellor scratched at his chin with a well-manicured claw. "The Dragons are marvels of engineering, but I would not risk such strain again, especially with the...unusual storm activity thus far. We should arrive in Sheynadwiin by tomorrow's dusk."

"Thank you, Chancellor. Your kindness eases my mind, although I must admit that I am not entirely eager to return." She leaned back stiffly in her chair.

They sat in silence for a while, relaxing into the slow rhythm of the ship. At last Neranda cleared her throat. "I had hoped that my legacy would be an enduring one, that future generations would see my leadership in the Sevenfold Council as the turning point in the creation of a promising future. Now everything is so muddled and confused." She hesitated, her voice thick with emotion. "Please forgive my impertinence, Chancellor, but I must ask you a question. Why did you help me sign the Oath after you voted against it with the rest of the Council? Do you not fear discovery?"

Blackwick turned to her, his eyelids heavy. All trace of the smile was gone, and in its place settled a deep sorrow. For the first time Neranda saw the burden of age bleed through the near-mythic reputation of shrewd diplomacy, political manoeuvring, and strategic machinations that had built up around the Chancellor over many long years. His was a powerful mind, but he was mortal, too, and bound by the same laws of mortality as the rest of his kith.

"Life is too often the unhappy path between painful choices, and this is the reality that besets us now. War would come to the Everland whether we signed the Oath or not; signing the document merely gives the appearance of tacit acceptance, an appearance that all involved know to be an illusion. Yet had the Ubbetuk turned away from our kindred and split the Council, the Folk would be torn apart from within, thus stripping us of any hope for withstanding the coming onslaught."

He shrugged and crossed his hands over the top of the staff. "Vald no longer has any need to use terror to compel us to sign; there may still be battles, but by signing the Oath you have given his crusade legal standing in the Reach, and no Human state will challenge its validity~not, at least, with force of arms. Without that hope to cling to, the spirit of resistance among the various Folk will be lessened, and emigration will be far more peaceful than it would have been if Vald had thrown his full fury upon us. Had that happened, we could have perhaps expected aid from the Humans of the Allied Wilderlands, Béashaad, or perhaps even Sarvannadad, and both the Everland and the lands of Men would have been torn apart by civil war and bloodshed. Vald will be cruel, certainly, and many of your people will die under the terms of the Oath, but more would have died if Vald had been defied entirely."

"You do not believe that the Dreydmaster will honour his word at all?"

Now a frigid smile passed over the Chancellor's thin lips, and his eyes narrowed to slits. "I am neither a fool nor an idealistic dreamer. Vald cannot be trusted~the Man is ravenous. He seeks blood and power, and each taste leaves him ever hungrier for more."

"But what would it benefit him to violate the Oath?"

"Have you heard nothing, Lawmaker?" he hissed, his soft voice almost too low to hear. "These treaties and agreements are fragile, written on paper that is easily burned. The Folk may regard words and promises as sacred, but Men have forgotten those truths. To them, treaties are merely convenient and efficient means of getting what they want while appearing to be eminently reasonable and conciliatory. There will be more agreements, which they will violate again and again, and then they will insist that we negotiate again and again based on the unjust terms of those same documents. They are some measure of protection, but only as far as Men are willing to honour them, too. Vald is a liar, a thief, and a murderer. Eromar is drenched in the blood of his own people, and the blood of the Folk will flow there before this storm passes. There is no hope for fidelity from such people. Our only hope rests in his belief that we are no obstacle to his ambitions. You have given him reason for that belief."

Neranda leaned forward, her face stricken. "Is death, then, the future you see for your own people?"

"The Ubbetuk live in every Human nation throughout the Reach. No general goes to war without first consulting his 'Goblin' tactician. No wealthy maiden attends a party without asking her 'Goblin' retainer for advice on etiquette and the latest fine fashions. There is no house of power in all the Reach of Men that is untouched by the hand or thought of the Swarm. Even Eromar itself depends on our machinery and iron-crafting for their great foundries and factories. Do you think this is mere coincidence? We survive by making ourselves so necessary to the functioning of this Melded world that we cannot be removed. If a new Purging begins, everything Men have crafted will collapse. They cannot kill us without killing themselves. Their survival depends upon our own. The Ubbetuk have no need of the Everland to endure."

Blackwick held up his walking staff and examined the carved head intently. "Do you know why the wasp is the symbol of the Swarm, Lawmaker? Above all else, the Ubbetuk are a people dedicated to survival~there is nothing more important than that. We will always survive. Your people, too, are swift and beautiful, with duties and passions of your own, but you are more akin to bees. Your hives are lovely, your honey sweet, and you are fearless when enemies attack. But a bee can sting only once, and then it dies.

"The wasp, however, is different. It may not have the golden comb and flow of honey, but it can sting again and again and again. It is merciless in its defence of home and nest. And there is no place that a wasp cannot make its home. No place at all."

His words hung in the air. Neranda grew pale as she studied the alien visage on the staff. "If such is the case, why not simply vote with your conscience and against consensus?"

Blackwick laughed, a thin, dry sound, like torn birch-paper. "I did vote with my conscience, Lawmaker. The Folk will be driven to the shadowy West, but they will do so with a feeling of righteousness, and this will give them strength to survive in the dark days to come. Had I voted in favour of the Oath, the other Folk would see the Ubbetuk as the architects of their suffering, with unnecessary death as a result on each side. I did not lie at the Council. We are kith yet, and though your peoples' dependence on the Everland is a terrible weakness that we do not share, we still acknowledge our bonds of kinship. If the Folk saw us as enemies, the enduring hatred and deaths that would result could never be made right. Such division could bring nothing but suffering. I would not have that burden on my shoulders, Lawmaker."

"But I signed the Oath. Will not that create division? Will not...." She suddenly stopped, her eyes widening with dawning horror. It was all becoming terribly clear.

"No, it will not." The Chancellor shook his head. His expression was impassive, emotionless. "That division already exists among the Kyn. Once the dying starts, once the elders and young ones fall, your betrayal will bring your people together as one again. They will look past the silly squabbles between the Old Ways of the forest and the New Ways of the sky, for a while at least, and turn their attention to survival. Their rage and sorrow will fall upon the Oathsworn, and as your blood falls, the Kyn Nation will be reborn."

"But you..." she whispered. "You helped me. That Wielder saw you. They'll know...."

"What will they know? I never stepped into the Hall; indeed, I never once left the galleon. I came to Eromar City simply to ensure the safe transport of two high-ranking Goldcap trade merchants back to Sarvannadad, both of whom are now aboard and resting comfortably; I was both shocked and saddened to discover that you used my generous offer of transportation to engage in such unlawful activities. Such betrayal particularly grieves me because of my very public opposition to the odious terms of the Oath of Western Sanctuary."

Blackwick stood and gently smoothed the wrinkles from his robes as he stepped to the door. Without turning, in a voice little louder than a whisper, he said, "It seems that you have left your sting behind, Lawmaker. But do not fear: your betrayal may yet ensure the survival of your people. In years to come, they will speak your name, and those of your compatriots. The Oathsworn will be known for generations, and the Kyn will curse your names. Rest assured–your legacy will most certainly endure...Shakar." The lamps in the hall dimmed, and when they flickered back to life, the Chancellor was gone.

Neranda buried her face in her shaking hands, her nails scoring long, jagged lines down her cheeks. She rocked back and forth silently as the lamp-light danced around her. The only sounds to be heard in her chamber were the mechanical groans of the great Dragon as it cut smoothly eastward through the clouds.

The horns continued to bleat, even as the massive cloud-galleon vanished into the clouds and the storm raged around the tower. The hail had ended, but the rain that drove down continued pummelling the earth. Tobhi and Daladir could still see Tarsa on the parapet, her hands tightly clutching the wyrwood staff.

"Why isn't she coming down?" Daladir yelled, trying to be heard over the peal of thunder and the maddening burst of the horns.

Tobhi peered through the rain. "She can't. There en't no way down but the tower stairs, and I'll bet m' knock-kneed deer that Vald's Men is blockin' that route." He looked around. "I guess we'll just have to figure out some way up there ourselves."

"We can't go back into the Hall." Daladir shook his head. "There isn't any way."

The Leafspeaker turned to the he-Kyn, his face beaming, and pointed. "Oh, I en't so sure 'bout that." Daladir followed the gesture to a handful of golden-capped Ubbetuk rushing around a large shape that lay indistinct in the raging storm.

Before the he-Kyn could say anything, Tobhi unslung his hatchet and rushed out into the rain. With an exasperated sigh, Daladir followed after.

Fight on, spirits of the raging sky. Share your fury with me for a while longer, I beg you. Let your cleansing wrath fall upon this poisoned place.

Tarsa felt the *wyr* surge through her body in response to her desperate appeal. Blue-green fire danced across her skin to arc in a blistering burst across the swords that hovered over her. The first Man fell, followed by the second, and a third, but Tarsa knew that she wouldn't be able to stop them all. The tower doorway was too wide, and she was weakening fast. As her

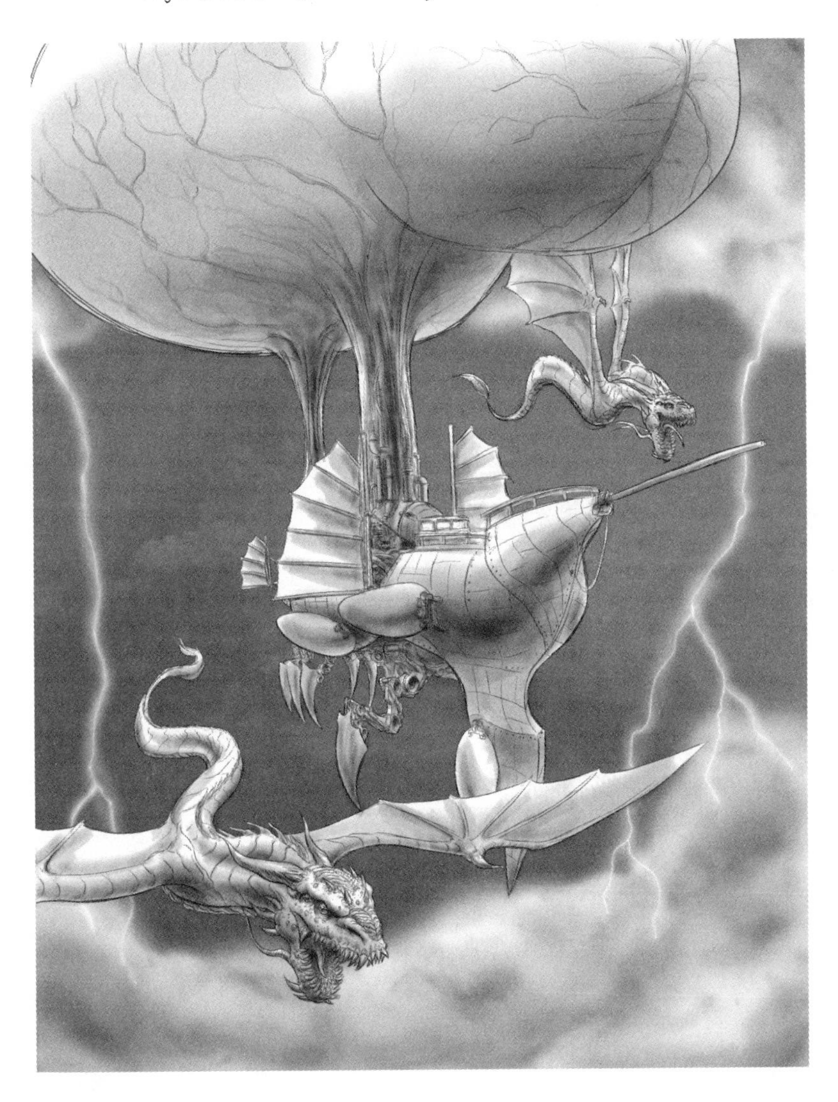

Dragon

thoughts wandered, the flash of an iron crossbow bolt shot past her head. She heard the click of another bolt being readied. The Men were preparing for the final assault, and this time she didn't have the strength to stop them before they brought her down.

Very well. If this was the way death would find her, she'd make sure that it would haunt Men's darkest dreams for years to come. The Wielder took a deep breath and flung herself forward again. They were ready. A club clipped her in the shoulder and she stumbled backward. Her staff shot out, parried, smashed into an arm, a jaw, caught the edge of a sword and snapped the arm holding it. A blade tore into her free hand; a bolt pierced her upper thigh. The storm grew in intensity as her own blood glistened in the flashes of sky-fire.

Tarsa smiled grimly. She could feel the *wyr* drain from her as a wreath of lightning suddenly crackled around the tower and crashed into the parapet, sending stone shards flying and Men screaming. The wood on the east side of the tower caught fire from the intense heat, in spite of the pouring rain.

Another explosion of thunder shook the tower. Buffered by the *wyr*, Tarsa felt nothing more than a sudden shift beneath her feet, but the Men around her covered their bleeding ears and crouched screaming on the trembling planks. The horns stopped. A groan crawled across the structure's stones and timbers, growing louder from below, as though a creature of the deep earth was rising up, tearing its way to the surface. The tower trembled and began to buckle. Those militiamen unbroken by the storm jammed the stairwell, trying desperately to escape. The she-Kyn Wielder was now forgotten.

Tarsa leaned wearily on her staff as another burning blast of lightning illuminated the tower like sudden daylight. It was over, or soon would be. She slipped to one knee, her flesh tearing on the jagged plank, as the tower shifted again. She couldn't do any more. The *wyr* had left her. Though the tempest remained, the spirits of this strange land had slipped back into slumber, and she didn't have the strength to call upon them again.

Then, as though stepping from mid-air, Tobhi appeared out of the storm-shrouded darkness.

"Tarsa! Grab m' hand!" And he was gone again, lost in the smoke and rain. But only for a moment. He swung wildly in the air, tied to the end of a thick rope that hung off a small Ubbetuk cloud-skiff. Tarsa could see the small ship through the flashes of fire and lightning. It bounced and fluttered like a giant moth, buffeted by ferocious winds and driving rain. Tobhi swung back into view. His hat was missing, and his long black hair whipped around his face and neck.

He thrust out his hands again, and this time Tarsa tried to grab him, but the tower moaned and the planks moved under her feet, sending her sprawling. Breathing heavily, she pulled herself up on trembling legs, holding her free hand to the sky, reaching out to his flailing hands.

"Down!" Tobhi screamed to Daladir and the young Goldcap Ubbetuk beside him. The winds were dangerously erratic. The Tetawa cursed loudly as the little Dragon dipped and shot up again, sending him spinning in a wide, uncontrollable arc.

"Tarsa, hurry!" he cried out to the wind, not at all sure where she was, where he was, or whether she could even hear him. His stomach twisted into a knot of nausea as he reached out one more time.

The tower's groan shifted in pitch, rising to a thunderous roar. The screams of the Men in the stairwell were lost in the raging noise, and at last the structure crumbled. The shattered mass plummeted to earth, and a choking cloud of dust and ash burst up from the ruins.

In the air above the broken tower of Gorthac Hall, a cloud-skiff bobbed awkwardly. Below it, hanging from a heavy rope, were an airsick Tetawa and a worn and weary she-Kyn. Half-conscious, Tarsa clutched at Tobhi with one hand; in the white-knuckled grip of the other, she held Unahi's wyrwood staff, its amber head aglow in the new dawn's light. Daladir tugged at the rope, slowly drawing them upward. The small Dragon jerked in the air, wounded by the storm but not broken, and limped its way east, toward the Everland.

CYCLE FOUR

THE HILL OF BROKEN PINES

The Dreyd were not the first gods of Men. They were usurpers, unsatisfied with the knowledge given to the ever-dying world, unwilling to accept the Chain of Fate as it was forged, link by link, within the great soul-foundries of the Immortals of Old. Chaos was the bastard child of the Old Ones, and Men despised and feared Him, for He gave honour to none, and He loved many, cruel and kind in turn. None stood high in the eyes of Chaos, so Men created Law, and She brought Chaos to heel and sought to bind Him in walls of stone and shackles of iron. Law was cruel, but She was predictable, and Men loved Her even as they feared Her. But Chaos could not be contained, and He slipped free of Law's embrace and laughed at Her fury. And He returned to the world of Men, unchanged, bringing joy and pain with every step, caring no more for one than for the other.

The Old Immortals were drinkers of blood and wine, slaves to sacrifice and adoration. They indulged their wild son and scorned the hard-eyed daughter of Men. And they laughed when the Dreyd sought the hidden mysteries of the Veil Between Worlds. But their laughter was short-lived, for Kaantor, the Great King of the fertile valley of Karkur, had penetrated into the mysteries and returned again with their secrets. The Veil tore apart, the Old Immortals fell screaming to earth, and the Dreyd rose up to take their place. These priests and alchaemists thought to bring Law with them into eternity, but they were deceived, for when the Blind Lady removed Her mask, the Dreyd wept in despair: it was Chaos who looked laughing upon them.

And yet the Dreyd still seek to trap the bastard son of the Immortals of Old, but they know now that Law is a lie crafted for Men's comfort. So they try to give Her flesh, to place life in those nerveless fingers, and the greater their efforts, the greater the mirth of Chaos. So it has been for a thousand years, and so it will always be, as long as the Dreyd reign and the memory of the world remains lost.

CHAPTER 8
THRESHOLDS

Even with her eyes pinched tightly closed, Denarra couldn't avoid the dawn, as the single sun's first light cut through her consciousness like forge-heated needles. She groaned with over-dramatic emphasis and pulled her pillow over her head, but there was no escape—she'd forgotten to lower the curtains before falling into bed, and now the morning's brightness was everywhere. She couldn't quite bring herself to face the dawn today, or any day for that matter; she normally slept until mid-morning, or early afternoon if she'd had spirited company the night before. Once awake, she generally found it impossible to go back to sleep, at least until later in the day, when the lush interior of her brightly-coloured wagon would be a welcome respite from the prairie's afternoon heat.

Though the cool shadows of twilight were long gone, and though she was well aware that sleep was past, the curvaceous Strangeling lingered in bed for a little while longer. When she mustered the courage to finally open a bleary, sleep-crusted eye, she let out another groan and slid back under the silken coverlet. The wagon was a mess. Overturned crockery, half-drained jugs of various local and regional wines, a partially-eaten loaf of bread and a rather pungent piece of white-skinned cheese covered the narrow table and bench, and miscellaneous articles of bright, perfumed clothing were scattered on the floor, chairs, tables, with the most intimate articles hanging from her cabinet doors and draped over the head of the small statue of a strutting peacock.

As her thoughts came together through the haze of wine-addled sleep, the last items brought a flash of recognition to her face. She sat up, slowly, and stared at the three shapes slumbering in the bed beside her, their well-muscled chests rising and falling softly, sun-bronzed limbs wrapped together, slightly damp locks curled and pasted to their foreheads. As the pleasing memories of the previous night's events slowly returned, Denarra shook her head, wincing as a pounding headache announced itself with the force of Gvaerg war drums.

Farmhands, she berated herself. *Suns save you, Denarra Syrene, what's the appeal?*

She lifted a corner of the blanket and gave the young Men a more thorough appraisal. She couldn't help but grin; it all made perfect sense now. Gorgeous farmhands and triplets.

Of course.

It took her a while to disengage herself from the firm, sweat-moistened knot of arms, legs, and other fleshy appendages~a struggle she didn't particularly mind~but she eventually managed to stumble to her wardrobe and into a tight-fitting emerald dressing-gown that she'd chosen specifically because the striking hue matched her eyes and complemented her dyed auburn hair. While her guests remained soundly asleep, Denarra stepped outside into the already warm day and walked barefoot to the oak-staved barrel at the back of the wagon. The water within was ice-cold and clear. She squeezed her eyes shut and took a quick breath before dunking her head. She rose up again, sputtering and gasping, and finally felt the morning's mind-fog clear away.

She'd forgotten to bring a towel, so the water streamed down her face and neck and pasted the clinging gown to her skin. Now fully awake, she idly considered waking up her young guests to show them how transparent and form-fitting the wet cloth actually was. Given their performance the night before, she had no doubt that they'd be more than eager for a frolic before breakfast. She was half inclined for a pinch and giggle herself. But with full awareness came a sudden knot of unease in her stomach that had nothing to do with the glistening tangle of luscious Man-flesh in her wagon.

Denarra turned to the east, toward the Everland. The caravan was in the southern stretches of Eromar, miles away from the southern edge of that ancient territory of shadowed forests and reaching peaks, but she could always feel the green lands calling her back. It had been years since she'd been home; she shared her parents' mutual restlessness, and she'd long ago given herself to the road and all its unpredictable ways. Hers was a sometimes wearying life, with too few opportunities to sit and enjoy the quieter side of sociability. Her temperament wasn't much suited to domesticated pleasures, nor to tradition, and her father's people had no great love for a Strangeling who seemed bent on following the wild ways of her Human mother far more than the grounded Kyn teachings of her father. Over the years she'd found many places to call home, at least temporarily, and Bremen and Crowe's Medicine Show and Repertory of Thespian Delights was among the better of them; she didn't stick out as particularly freakish among this motley company of actors, acrobats, musicians, and minor miscreants, and her various mundane and marvellous skills were quite useful for a group of wanderers who, on occasion, skirted both propriety and legality. This life would do for a while, at least until she could get back to the marble-lined streets and gilded domes of Chalimor, the greatest city of Men in the Reach. It was the one place besides the Everland that always called to her, and it was the only call she happily answered. The ways of the road could be lonely, but it was better than feeling a foreigner in your own homeland.

Still, as the tightness in her stomach reminded her, Denarra would always be tied to her birth-home through blood and history. She could keep running for the rest of her life, but she'd never be free of the Everland; it would always inhabit her, twisted deep within spirit and memory, no matter how far the road might stretch. And the closer she came to the often unseen barrier between the Reach of Men and the lands of the Folk, the clearer that link became.

Yet as she looked off to the eastern horizon, squinting her eyes against the hot sun, a trickle of fear crept down her back. The boundary between the haven of the Folk and the world of Men wasn't unseen any longer. She could see it just fine now.

It was smoke. The border of the Everland burned.

The dream always begins the same way. It's a soft purple evening, the spice of pine sap heavy on the drowsy air. Quill sits in her bent-root chair beside the fireplace. The apple-head dolls crowd around her, singing a low, soft melody, their distinct voices melting together, deep as taproots, old as stone. The Tetawa doesn't sing, but she listens and taps her foot in time to the song. The dolls nod approvingly and their voices grow stronger, the words fading beneath the rhythm. Soon the entire cabin is alive with the sound–every tile, every swatch of cloth, every kiln-fired plate. It's an ancient song, with words unknown to any but the dwellers of the Spirit World. It ties the Dolltender to her memas and grannies, all those firra before her who spoke to the dolls and knew of those ancient days in the Eld Green, when the world belonged to the Folk alone, when there were no walls between the Folk and their Spirit cousins. Those days are lost to all but memory now, and to the dolls, who remind her.

Quill sits in her chair, listening to the song, and finishes sewing a tight edge on the long red sash in her lap. The sash is the colour of old blood. She has double-stitched black trim to the edge, from which emerges the silhouettes of badgers dancing across the long red field. It's a gift.

She feels the knock more than she hears it; it's too soft to be heard over the song. The dolls move aside, singing still, as the young firra drapes the sash across her arm and steps to the door to welcome her visitor. The door swings open, but it's not a welcome guest who stands in the doorway.

A claw slashes forward and catches the sash, tearing a jagged hole through it with a single motion. Quill sees yellow, watery eyes, and hears the bubbling giggle, and the figure stands tall, looming above her, its jagged teeth dripping with slime and blood.

She sees the clawed hand rise again, and she tries to scream, but her voice is lost in the song, which goes on and on and on…

Quill jerked awake. She gasped and clutched at her hand, where the bone embroidery needle dug deeply into her palm. Pulling the needle from her flesh, she lifted her hand to her mouth and looked down at the sash. A thick droplet of dark red blood glistened for a moment on the surface before vanishing into the thirsty cloth.

Someone was at the door. She looked around, her heart suddenly beating wildly. The dolls were again on their own shelves, where they'd been since Medalla and Gishki helped her put her own house back in order. Those *firra* lay in Quill's bed, sleeping soundly after the stress of recent days, but the Dolltender couldn't sleep and had chosen to sit beside the fireplace and continue working on the sash. She'd slept in her chair for the past three nights, unable to find comfort in her own bed. A few logs crackled softly in the hearth; a kettle steamed from its hook above the flames. Otherwise, all was silent.

The knock sounded again, more insistent now. Her heartbeat drummed loudly in her ears, but she stood anyway, bare feet dragging slightly on the stone floor. There was desperation in the sound, a need calling out to her. Quill glanced up at the dolls, but their eyes were dull and vacant, nothing like the brilliant black stars they'd been in the dream.

One brown hand closed firmly over her stout, smoothed-pine walking stick beside the door, while the other slid hesitantly over the door latch. Her breath rose and fell in quick, short pants. There was silence beyond the door now, waiting for her to open the threshold wide. She clutched the walking stick until her knuckles went white, and then the door was open, and she was standing with weapon raised against a trio of figures barely illuminated by the light streaming out from the cabin. Quill froze as she stared at one figure in particular, the mundane world suddenly lost in impossibility, and the staff was on the ground and she was in his strong arms, crying with joy and relief, her words nearly lost in sobbing breaths as the words she'd dreamed of saying for so long at last found voice.

"Etobhi, my love, where have you been?"

«Only one this time?» the Woman asked impatiently, her thin voice already grating on him. «You seem to be losing your touch, Vergis.»

The Seeker watched the guards drag the Deerman toward the holding pens, where the creature would be kept until the wagons to Eromar were full and ready to transport. Thane and his prisoner had arrived at the assembly hall in the early afternoon, and now he was finishing the obligatory interrogation. «The Fey-Touched are getting harder to find these days, Carinne, especially in the outer reaches. I caught the trace of a few others, but I wanted to deliver this one before following after them.» He leaned back in his chair, his mud-stained boots propped up on the Binder's desk, and drew deeply on his pipe.

After casting a cold eye at Thane's breach of etiquette, the old Binder nodded and returned to scribbling in the voluminous tome shackled to her bony wrists. «It's a good thing that you arrived when you did. The Dreydmaster has called for all the faithful to prepare for the Unhuman Expulsion. This should make your Seeking that much easier.»

«No, it won't.» Thane spat out a loose piece of tobacco. «The last thing I need is for a bunch of hot-headed flatlanders to be pushing my quarry deeper into those damned hills. It's hard enough to find them in their villages without having to ferret out their hiding holes.»

«It can't be as bad as all that.»

«I don't tell you how to Bind, Carinne, so don't try turning Seeker on me now. I've been over more of that land than any Man I've ever met, and I'm telling you that this latest plan of Vald's is going to cause us all a lot more trouble than he knows.»

Carinne's bird-like features jutted forward. «That's Dreydmaster Vald, 'Seeker' Thane. You've been a little too independent for too long, I think. Your impertinence is going to get you into trouble one day. The Purifiers are always eager to bring the proud and haughty to the High Hall in Bashonak. Talented you certainly are, Vergis, but don't count yourself too precious. Perhaps you could use a reminder about the proper respect for our honoured leaders and their inspired dictates.»

Thane's lip curled slightly, but he knew that this was a losing battle. Carinne may have looked like a half-drowned buzzard, but she was the undisputed voice of the Dreydcaste in the Half Moon Hills and the southern edge of Eromar, and her fidelity to the ambitious Dreydmaster of Gorthac Hall was unwavering. This was an argument for another time. For now, Thane merely nodded and continued smoking his pipe.

Carinne smiled as she finished writing in the book. She motioned to the Seeker, who read over the transcribed account of his latest assignment and signed at the end with the ink-stained quill. The Woman sprinkled a handful of sand liberally over the wet ink, blew the excess back into the sand-bowl, and shut the great scarred tome, her Binding chains rattling loudly in the largely empty room.

«We may not have many more opportunities to find them in their wild places, Vergis, while they're still pure in their powers, so I'm sending you out again as soon as you're ready. We haven't much more time. Do you, perchance, have any objection to that proposal?»

Even if he had, it wouldn't have made much difference, as the Binder permitted no defiance, even while pretending to give choices. It hardly mattered. Thane had little interest in remaining in Chimiak for any longer than a bath, new travel gear and hardtack, maybe a little fun with a wide-hipped whore, and a good night's sleep.

He finished his meeting with Carinne and headed to the barracks behind the hall, where he could begin with the bath while a novice filled his supply order. The whore and sleep would come later.

The barracks included both a communal bathing room and, particularly for Seekers, a series of smaller bath chambers for unsociable individuals. It was the latter that Thane sought, and he found an unoccupied cell without difficulty. The white stone walls of Chimiak were built on the site of natural hot springs, so most of the public buildings and all of the Dreydcaste structures had a plentiful supply of hot water. Thane undressed and eased himself into the small stone pool, feeling the tensions of his latest journey slowly work themselves out of his muscles.

He pulled the patch away from his eye and slid under the water, feeling the burning tingle of water envelop his body. It wasn't quite so intense that it blistered the flesh, but it was just hot enough to drive the flesh to its sensory limits. He didn't mind the sulphurous smell, nor the gritty residue that remained after even a short bath in the springs. It beat the mud, sweat, and other accumulated grime of the traveller's life. He surfaced and floated to the side of the pool, his thoughts wandering on the water.

Though the lowest of the Dreydcaste, the Seekers were also the most vital to its survival, for it was through their clarity of purpose and diligence that the Fey-Touched were found and captured. Without the Seekers, the Binders would have to draw upon their own lifeblood in their alchaemical incantations, and they would wither away to ashes much too soon. As it was, the soul-tomes shackled to their wrists were the only true defence they had from being consumed by their manipulating powers.

Seekers had no such weaknesses. The greatest risk a Seeker faced was sympathy; the many faces of their captured quarry rarely faded with time.

Thane had little worry about this failure. If he'd ever needed a reminder of how dangerous the Fey-Touched could be, the eye-patch and a grotesque series of scars on his belly were enough. No matter how many tears his quarry shed, no matter how great the ransom promised or brutal the vengeance sworn, they rarely found an escape from Vergis Thane. None but a small handful had ever successfully evaded him: a Fey-witch and her other Unhuman friends who'd long ago scarred and cast him down into the darkness from which it took him years to emerge. Already one had fallen to swift, certain death at the merciless edge of his blades. Another he'd mutilated and left more dead than alive; if she'd survived, hers was no doubt a greatly diminished existence. As for the last one~well, he would never cease that hunt, even into the next life, if necessary.

But that wasn't the mocking face of his long-sought quarry that floated before him now. Instead, the sandy-haired image of a young Brownie maiden returned to his thoughts. Brownies, though so inconsequential on the surface, had often been the most nettlesome of the Unhumans to the Seeker. Thane didn't understand why, but those little people had a strange ability to shroud their Fey-Touched radiance, and he had few hunts in Brownie country. Still, the little maid with the dolls had lingered in his thoughts long after he left her house, and Thane was sure that this feeling was more than simply the disquieting feeling left by the strange, hunchbacked hound with yellow eyes that scampered away from the household's slaughtered pigs. He'd long ago learned to trust his hunches. The Brownie was Touched, of that he was certain, but she was different from anything he'd encountered before. That alone was enough reason to return.

But there was something else. Whatever that dog-shaped creature was, it was there for more than fresh meat. It was looking for something, too. Thane knew well the sweet, tangled scent of a hunter and its prey.

He reached into a copper urn resting on the side of the pool for a handful of coarse soap flakes. The mystery would resolve itself soon enough. For now, he turned his attention to the bath. In his long experience, no whore liked a dirty Man.

Quill's happy cries had woken Medalla and Gishki, and they now sat with the visitors~young Tobhi, whom they had known for many years, and the two grim, silent Kyn with him~eating a makeshift dinner of rice stew, deer-milk cheese, thick bread, and winter willow tea. Quill glowed as she sat beside her travel-weary lover, her fingers twined in his long hair, her head leaning softly on his shoulder. Tobhi pulled her close to his side as he ate, content in spite of the deep circles under his eyes and the ache in his muscles. After hearing about Tobhi's recent adventures, the Dolltender told the visitors about the recent events around Spindletop, the Skeeger who'd seemed to hunt her after slaughtering a Tetawa cub, and of the strange Man who'd driven the Skeeger away and left before dawn.

Tobhi nodded. "I en't surprised, givin' what's been happenin' throughout the Everland lately. Men are gettin' bolder than ever, and all sorts of monsters is comin' out of the shadows of old stories. We'll see more of these beasties afore the end, I reckon." He glanced at Tarsa and Daladir, but they'd long ago lapsed into a dark silence.

The Leafspeaker shook his head. Had it really been only five days since they'd fled Eromar? The damaged cloud-skiff had borne only enough fuel to reach the far western edge of the Everland, on the southern edge of Meshiwiik Forest. It was far from the best site for landing, as the territory was still dangerously close to the grasp of Eromar, but the Ubbetuk had refused to push the small Dragon beyond its strength. When they'd landed, the youngest and most sympathetic of the merchants, Lowknobbin, gave Tobhi some travel rations and offered them various oils from the ship's hold, but he couldn't convince his five companions to assist the travelers any further. Tobhi could hardly blame them, as he and Daladir had forced the Ubbetuk into this sudden and dangerous journey when they'd commandeered the ship. While he'd have preferred to have taken the skiff all the way to Sheynadwiin, he knew they were lucky to have gotten as far as they had already.

Still, good fortune had been with them, for although they were farther away from the heart of the Kyn Branch-hold, they'd landed quite closely to the wild, tree-thick country that Tobhi called home: Spindletop, the Edgewood, the Hollow Hills. They would find help here, and then they could hurry to Sheynadwiin.

Besides, he'd had a long-overdue visit to make.

It had been nearly two years since he'd set out from the forested hill-country near Spindletop to meet with his aunt Jynni Thistledown at the Gathering of Clans in Mossydell. That was where everything began for him. But before he'd left on that snowy morning, he held a sandy-haired *firra* close and kissed her full lips with the promise that he'd return. He'd sent letters and gifts with the occasional traveller heading that direction, but it wasn't as much as either of them had wanted.

So tonight, he kept the full measure of his promise.

But what now? Tobhi turned to look at Quill. Her dark eyes were warm, and they drew him deep. Yet he knew that he couldn't stay. And he also knew that, if things went as badly as Tarsa and Daladir feared, he might never be able to come back. He might not even have anything to come back to.

Medalla stood and clapped a hand on his shoulder, interrupting the Leafspeaker's troubled thoughts. "Welcome home, Tobhi. We'll leave you now; I'm sure you've got plenty to talk about." She glanced sadly at Quill. *She knows*, Tobhi realized as Medalla moved toward the door and motioned to Gishki. "It's nearly dawn," she said to the Dolltender. "We'll check back on you around mid-day."

Quill smiled and held her cousins' hands tightly as she walked them to the door. "Can you believe it? Tobhi's back! I told you he'd be home again." She could barely keep her eyes off him as she spoke. "We'll have a welcoming feast tomorrow night to celebrate!"

"I'm so happy for you, Quill," Medalla said, her voice hoarse. With a doubtful glance at Tobhi and his companions, she slipped into the darkness beyond, followed silently by Gishki.

After bolting the door, the Dolltender turned to her visitors. "My room is on the left, and my spare room is on the right. You're welcome to either one."

Tarsa looked at the Tetawa and nodded, smiling in spite of her exhaustion. "Thank you, Quill. It's been a long time since we've slept without fear or cold as our companions. I'm only sorry that we can't be better guests."

The *firra* shook her head. "You're welcome regardless, Tarsa. If you're Tobhi's friends, then you're mine as well. Please, make yourselves at home. I'll have hot water ready for a bath when you wake up."

Tarsa headed down the short hallway, then stopped and turned to Daladir. "You'll need your sleep, too, Ambassador. We can share the room and give them some time alone."

He looked up, his green eyes heavy. "Should I take the floor?"

She laughed, the shadows momentarily slipping from her face. "No need, so long as you're less selfish with the blankets than you've been with the bedroll these past few nights! Given our past tenday together, modesty doesn't hold much between us, Daladir. I think you've been too long in the world of Men. You're back on home ground now, or near enough to it. Things are different here."

Daladir smiled thinly and followed her into the guest room.

The Tetawi were alone now in the main room of the cabin. It was still dark outside. Tobhi stood and scratched his chin nervously. "Well, I s'pose I can lay m' bedroll here aside the fireplace. Ye reckon I might have a bit of that hot water later, too?" He cleared his throat.

The Dolltender didn't respond. She stood and walked around the room, blowing out the oil lamps, leaving only the dancing flames of the hearth to light the room. Then she returned and took his hand as she led him to the fire, where she slowly unlaced his sweat-soiled jerkin. Tobhi trembled at her touch.

Quill left him again, but only for a moment. The Leafspeaker heard splashing, and then she was beside him once more, a washcloth draped over her forearm, a large wooden bowl in her hands that was half-filled with cold water and a handful of dried flower petals. She filled the bowl now with hot water from the steaming kettle. Pulling the *fahr* closer, the Dolltender slipped his jerkin off, dipped the rag into the fragrant warm water, and ran it over his skin. Tobhi moaned.

"Quill, ye don't have to…." Her finger pressed against his lips, and then her own lips were there, soft and full and warm. She brought the moist rag against his chest and felt his nipples harden beneath her fingers.

They sank together onto the tiles before the hearth. Quill's own garments joined Tobhi's on the floor, and soon their unbound bodies shimmered and moved with a gentle rhythm, brown skin glistening like liquid bronze in the firelight.

Vald examined the ruins of the tower impassively and with little interest. The centre of Gorthac Hall had been crushed by the falling stones and timber, and with it, remarkably, only eighteen members of the household, not counting the score of soldiers who'd been killed in the attempt to dispatch the Wielder and her friends. It hadn't taken long for Vorgha, the

Dreydmaster's personal attendant, to organize both labourers and militia together in repairing the breach in the Hall, and even now, in the darkest hours of early morning, there were hundreds of Men and Women swarming over the broken structure like so many dusty ants, desperate to appear busy under the Dreydmaster's unyielding gaze.

The Man turned back to the stable yard, where the bodies of the Kyn Shield and the Redcap Goblin lay swollen and crumpled, now five days dead. The terrible storm invoked by the Fey-witch had continued long after her departure, turning the yard into a pasty mass of mud and slimy dung, but Vald cared little for such trivialities. He looked up again to the site of the tower, which was brightly illuminated by hundreds of torches jammed here and there in the ruins.

«Your Authority?» Vorgha slipped across the muddy yard toward Vald, limp hair sticking to the thick sweat on his pallid brow. The attendant was unused to such labour, but he didn't dare to complain in word or deed. The Dreydmaster had no patience with laziness.

«What is it?»

«We've completed our search of the rubble, and it's certain that both airships escaped intact. However, by all reports the smaller craft was heavily damaged in the storm, so it's quite likely that they crashed somewhere between here and the Everland. I've ordered seized some of the city's remaining airships and loaded our soldiers into them; they began a broader search for the witch and her associates last night.»

Vald looked to the darkened east. «Don't waste your time–we have more important matters at hand. Let the Fey-witch go, for now. We will see her again soon enough. At dawn, use those ships to deliver leaflets announcing the details of the Oath to all cities within three days' march to the Everland. Make it clear that the spoils of Sheynadwiin are mine alone, but everything else is free for the taking; I won't punish anyone protecting what they claim by right of conquest.»

«Yes, Authority.» Vorgha moved slowly backward, careful to avoid plunging into the muck. «Will there be anything else?»

The Dreydmaster's attention was focused on the ravaged tower. His thoughts drifted back to the sight of the Wielder in the storm, her dark hair wreathed by blue lightning. Spear-breaker, she called herself. Such power--and such potential.

He turned to his attendant. «No–go on. I will take care of the witch myself.»

As Vorgha crept back to the Hall, Vald strode to the western walls. The mud was no obstacle to the Dreydmaster–it hardened beneath his stride before each boot struck earth. Under the sun, one could see that the sky was black with storm clouds in the eastern sky, a perpetual wall of gloom that now rose up on the border of the Everland. Night's fading darkness now held sway over Eromar City. The damage to the Hall looked terrible now, but it, like the sky, was revealed to be so much worse in daylight. A massive pile of rubble as tall as a Man lay in the centre of the Hall; those that had been scattered in the collapse were gone, swept away by Vorgha's efficient organization. Half of the eastern wing roof collapsed two days after the tower's fall, but the only casualties were some maidservants, and a cowherd who had snuck into the house for a brief liaison–an insignificant loss, and a fitting end for such lechery.

The western wing, where Vald's family chambers were located, had never been in any danger. The Dreydmaster had long ago ensured its stability with blood and Crafting. The world itself would crumble to dust before that part of Gorthac Hall fell.

Vald ignored the Men who saluted him as he passed through the western doors and through the north-leading hallway toward his private gardens. Three more soldiers–all picked long ago by Vald himself–guarded this doorway. The Dreydmaster held up his right hand, bending the middle two fingers into his palm, and whispered a few words under his breath as his other hand released a handful of ash into the air. The Men nodded, their eyes glazed, faces pale and drawn tight like the skin on a drum, and stepped to the side of the door, their muskets still held high in eternal defence of their post. Vald walked through the door.

The garden was as dead in summer as it had been in the spring. None of the trees bore a sign of leaf or greenery. The tangled weeds that choked the dried fountain and broken garden pathways were brittle and desiccated. The acrid stench of sulphur~and something worse~hung in the air, a yellow haze that singed the Dreydmaster's throat and eyes and left an unpleasant film on the flesh. The place burned, not with the blistering heat that often accompanied his visits, but now with a preternatural cold. This chill oozed with slow deliberateness from the pulsing hole of shadow that the Dreydmaster had opened months before. It was from this rift that he'd sent the first shadow-stalkers, all dark feathers and claws, after the Sevenfold Council's messengers and some of the more troublesome witches. Seekers took care of the minor Fey-Touched. Other shadow-servants he'd pulled from this dark nether-region, each bound to Vald's will through freshly-shed blood and words of great power.

He generally showed restraint in bringing these creatures forth, as he never knew what would answer his bidding, but his visions had become progressively clearer over the last few months, and he knew now that he was on the cusp of achieving the ambition that had so long evaded his grasp. Hesitation now might well undermine his resolve: he was, after all, a Dreydmaster, and it was both his right and duty to bind these creatures to the will of Men. The words of the Dreyd were so much clearer now with the gate open, and it was their words that pulled him forward. It was their words that haunted his nights and left him gasping in exquisite fear and pain. It was their thoughts that bled the living world of joy, promising so much more in the shadows beyond than mortality could ever offer.

They promised him ascension. They promised him everlasting life.

The first message came to him years ago, when he'd first joined the Ruling Council of Eromar, a dark-eyed lawyer from a merchant family with more money than influence. The other Councillors had ignored Vald, dismissed this young, kinless upstart without connections or a lineal heritage of significance. It was one night during that humiliating time~while fiercely mounting his unwilling young wife and ignoring her tearful pleas as he took what was his by marital right–that he'd first heard the voices. He'd screamed and clutched at his head, falling backwards from the bed, and the voices had vanished in the commotion. But they returned, over and over again, year after year. He'd soon grown used to them and longed for their presence, for their words were like golden honey, an all-too-brief sweetness that lingered longer in memory than on the tongue.

And they *always* came back.

Do not fear. You will be among the Foremost, the Dreyd. We were once Human like you–frail and easily broken. We knew the frustration of mortality, of giving fealty to the Immortals who cared little for your people, except to use you for amusing playthings and then to discard you in petulant boredom. We knew hunger, and pain, and loss, and we watched as the Immortals of Old played their games and hid their glories in other worlds.

It had been the Dreydcaste who'd offered young Vald the quickest route to power. With disease and famine spreading like fire through the land, the purifying rites of the Dreydcaste brought comfort, and the people had rallied to the cause. Vald had reminded them that witches and conjurors were everywhere among Men; only a ruthless cleansing could bring back hope. Fear had given strength to the rising power of Dreyd-law, and Vald had been well-suited for bringing order to a lawless land.

The lawyer became a judge, and the judge became the name of law in the province.

So we watched, and we waited, and when our strength was at its peak, we sent Kaantor into the Fey World, and on the night when he drove cold iron into the Veil Between Worlds, we drew upon the Power he unleashed, threw down the Immortals of Old, and took their place at last.

He'd orchestrated the First Cleansing that had swept away the old Ruling Council. Soon after, the High Hall of Bashonak, the centre of Dreyd power in the Reach, had sent word that Eromar would know its first Dreydmaster, the great Purifying Authority and defender of the Dreydcaste and its principles: Lojar Vald. The Man who had once known only frustration and dismissal was now the most feared and respected figure in the northern Reach.

The people had loved him then, and they overwhelmingly chose him to be governing Prefect of Eromar.

We are the Dreyd. We are more than the new Immortals~we are the unyielding certainty of Power.

The Reachwarden of the time, Kell Brennard, had protested from the safety of far-away Chalimor, claiming that no Man should hold the power of both the Dreydcaste and the Prefectorate, but he'd been powerless to intervene. Chalimor was the great gaudy jewel of the Reach, but its grandeur masked its impotence in these hard lands. The people of Eromar had chosen: the Dreydcaste would oversee their lives, in this world and those to follow.

Vald had immersed himself in both the political life of his harsh province and the deeper studies of Dreyd-Crafting. And he became an efficient master of both.

You are meant to be one of us. You must sacrifice. You must give for what you receive. Do not fear that the cost will be too great.

And in the years that followed, the voices had pushed him further. When his temporal ambitions became so manifest that the Reachwarden's army finally threatened invasion, Vald conceded the authority of Chalimor, then turned his attention to Crafting, where fearful, small-minded Men could never interfere. Though he had no doubt of the strength and martial skill of his militia, he had too much work to finish, too many plans to put into place to risk being distracted by a yet unnecessary war.

Finally, after over thirty years of unyielding discipline, the voices revealed the path to him. He knew at long last what the Dreyd required of him, and he was more than willing to surrender to his destiny. The Melding of a thousand years past hadn't finished its work. Remnants of the first power remained scattered across the Reach, that power the first Dreyd had unleashed to fuel their own ascension.

Be the master of your fear. Strike hard, strike fast, and be merciless. There is no room for the weak among the ranks of the Dreyd. Only power will be remembered.

The Everland.
Remember our legacy.

Vald called into the rift, and from it flew a great flock of creatures, each as large as a small Human child, with ragged garments that seemed at times feathered wings and at other times the shredded black remnants of grave-clothes. Their bald and wizened Men's heads were too large for their fluttering bodies, and they had wide mouths ringed with scores of sharp teeth. Slimy holes gaped wide where once eyes might have glimmered with life.

The Not-Ravens hopped around the Dreydmaster's feet and cooed affectionately while they rubbed greasily against his legs and each other. They gladly served him; the blood he provided was intoxicating, and although they didn't belong in this world, there was still joy to be found in its unpredictable shadows. Vald waited for a few moments, until no more of the creatures emerged from the gate, and then he lifted his voice in a series of low cackling whistles and grunts, which the Not-Ravens echoed enthusiastically.

Within moments they were aloft in the early morning darkness, hundreds of the creatures flying with grace and purpose toward the storm-shrouded Everland. They would find and watch the Fey-witch who'd destroyed his tower until he was ready to claim her and her power. And that would be a day this long-cursed world would never forget.

They lay together in the indigo twilight before dawn. Half-covered by a supple white deerskin, Quill nestled tightly in the crook of Tobhi's arm, the clean smells of sweat and passion filling her senses as she listened to his strong heartbeat. Tobhi softly stroked the damp hair on her forehead, marvelling as he did so that she was now so much more beautiful than before, when she'd already seemed the most beautiful firra in all the Everland.

Sunrise was coming, and the thought chilled them both. When Tobhi shivered, Quill held him tighter and ran her fingers along the line of sparse black hair that traveled from his chest to his most delicate parts. She wanted to talk to him, to share all her dreams and fears, to remind him of their vow and beg him to stay with her to protect her from the gathering storm. But even as they made love that night, their promises at last more than mere words, she'd known that he wouldn't stay with her. He couldn't, not now.

As Quill thought about the tender truth of this moment, anger blinded her, and she stiffened at his side. Tobhi looked down at her face. There were tears in his eyes, pain that she didn't expect to see. He swallowed thickly and opened his mouth to speak, but Quill leaned over and kissed him, taking his words into her, knowing now how much he wanted to stay at her side. She didn't need to hear the words spoken.

As the sky brightened through the windows, the room grew warmer and the shadows receded. The Tetawi lay under the deerskin in a tender embrace, unwilling to let go, but knowing, too soon, that they must.

Dawn came and went in Spindletop. Daladir still slept in the guest room, lost in long-needed sleep and adrift in the thick feather bedding. Tarsa sat, freshly bathed, on a large rock near the door of Quill's moundhouse cabin, drinking a steaming mug of mint tea and relishing the sunshine of an early afternoon. It had been far too long since she'd enjoyed the daylight for its own sake, and it was almost enough to drive the fear and anger of the events in Eromar from her heart.

"May I join ye?" Tobhi asked softly. Tarsa looked up. The Tetawa's hair was dishevelled and tangled, and his eyes were dark with grief. He plopped down on the mossy ground beside her. They sat together listening to the sounds of the day.

The Leafspeaker broke the silence. "First time I ever seen her, we was at a turtle dance." He smiled at the memory. "M' pepa, Jekobi, took me with him to Spindletop, where we was gonna sell some of our tobacco and pick up some fresh supplies. I'd never gone with him afore, as our settlement was so deep in the woods, so it was a real treat. We worked real hard all day, and that night, when the work was done, we heard that there was gonna be a dance. Well, Pepa wasn't about to dance 'round the fire without m' mema, but he didn't have no worry about me joinin' in. Prob'ly thought it was about time I enjoyed m'self with others m' own age. So, I slid into the stompin' line and started to dance, a fresh-faced cub from the hill country. M' old-fashioned britches prob'ly made me stick out in that place like a third ear, but nobody said nothin'. Quill's pepa, Mungo, was leadin' the dance and shakin' his turtle rattle. I followed along with the other *fahr* as they sang back to Mungo's song, him startin' the songs and us continuin' the tune. The *firra* slipped in between each of us, alternatin' one after the other. It took me long while, but I eventually caught on that the same light-haired *firra* kept movin' into the line right ahead of me with each dance. Once I finally figured that out, I started noticin' little things, like the way her hair smelled like fresh apples, the way her silver earrings shined so pretty in the firelight, the shape of her hips and the sweet slow way she danced. Finally, when that last dance was over, she turned and smiled at me afore runnin' off to catch up with her cousins. I tell ye, Tarsa, I en't never seen nothin' prettier than that smile. I fell in love with her that night, and I made it back to Spindletop every chance I got. Though I've held a fair share of soft flesh in m' time, in m' heart there en't never been nobody else; never will be, I reckon."

He sighed. "I never forgot about her, ye know, even though I been gone such a long time. Every dream of every night has been 'bout her. I just never knew how deep and empty m' heart's been since I left. It en't too hard to put that aside when ye keep yer thoughts busy elsewhere. But now I'm back...." He pointed at the roof. "Them tiles could use a bit of care. That chimney smokes a bit too much for m' likin', too. She sure could use a bit of fresh venison hangin' in the cold room. That stuff ye trade for at market is too often just the fatty leavin's the hunters don't want 'emselves."

Tobhi's face darkened. "She shouldn't have been alone here with all them Men and monsters about. She shouldn't ever have to be alone." He turned to his adopted sister. "I en't told her I'm goin' yet."

Tarsa nodded and looked side-long at the Tetawa. Tears shimmered in his dark eyes as he stared, unseeing, into the distance. The Wielder reached down and squeezed his hand, and they lapsed again into silence. After a while, she said, "We'll understand if you stay, Tobhi. You've done so much already. You don't have to go on."

"Yes he does, Tarsa," Quill stepped out of the cabin, her eyes sad but clear. Tobhi looked down, unable to meet her gaze, even when the *firra* stroked his cheek with her hand. "He can't stay here. Tobhi's given himself to this path, even if it wasn't of his own making~I've seen it in his eyes, a shadow behind his love for me. He'd stay if I asked him, but that would be asking him to turn his back on everything he's fighting to save. Besides, if things are getting as bad as we've been hearing, Spindletop won't be any better than Sheynadwiin pretty soon. And if it can be stopped, that's where it's going to happen, not here. I understand that."

He looked at her now, and she pulled him close, draping the newly-finished badger sash around his neck. "I'll be okay, but you've got to come back to me, sweetness," she whispered. "I'm letting you go now so I can keep you later. Promise that you'll come back."

Tears trickled down her round cheeks as he buried his face in her shoulder. "Keep your friends safe, and keep yourself safe, too, my sweet, strong *fahr*. Don't forget your black-eyed *firra*, Tobhi, because she won't forget you."

Medalla and Gishki returned to Quill's home after walking Tobhi and his friends to the edge of the forest. Quill sat beside the cold hearth. Her cheeks were swollen, but there were no new tears in her eyes. She'd tried to be cheery and strong as the travellers gathered supplies for their departure, and although everyone could see her grief, they'd played along. The farewell seemed easier to bear that way.

"Do you want us to stay?" Gishki asked.

"No, *mishko*. I think I'd rather be alone right now, if you don't mind."

Medalla squeezed the Dolltender's arm. "We'll be back in the morning. It's market day. It'll be good to get out of the house again." They slipped out the door.

Quill remained beside the hearth until late in the night. Her thoughts spun wildly, and they kept coming back to Tobhi's story the night before, when he'd recounted his adventure. She felt so helpless. She couldn't go with Tobhi; his path was dark to her. But there was another option, a path that grew clearer even as her heart grew heavier from the thought of it.

She turned to look at the dolls on their shelves, their puckered faces pinched into looks of disapproval. Her own lips tightened defiantly. She was tired of sitting and waiting for things to happen. She was tired of feeling so scared and helpless. Tobhi was willing to sacrifice so much to save their people. He needed her, now more than ever. Maybe she could do something to help, even if she wasn't by his side in Sheynadwiin.

"Yes," she whispered. "Somebody's got to tell the Reachwarden about Vald's treachery. He's the leader of all the Reach, more powerful than Vald, even. I know that good people won't let this happen. They've got to be told the truth." She stood up. "And I guess I'll just have to go to Chalimor to do it."

CHAPTER 9

HUNTER AND HUNTED

The first thing that Vergis Thane noticed was the smoke. It rose in long columns throughout the Everland, creeping skyward like hundreds of oily eels, thick and black against the afternoon suns. His brows narrowed. Such a waste. This bountiful land was more than adequate for all the settlers; there was hardly any sense in burning the crops and houses to useless ash. Such was the foolishness of land-hunger. Silly, weak-minded Men without any purpose beyond greed and the cowardice of mob force, gathering together to take what they could and destroy what they couldn't. The Seeker cared little about the Unhumans themselves, but he saw no reason for unnecessary devastation ~ it would merely strengthen the creatures' resolve to remain in the Everland, and stiffen their resistance to the inevitable. They would die, Men and Women would die, the land would be torn and broken in the conflict, and everyone would suffer ~ all but the politicians, those Men who'd set this conflict into motion.

He didn't need to make his way to the forest to know that Spindletop, too, was aflame; it wasn't likely that the little Brownie he sought would still be in her cabin. This would make his job much more difficult.

«Dreyd-damned fools,» he growled under his breath, sliding his battered hat back on his head and spurring his sure-footed horse forward. If the Brownie still survived, she'd probably be seeking refuge in the forest, or else be among the prisoners in the slaving wagons. Either way, she was now bringing him a great deal of trouble. It would take time and talent to find her. If she was Fey-Touched, as he thought, she'd be well worth the effort; if not, at least he had the opportunity to further hone his hunting skills.

He was at the ruins of the cabin by nightfall, and it was as he had expected: she was gone. A quick search through the rubble revealed little. Looters had taken everything of value and ruined the rest. None of the cabins in this part of the settlement remained standing; even the stables and barns had been destroyed. He found nothing of interest in the rubble he'd come to that first night, so he walked down the hill to what remained of a small house at the base of an old, fire-scarred pine. In the broken wood and embers of what had once been the main room of the cabin, Thane found the smashed remnants of one of those strange dolls he'd glimpsed for just a moment during his last visit, half of one apple head now glaring reproachfully at him with a glittering, polished-stone eye. He removed a glove and slid his hand over the piece.

The prickling burn on his fingertips confirmed his suspicions: the dollmaker was Fey-Touched! Whatever the purpose of these dolls, they were a powerful part of her witchery. So much stronger than the Deerman he had captured, yet she'd been able to veil her powers from the Seeker with little apparent effort. The corners of Thane's mouth creased slightly. He had to admit an increasing admiration for the little Brownie; whatever else she was, she clearly wasn't stupid. Whether she'd known that he was a Seeker or not, she'd certainly understood upon their meeting that he was a threat, and she'd kept him from sensing her secret.

But the secret was his now. He slipped the broken apple-doll into a pocket and looked around again. No body or bones, no bloodstains. No more dolls. She hadn't died here, that was certain. The place was empty of her presence, other than the lingering memory clinging to the blasted and torn roots of the trees that reached into the base of the cabin from the east. His bare hand rested softly on the roots. They still remembered the Brownie, even through their dying ache. His palm twitched slightly in response. He slipped on the glove and headed toward his horse.

He looked toward the direction of the still-smouldering village of Spindletop, some distance from the Brownie-witch's house. That would be the start of the true hunt. He rode quickly away from the ruins of the house, closing his ears to the trees, their whispering voices calling endlessly for the she-Brownie, wondering where she'd gone, why she'd left her cozy little cabin behind.

Come home, Spider-child, they wept. *Come home.*

The most difficult decision about leaving home was deciding which dolls to take and which to leave behind. Quill had gathered them together near the hearth, all seventy-three, their dried apple faces pinched with worry and corn-husk garments rustling nervously, and told them of her plan. There was no changing her mind, so the debate would centre on which dolls would go with her. That was a decision that only the dolls could make, so Quill had left them in council and busied herself with the final preparations for the journey.

She'd returned to the common room to find only three dolls together beside the hearth. The others were back on their shelves, their eyes cloudy with grief. Holding back her own tears, Quill sat on the tile floor and pulled the three dolls to her. They were all from her Granny Pearl's days as Dolltender: Cornsilk, the quiet, sleepy-faced doll whose contemplative spirit helped ease the thoughts and body; Green Kishka, a dour doll with a feather skirt and multicoloured corncob body; and Mulchworm, the oldest of the dolls, whose white-capped head was so deeply etched with age that his features were almost lost in the wrinkles. Old friends all; brave friends, too. Their willingness to join her was more of a relief than she'd expected. This wouldn't be a midsummer trip to market.

For the first time, she was beginning to understand just what her decision to leave truly meant, and a wave of grief and longing hit her. It was more likely than not that she'd die out there, far from home, and the other dolls would never know what happened to her. Cornsilk, Kishka, and Mulchworm weren't just going along on an afternoon stroll—they were risking themselves and likely giving up their life-long fellows to accompany her on this mad quest into the heart of the Men's Reach. The pain in Tobhi's eyes returned to her then, and she now understood the fear he'd tried to keep from her. *Oh, Granny Jenna, Mother Turtle, help us.*

Quill left in the early hours of the morning, when the fragrant dew still lingered on the pine boughs of Edgewood. A note tacked to the front door explained everything; Medalla and Gishki would find it when they stopped by to walk to market in the early afternoon. She'd struggled with the note, wondering if it was cowardice that kept her from telling them goodbye in person, but she also knew that they'd try to convince her to stay home. Her resolve was already shaky; if she was ever going to leave, she'd have to do it now, before new fears overwhelmed her. At the end of the note, she left feeding and care instructions for the dolls who remained behind. They'd be well cared for in her absence.

The first two days were more fun than she'd expected. Although her knowledge of the lands around Spindletop was limited to the main dirt roads and favourite harvesting paths she used for doll materials, she was surprised at how little discomfort she experienced. Some of this was certainly due to her foresight in choosing traveling clothes. Thick-soled leather boots and a high-collared, oiled-leather coat protected her from the worst of the elements. Her hair was bound into a tight topknot and away from her eyes, and the neck and chest of her blouse were covered by a long scarf studded from end to end with small white shells that clicked softly together as she moved. Gloves, rope, a small knife, fire-stone and tinder, two more blouses and another pair of cotton breeches, soap and menstrual rags, tooth-cleaning sticks, and a thick blanket joined a full week's worth of thick pan-bread, dried fruit, and a water-skin in the travel satchel on her back. Across her waist hung the leather purse that carried the dolls and a gourd hand rattle, each wrapped firmly with red cloth. She carried a farewell gift from Tarsa in her hand—a stout cedar walking stick, its shape etched by the *wyr* with trailing vines and blossoms. Quill marvelled at the delicacy of the wielded wood; it looked as though the flowers had grown along the wooden shaft of their own will.

Two days had taken her beyond the southern limit of the Edgewood. She'd guessed it would be a few days to the southernmost edge of the Everland, although she couldn't know for certain, as there were no maps in her cabin, and she had to rely on the dim memory of traders' conversations and the growing beyonder rumours that had so haunted the region in recent months. Still, she knew that the Old Windle Road stretched across the entire south of the Men's Reach south of the Everland, and the easternmost point of that ancient roadway was Chalimor, the political and cultural heart of the lands of Humanity. All she had to do was continue south and she'd eventually find it. It would be quite simple, really~little more than a lengthy hike. She might even be back home again before the first winter snows.

Quill awoke on her third morning from Spindletop to find a giant, sharp-toothed raccoon with pale fur ravaging her pack. She screamed in surprise, then fury, as the creature crouched backward with Green Kishka in its mouth.

"Put her down," Quill hissed, but the raccoon simply stared, its yellow eyes regarding her with something like amusement as it crunched down on the doll's corncob body.

The Dolltender flinched. A red stream trickled from the pierced kernels.

She stepped back, trembling. Blood. The doll was bleeding. The raccoon remained still, its jaws clenched tightly around Kishka's body. A noise from behind caught Quill's attention, and she turned to see the other two dolls standing beside her, their eyes fixed on the raccoon and poor Green Kishka, whose face was now twisted into a grimace of pain. Quill's mouth went dry.

The Dolltender reached down slowly, hoping to wrap her hand around a rock, or a stick from the burnt-out fire, but she stopped when the raccoon slowly lowered its head, its gaze fixed on those of the dolls, and gently dropped Kishka to the ground. With agonizing slowness, the creature crept backward into the undergrowth, its yellow eyes never turning from the dolls, before disappearing into the foliage.

The weight on Quill's chest relaxed, and her vision cleared. It was over.

Looking down, she saw Cornsilk and Mulchworm lying side by side on the ground, no longer standing in bold defiance. The Tetawa took a deep breath and picked them up, then lifted Green Kishka and wrapped a cleansing cloth around the doll's wounds.

"I don't know if this will be enough," she whispered, her voice laboured.

She never doubted the reality of the dolls' spirits~they'd spoken to her too many times to deny that~but this was the first time she had ever known one of them to bleed. She wasn't entirely certain that the knowledge was welcome. It was one thing for the dolls to be filled with a life spirit; it was another thing entirely for that life to include such mortal realities. If Kishka could bleed, then she could die, too. The thought stripped the journey of any fleeting romance.

The rest of the day wasn't much better. Quill returned to her satchel to find that the raccoon had eaten most of her travel food. One of the gloves was missing, and the cake of soap had been chewed into a half-dozen small pieces. After kicking out the remains of the fire-pit in a tantrum, she gathered everything together and stomped southward in the late morning, now fully submerged in her foul mood.

The rain started as a light, easy drizzle, but it soon swelled into a downpour that soaked through coat and boots alike. Her topknot drooped down her back, and her blouse clung to her skin. Lightning regularly split the dark rain, and the thunder was so loud and so close that Quill cried out in terror more than once.

She was now in the Downlands, a series of rough, rocky hills that took up where the Edgewood left off. The thick pine and cedar forest gave way to broken country, covered with low, bushy pines and scrub oaks, knee-high thorn bushes with dagger-sharp thorns, wild roses in late bloom, and prickly raspberry plants still far from ripeness. Occasionally the sound of tinkling bells echoed across the open hills, its source unknown but welcome. Even through the driving rain Quill could see that the land had a harsh beauty to it, and she could hardly help but be impressed by the sight, especially the towering stones that stood all the way to the horizon. They were rough and worn, nearly featureless, painted by the elements and layers of grey-green lichen. Some were only as tall as the Tetawa, while others stood six or seven times her height. Many were carved with shapes that had long since lost their meaning to the wind and ages. She'd never seen the Downlands before, but as she crouched beneath an overhanging stone to avoid the worst of the storm, she recalled that she'd heard stories of the place when she was a youngling cub.

She froze. Yes, she *had* heard stories about the Downlands, and now she was beginning to remember what they were. The Downlands had another name, one best known by grannies and cubs during dark-night stories: the Barrow Hills. Quill looked at the stone that leaned over to protect her from the rain. It was a barrow stone of the ancient days.

She was sheltering in a boneyard.

Lightning pierced the storm again, and the Dolltender crouched quivering in the rain. Had she seen something out there in the storm, in that momentary flash of sky-fire? Was it tall and thin, with fierce eyes, glistening white flesh, and the blood of a Tetawa cub still burning in its hand? Had it followed her here, to this land of ghosts and death? Her fingers tightened on the walking stick, but she lowered herself down to the muddy earth and pushed as far against the side of the stone as she could.

The dolls shifted in her pack, but she ignored their discomfort. She couldn't risk unwrapping them from their bindings and revealing her presence to whatever waited out there.

Thunder shook the ground. Quill slid her hands over her ears, but not before she heard another noise, a squelching sound, like broad feet moving slowly through mud. Her hands dropped back to the walking stick. Whatever was making the noise, it was close.

A shape moved out of the plummeting rain, followed by others, but Quill didn't relax. If anything, her heart beat even faster as figure after figure now moved past her hiding place. Six, then ten, twenty or more, some on horses, others on foot, all heading north through the Downlands.

They were Men. Men were marching through the Everland.

The dolls twisted violently. Quill bit her lower lip. She could feel it too: the Men carried iron. Swords, flintlocks, even the iron buttons on their jackets, the nails in their thick boots and the shoes of their horses seeped out and burned the air around the trembling Tetawa. But there was more, far more;

it made her stomach cramp and eyes water. A ponderous wagon moved into view, the creaking whine of its axles shredding the dull rhythm of the rain. It was a massive structure, large and unwieldy on the back of a wooden pallet. Iron bars glinted dangerously in the flashing lightning, and Quill saw shapes huddled inside the bars, shapes of captive Folk.

"A slaving wagon," she whispered, more to herself than to the dolls.

Terror swept through her. Here she crouched, not even thirty paces from the Men; all it would take to join the poor Folk in that wagon would be for one Man to turn and look her way. *Please, keep going. You don't see me. Keep going. Please....*

But one Man did turn, and he saw her. He lifted his hand to his eyes and peered into the shadows of the rock, stopping his horse as he did so, and called out in a harsh language the Tetawa didn't understand. Quill didn't stop to think. Like a panicked mouse, she burst from her hiding place and skittered around the side of the rock, boots slipping in the muddy earth, her thoughts on one thing only: escape.

The rumble of hooves shook the ground around her. She spun around to see the Man riding hard, a long knife in his hand. Quill lurched back again, but she slipped on the soft earth and landed hard, mud filling her eyes and mouth. She was too frightened even to scream.

And again she heard the sound of bells, the same sound that had echoed throughout the hills in the early afternoon. It was closer now. The Man's voice roared out again, almost on top of her, but it lifted into a howl when a blast of heat swept like a curtain in front of the trembling Tetawa, choking the air with the stink of burning hair and flesh. The horse shrieked, the earth trembled, and another burning burst split the air. All was chaos. Quill tried to lift herself up and wipe the mud from her eyes, but something hard smashed into her, and she rolled to the ground again. She couldn't breathe. From the other side of the barrow-stone she could hear the roar of the muskets, and then more screams and shouts. The tinkling bells rang again, now directly above the flailing Tetawa. In between the explosions and cries, Quill thought she heard laughter. The gentle sound was so out of place in this strange, terrifying moment.

The Dolltender wiped furiously at her eyes, enough to clear the gritty mud away, and sat back on her knees in wide-eyed astonishment. The Men had been routed. Those who remained were dead or wounded, their horses racing off in various directions. But it wasn't the Men who had her attention now.

A small train of brightly-coloured wagons stood in a semi-circle around the Tetawa. Wandering through the ruins of the slaving train and looking after the imprisoned Folk was a motley group of figures, all dressed in strange and colourful clothing. Some were impossibly thin and tall, others as short and squat as toadstools, while others seemed of average build. Most were Humans, but they looked and sounded nothing like the slavers: the tinkling sound Quill had heard came from the rows of bells and tambourines hanging from bright cloth belts around their waists or bracers on their wrists and ankles. Men and Women alike moved to the slave wagon and pulled the prisoners free, tending to their wounds and gently administering medicinals and fresh water.

"By Bidbag's hairless goat, you're an awful mess, darling." Quill had heard the voice before; it was the source of that laugh, the merry sound that had cut through the storm during the attack. She turned around and her mouth flew open as a buxom, bronze-skinned figure knelt down and wiped the mud from her face with a soft silk cloth. The stranger wore a billowing lavender dress, its bodice cut daringly low. Her thick auburn hair was held back by a wide-brimmed white hat fringed boldly with iridescent, blue-green feathers. Bright emerald eyes sparkled as they examined the Tetawa for injury.

"What happened?" the Dolltender coughed, spitting mud and grass out of her mouth.

The stranger laughed. "Why, we rescued you, of course," she said. Her accent was fast and oddly lilting, but pleasant. "To be absolutely honest, my dear, it was a truly magnificent sight, one of the most dramatic rescues I've ever attempted. I've rarely impressed myself so much, and that's hard to do, believe me."

"I'm a bit confused."

"Of course you are." The figure slipped her hat off to reveal four knobby protrusions that swayed gently from within the thick hair at her temples. Pulling the curls away from her ears, which slightly resembled oak-leaves, she grinned. "But you needn't worry, my mud-stained wanderer—you're among friends!"

"You know Folk-speech. You're a Strangeling!" Quill whispered in awe.

Again the stranger laughed, and the sound was so carefree and infectious that the Tetawa couldn't help but smile in response. "It's been so long since I've heard that quaintly antiquated term! Yes, darling, my father was Kyn, my mother Human." She held her hand to her chest in proper Folk greeting. "Love worked its sweet, sweaty magic, and not long thereafter I was born. You are now in the presence of the radiant, green-eyed beneficiary of their inspired enthusiasm: Denarra Syrene, daughter of Walks-With-the-Winds and Zoola-Dawn Bandabee."

Nearly overwhelmed by her talkative rescuer, Quill hesitantly lifted her own hand. "Quill Meadowgood, Spider Clan of Spindletop at Edgewood. Many thanks."

Denarra stood and wiped the mud from her dress. "Please don't mention it, darling. Always glad to help out, especially with these boorish and unhappily unhygienic brutes lurking about. Can't have a wee, wide-eyed maiden like you wandering around alone in such a dangerous place, now can we? Come along, then—you'd better stick with us for a while."

Looking around with some trepidation, Quill asked, "Who are these Humans with you?"

Denarra grinned. "You're in for a magnificent treat, my dishevelled friend. You've been personally rescued by the illustrious, Reach-renowned traveling company known to all and sundry as Bremen and Crowe's Medicine Show and Repertory of Thespian Delights."

"Repertory?" Such a strange word. The Tetawa's eyes lingered on the wagons. She could see large letters, painted brightly with vines and strange sym-

Rescued

bols weaving their way around the characters. Their meanings were unknown, but the pictures themselves were quite attractive. "Is that what you call your army?"

The Strangeling giggled and pulled Quill along behind her as she moved toward the gaudiest wagon of all, a bright pink and yellow structure with broad-tailed birds painted in gold on the walls. "Our 'army'? Oh, my dear, you are a peach! We're no army, Quill–we're entertainers! Some are actors, others jugglers, some singers and dancers, all performers of rare and exceptional talent. I'm rather versatile myself–a little of this, a little of that." She winked conspiratorially. "And let me assure you, with all due modesty, we may be a small company, but there are none better anywhere–not in the Everland, and certainly not in the Reach."

Quill looked back to the shattered slaving train, where the cooling bodies of the slower slavers lay scattered in the mud and rain. "I've never heard of actors being able to do something like this."

Denarra nodded sympathetically. "No? Ah, but then you've never performed in Harudin Holt, either. They hang bad actors and off-tune troubadours naked in the city square and let angry critics skewer their backsides with heated pins–a lenient sentence for such aesthetic heresy, in my humble opinion. If you can handle the audiences there, then scattering a little gang of high-smelling thugs is no difficult matter. Besides, I have a few tricks that come in quite handy from time to time." The Strangeling held up her hand. A sheet of shimmering lavender flame danced across Denarra's fingers.

An actor *and* a Wielder, Quill mused–an unusual combination.

Smiling broadly, Denarra led Quill to the wagon door. "Now, let's get you cleaned up and get some dry clothes on you. This rain is starting to soak into my boots. I imagine that underneath all that grime you're actually rather charming to look at. Maybe we'll do something with your hair while we're at it, if you don't mind. No reason to look like a waterlogged prairie dog, even if you feel like one, don't you think? I've got an extra cot; you can sleep there for now, at least until we can figure out more appropriate and certainly more comfortable sleeping quarters."

Too tired and bewildered to protest, the Dolltender followed Denarra into the wagon, where she found a hot bath, a clean robe, and the endless but pleasing chatter of her flamboyant host, until the day's fears drained away and sleep found her a few hours later. Denarra smiled and snuffed out the lantern before snuggling deeply into her own bed, drifting asleep to the sound of the rain falling on the wagon's cedar shingles.

In the darkness and the rain, far beyond the reach of the caravan's night lanterns, yellow eyes peered hungrily at the brightest wagon. The creature had been interrupted in its hunt three times this day~first by the Brownie herself, then by the Men, and finally by the newcomers and their sky-fire. He'd hungered for the little sand-haired female for a very long time, since she and her dolls interrupted his feast those many months past. But he didn't mind too much; the wait made the kill that much sweeter. He held her lost glove up to his nose and breathed in, savouring the smell of her salty skin and imagining its taste on his serpentine tongue.

There were other ways of getting to her; he could make a game of it. It would be fun. After all, her new friends couldn't watch her forever.

CHAPTER 10
GHOSTLANDS

The news of the Oathsworn's betrayal swept through Sheynadwiin like a brush-fire. Few knew how the news reached the city before the airship arrived, but there were rumours that strange Ubbetuk machinery helped to relay the message. It didn't take long for two large crowds to gather at the landing in anticipation of her arrival. The first was an armed group of Shields and their supporters, thirty strong, with a fitted carriage and four swift horses waiting to bear the Oathsworn to safety. They stood nervously against a much larger group of at least two hundred angry Kyn and Tetawi from across Sheynadwiin who milled around in agitation. The Shields were closest to the landing, but they weren't the only ones with weapons. The air was hot with rising rage.

It was early evening when the great wasp-faced Dragon emerged slowly from the storm-torn sky, gears whirring and bellows groaning from the exertion of the long journey. It hovered for a while over the landing, its four great canvas-covered wings moving with slow, rhythmic precision, finally descending on the far edge, where a dozen Ubbetuk swung on ropes from the upper deck to finish mooring the ship. When all was secure, the gang-plank slid to earth, and Neranda Ak'Shaar emerged alone, her head held high, her face pale but proud. Three long red scars burned on each cheek. No one else exited the ship with her, but the plank remained lowered.

"Shakar!" someone hissed, and others took up the chorus. "Traitor!"

The Shields closed the circle tighter around the Lawmaker, holding their ornate bladed staves and pole-arms against the crowd. No one tried to break the circle, but the chant grew in intensity as the numbers of the opposition swelled. *"Shakar!"*

Neranda stared straight ahead at the carriage as she walked. They would not break her poise. *I did only what others were too cowardly or foolish to do. We had no choice. One day they will see this, and they will honour me.*

They will understand. It was why she returned, even knowing that her life was likely forfeit--she would make them understand why she had to make this difficult choice. She wouldn't hide like a coward in the shadows, like the others who remained cringing in the ship, but would instead face her people proudly, defiantly, and they would see that she'd had no alternative.

She moved forward with renewed determination. The voices of her enemies faded beneath this certainty. She'd been preparing for this moment ever since leaving for Eromar City, speaking the words to herself over and over until they became a kind of armour, pushing away the nagging fear that clutched at her stomach, the memory of the Dreydmaster's chilly smile as the she-Kyn Lawmaker took the quill in hand and signed her name to the Oath of Western Sanctuary. There was poison in that smile, and the memory burned deeper every time she thought of it.

We had no choice. They will understand.

We had no choice. My people will listen.

The copper-haired Lawmaker was vaguely aware of a shift in the bodies around her, the swelling numbers pushing against the knot of frightened Shields, but she paid them little attention. The carriage door was open, and she drew her shimmering white robes away from her legs as she moved to enter.

The first rock hit Neranda in the small of her back. Pain brought her attention back to the moment. A second stone smashed into the carriage door beside her, while another struck her shoulder. She cried out and turned. Something wet and foul spattered in her face. Gagging, she wiped it away to see the Shields lashing out at the crowd that pressed against them. Bleeding shapes fell to the cobbled street. Shouts and screams rose up as the dam of bodies broke, and the Shields were overwhelmed by the mob. The carriage shot forward. Neranda had just enough time to fling herself into it before the angry Folk swarmed over the carriage, rocks, clubs, hatchets, and hands striking its sides. The driver shouted and lashed the fear-maddened horses forward, crushing a dozen bodies beneath hooves and wheels before shooting free of the furious crowd.

Neranda shook with terror and humiliated rage. The windows of the carriage were broken. She looked at her dress, soiled with spittle, dirt, and mud, along with unidentifiable filth that filled the carriage with its sharp stench. The carriage careened through the streets, but not without difficulty, for the people of Sheynadwiin now knew who rode in the coach, and they were rushing to share their displeasure. Rocks, sticks, clay pots, root vegetables, arrows, spears, and other weapons struck the vehicle and open window, but Neranda remained largely uninjured.

It was the voices that tore into her, each screaming a single word that burned like pitch-fire in her mind.

Tobhi always preferred dawn over any other time of the day. It wasn't simply that the arrival of the new suns over the eastern horizon was a sacred time to all the Tetawi, although that certainly had something to do with the joy he felt in the morning. Rather, it was a moment of renewal, a reminder that each day brought with it unknown possibility and promise. Tobhi's heart was lifted by daybreak, and he generally tried to greet the sister suns with a prayer of welcome and a bit of cedar-sweetened tobacco.

This morning brought with it no dawn, only storm clouds, and the Tetawa's spirits were as soggy as the day's promise. But he nevertheless whispered his prayer and scattered the tobacco to the grey sky and red earth before returning to camp, where Daladir sat rubbing his hands over the small cooking fire, a small gutted trout skewered on the end of a green sapling hanging over the flames.

The he-Kyn looked up. "Another long day ahead of us, I think."

Tobhi nodded and joined him beside the fire. "We got us 'bout a tenday 'til we're there, if we move fast and don't run into any more trouble on the way, which en't likely." He pointed to a dark blur on the northeast horizon. "That's the Eldarvian Woods. If we can find ourselves a good road, we might cut it down to eight days or so. There's better roads up north than down in the south forest. Either way, we still got us a bit of a haul yet."

Daladir handed the trout to the Tetawa, who peeled away the blackened skin and began munching on the steaming pink meat inside. They sat quietly, looking off into the distance, until Tarsa appeared over the embankment. Her hair still dripped from the cold lake bath. Daladir held up another skewer, this one piercing a thick sweet potato that they'd brought from Quill's home.

"It's not cooked yet," he said, his eyes bright, "but it shouldn't take too long; the fire is quite hot." The Wielder smiled and accepted the stick.

"Tsodoka." Tarsa's turquoise gaze lingered on the he-Kyn for a moment, but she looked away when he shifted toward her. Looking skyward, she asked Tobhi, "Do you think we'll be able to make it to the forest before the storm hits?"

"Nah. We'll be lucky to even break camp afore it gets here."

As if in response, a low rumble of thunder echoed through the hills. The storm was moving fast. Tobhi sighed. It was going to be a long, dreary day.

The rain struck hard and lingered all morning and afternoon, but they pushed on, even when blisters burned through the drenched and bunching leather of their boots. Time wasn't their ally these days. It had been seven days since their flight from Gorthac Hall, and they would have at least as many to go through dense forests and the western heights of the Kraagen Mountains. Word of the Oathsworn's treachery had surely reached Sheynadwiin by now, but no one knew how long it would take Vald to send an organized force into the Everland, and the trio wanted to be in the city before that happened.

Tarsa felt a particularly heavy pull on her spirit. All Wielders were needed at this time–now more than ever, as the darkest days were riding with the clouds of war. The sooner they reached Sheynadwiin, the safer their people would be. In their more optimistic moods, this was their thought. In their less sanguine moments, they wanted merely to stand beside their people at the end.

The Wielder was lost in the latter thoughts when they reached the edge of the Eldarvian Woods, the vast forest on the western side of the Kraagens. She'd tried to not chastise herself for leaving, for abandoning the city and her people, but those thoughts returned again and again. *Unahi was right,* Tarsa thought to herself. *I'm still a youngling, too caught up with my own wants to pay attention to what's really important.* Then her eyes flickered to Tobhi and Daladir. *But they would have died if I hadn't have been there. Oh, Green Mother, will we always be forced to choose between death and devastation?*

The rain continued to fall steadily through the late afternoon, turning the world the dreary colour of slate. In spite of their aching feet, they trotted the last few miles into the trees, where the thick canopy gave them some degree of protection from the storm. The tree cover at the forest's edge was sparse, mostly thick pines, cedars, and some scattered aspen stands, but the woods would become much denser as they moved to the northeast, where the land was shrouded by the massive, green-bearded wyrwood trees, ferns, blankets of thick moss and mushrooms, and shadow-tangled undergrowth. This part of the forest provided little protection from the elements, but they could at least spot anything approaching them; that wouldn't be the case in the deeper trees.

Tarsa lowered her travel pack and stretched, wincing slightly at the catch in her back. "Should we try to go farther tonight, or should we find a dry place to camp?"

"I doubt there's any such place in all the Everland today," Daladir muttered. He was limping badly now. The other two were far more experienced with the rigours of such travel, and the he-Kyn had been weakened by his months as Vald's reluctant "guest." He was wounded now in both spirit and body.

Tobhi took off his new hat, given to him by Quill as a farewell gift, and looked around, his dark eyes squinting through the trees. "I en't sure we'd be able to keep goin' if we stop now; m' feet is hurtin' somethin' fierce. Let's keep on for a while, least 'til we find ourselves someplace to wait out the storm." He pulled his long hair over his shoulder and tried to wring the excess water out of it, but he quickly gave up and tugged the lumpy hat back over his pointed ear-tips.

Tarsa slowly slid her pack back onto her aching shoulders. "Do you think we'll make it in time, Tobhi?"

The Tetawa shrugged, his face troubled. "I don't rightly know. Vald don't seem like the kind of Man who takes well to waiting. Then again, he en't the kind of Man who rushes into trouble, neither. I don't think he'll do much yet, but it won't be long 'til he does. I'm pretty sure we'll get back to Sheynadwiin in time to find out just what he's got in mind."

The cawing of ravens in the trees echoed strangely through the rain. "That's what worries me," the Wielder muttered.

The sister suns cut a bloody swath across the darkening horizon, their red glow giving little light or warmth to the Everland as they surrendered day to the curtain of twilight. No one would sleep in Sheynadwiin this night. Already wails of grief echoed through Dardath Vale from every house, den, nest, and burrow.

Garyn watched the setting suns disappear past the great Eldarvian Woods to the west. He was alone in his bedchamber, sitting in the darkness with his narrow-backed seat beside the window. He had very few opportunities for quiet reflection these days, and he cherished each one with more than a little selfishness. Even now, with his people in mourning, all he wanted to do was sit by his window and watch the day pass away before his eyes.

He was tired beyond reckoning. It was over. They'd fought so hard for so very long, and now all their work had come to nothing. The Sevenfold Council stood firm against the raging greed of Eromar. The Folk had been unified as never before, and this might have once been enough to gain support from Chalimor and its enlightened Human leaders. Yet everything they sought to defend, all the lives and legacies of the Everland–it had all been unravelled in an instant by the treachery of his own niece and her associates.

Among Men, fathers gave guidance to their children; among the Kyn, it was the uncles who guided their sisters' children into the ways of the People. And with Neranda he'd failed terribly. She'd always been headstrong and wilful, more interested in her father's Human-leaning ways than those of her own people, traveling to Chalimor to live among Humans and learn their customs, even against the wishes of her mother's family. And she'd returned changed, her heart distant. Perhaps her betrayal was inevitable; perhaps all the guidance he'd tried to give had been useless. He wanted to believe otherwise, but she was Oathsworn now, and that spoke more about her than any teachings he'd once shared.

He could hear the weeping rise up from the city. This would be only the beginning of the grief. Soon the brigands, robbers, thieves, cutthroats, and border trash would descend, emboldened by the threat of Eromar. When they had taken away what treasures they could find, the militiamen would come for the Folk. The Kyn and their kith would stand strong in defence of their homeland—of that Garyn had little doubt—but they were so few, and the teeming hordes of Men were driven by a voracious hunger that would never be sated.

Such different ways. Were all Men like those who swarmed over the Everland? Was his father? Garyn had only a few memories of that long-dead Human, more sensations than actual memories, but they held no taint of fear or hatred. If anything, the Governor felt the lingering touch of love and laughter from those brief youngling days, before the raging fever took his father, and before his Pine Branch mother fell into the long grieving silences from which she rarely emerged.

What was it that made some Men so grasping, while others found contentment in the gentle joys of life? What had his father found in Thornholt to convince him to surrender his former life and choose that of Kei'shaad Mendiir and her people? Garyn didn't know. All he knew now was that Humans like Reiss Thalsson were rare beyond measure in the Everland these days, but he hoped that other Human leaders would respond to Vald's aggression with righteous fury. He'd written so many letters and appeals, making the Kyn case for Human politicians and policy-makers, intellectuals, moral leaders, social crusaders~anyone who could shift public opinion in their favour. It was the last, best hope they had, and Garyn hated it. He'd learned all too often how dangerous it was to trust in the kindness of Men.

A soft knock sounded at the pine-slat door. Garyn turned to see his consort, Averyn, enter with a mug of tea on a tray, which zhe placed on a small table beside the window.

The black-haired zhe-Kyn rested hir hand on the Governor's knee. "You'll catch a chill if you stay here too long, my love."

Garyn returned his gaze to the window. The suns had passed below the horizon. It was twilight. "Do you hear them?"

"Yes," Averyn whispered. "The night aches with sorrow."

"You know what is to come?"

"Everyone knows. It is why they weep. It is why they need your strength now, more than ever before."

Garyn's face darkened. "I cannot be the strength of the entire Everland. I am weak. I have failed."

Averyn knelt between the Governor's knees and took the silver-haired he-Kyn's face gently in hir hands. "Our people live still, Garyn Mendiir, and as long as that truth endures, so will your strength. You have not failed us, not yet. If you cannot find strength in yourself, find it in us...in me. Give us a reflection of our own strength, and that will be enough to sustain us in the times to come." Zhe kissed Garyn tenderly. "You are needed now, beloved. Pradu Styke is dead, as are most of the other Celestials who signed the Oath~all executed today by mobs of fear-maddened Folk." Seeing the grief rise up in Garyn's eyes, Averyn added, "Neranda still lives. She alone of the Oathsworn was able to escape the vengeance of the People, but I have had no word of where she fled. There are rumours that she is rallying her supporters, and the killings have added both fuel and fear to her cause."

The zhe-Kyn brushed a lock of hair away from Garyn's face. "Our Nation threatens to split apart from within. The People are in pain, and you must help them. It is your duty. It is the trust that they gave to you."

Garyn nodded and pulled the younger zhe-Kyn close. They held each other for a while, sharing grief and hope in their embrace, until a noise in the distant forest pulled Garyn away from his lover's touch. It was a strange sound, something like crows calling to one another in the night, but unlike any such bird either Kyn had ever heard before.

The Governor's eyes narrowed. "Not all creatures mourn this night." He stood and stepped to the bed, where his coat of office lay tossed across the thick blankets, its much-frayed edging a mark of honour and endurance. Averyn wiped the tears from hir face, stood up, and stepped forward to help Garyn make himself presentable. They could hear the gathering rumble of Folk in the room beyond, who waited for the reassuring presence of the stalwart Governor of the Kyn Nation.

Averyn slid a polished silver gorget over Garyn's head and let it rest on the Governor's chest, where it gleamed in the soft moonlight through the window. The silver-haired he-Kyn tenderly stroked his lover's cheek. Straightening his shoulders, he pulled the door open and stepped out to confront a growing throng of terrified Kyn.

"Be strong," Averyn whispered softly from the shadows of the bedchamber as Garyn spoke to the crowd. Already the Governor was easing their fears with his powerful words and solid presence.

The strange noise echoed again from the shadowed forest beyond the city. Averyn moved to the window and closed the shutters against the night. But before zhe headed to the common room to join Garyn and the others, hir thoughts lingered on that troubling sound, and the many enemies that crept ever closer toward Sheynadwiin.

"Be strong, beloved," zhe whispered under hir soft breath. "We have never needed your strength so much, and we will need so much more before these dark days are gone."

CHAPTER 11

NEW WORLDS AND OLD

Life among actors was very different from anything Quill had imagined. She'd seen few professional performers in her life, other than the occasional ceremonial mask-dancers who visited Spindletop and Harvesthome during the high-season festivals. Those dancers would appear from the night's shadows, their faces hidden by hideous carved masks, their bodies covered by long, shaggy reed cloaks that made them look even more beastly. They'd rush around and frighten the cubs and young *firra*, wheeling around the dance grounds and howling to the stars, before fleeing back to the darkness with relieved laughs following them into the night. The mask-dancers took the People's fears and anxieties with them, and when the young *fahr* stepped back into the settlement, the masks and cloaks hidden, they returned to a community that had faced its shadows and surrendered them to the mask dance.

Those Tetawi dancers were nothing like these peculiar Humans and the Strangeling who accompanied them. The Tetawa couldn't understand anything the Humans said, but their acting skill was such that she had little need of understanding their tongue, for they made their stories known through the delicacy of their movements, the passion in their voices, the pain and power in their expressions. Theirs was an exotic and mysterious world, but one that was, for all that, remarkably comfortable.

At first Quill was surprised that there were few Women among the main performers, but Denarra explained that in many Human lands it was considered indecent for Women to perform in public plays, so Men often assumed the feminine roles. "They don't give a dirty damn if a Strangeling or a whore steps on stage, just as long as a Woman of rank doesn't soil her tender virtue," Denarra said, turning to spit on the floor of the wagon. Thinking better of it, she pulled a handkerchief from her sleeve and bent to clean up the mess. Then she giggled and stuck her chest out. "Still, I've got to admit that these silly prejudices have worked out pretty well for me. I get the best roles, and our customers all know that when they see these great bulging mams on stage they're getting nothing but the best!" Quill blushed, and Denarra laughed even harder.

The Medicine Show and Repertory, about thirty strong, moved gradually south, then eastward, at a leisurely pace. They rarely remained in any one place for very long, preferring to share their stories with new audiences every few weeks. Their last few performances, however, had ended a bit abruptly, as the Strangeling had an uncanny ability to attract unwelcome attention with both her exuberant *wyr*-fed fireworks displays and her equally enthusiastic effect on leading male citizens of the towns. The troupe usually had a few days before a mob came looking for the Wielder who'd seduced one or more of their handsome young he-Kyn or *fahr*, and then the folk of Bremen and Crowe pulled up and headed to the next town. It surprised the Tetawa that Folk could be so inhospitable, but these lands were close to the danger-riddled border of the Everland, and they had long ago learned that strangers more often than not meant trouble.

Yet even with all the quirks and upheavals, Quill understood why the troupe never got rid of Denarra. As maddening as the Wielder could be, she was also a dauntless protector of her friends. The mobs always came looking for trouble, but they scattered like corn-crib mice when the purple fire started dancing on the Strangeling's fingertips.

The main entertainers generally kept to themselves, as they spent most of their time writing and rehearsing the extended performances that were their own specialty. Denarra spent some time with them, especially with an acrobatic young Man with pale hair and a charming smile named Kinnit, but most of her time was with the eccentric entertainers who appeared during intermissions. The Strangeling introduced Quill to some of them: Lartorsha, a painfully thin Woman with wide, sorrowful eyes and lifeless hair, who danced with such frenetic abandon that Quill thought the Woman's delicate feet might burst into flame every night; Colonel Bedzo, a scarred but distinguished Man with sweeping moustaches who swallowed wicked-looking long blades and performed lengthy, emotional monologues that brought tears to the Tetawa's eyes, even though she had no idea what he was saying; Mother Baraboo, the leader of the company, an immensely fat Woman who sang beautiful songs and smelled like winter-mint tea; and the harpist Adelaide of the Veil, whose renowned beauty was hidden beneath a series of gauzy, mist-like scarves that seemed to dance of their own power. Though not an actor, the most imposing member of the group was grim, silent Klaus, a huge bearded Man with dark eyes who was the troupe's main hunter, groom, and wagon-mender.

There were few grand performances now, as the lands they traveled through were sparsely populated by Folk, and the Humans weren't interested in performing for the animal tribes in the region. Quill figured that was for the best, as she didn't think the plays were quite suited to the tastes of sage deer, coyotes, or burrowing owls. Still, whenever they met travelers, hunters, traders, farmers or herders on the way they generally stopped the wagons and gave a brief show, asking in payment only what the viewers believed to be fair. As a result, the troupe was always well-stocked with fresh meat, nuts, fruit, an acorn-fattened piglet, and even a freshly-woven fishing basket from an old Tetawa *fahr* and his grandson. It was a fascinating time.

Denarra woke Quill in the early morning of her third day with troupe. The Strangeling was dressed in an uncharacteristically drab grey gown and forest-green cloak. Her unadorned hair was pulled back in a simple braid, and her face was solemn. The heavy air was unusually humid.

"What is it?" Quill asked, instantly awake. She reached for her leather purse in the bed beside her. The dolls were still there, but she could feel them twisting in unexpected discomfort.

"We're about to leave the Everland." She handed Quill a small beaded bracelet. "We're coming to the Human lands, now, and you'll need this handy little accessory. Keep it on you at all times, and it'll guard you from most of the iron sickness. I'm afraid it can't help with what's coming up right now, though. It's not a very good experience, so I thought you might want a bit of warning. Don't worry; I've left and returned many times, and the feeling won't last for too long."

"What feeling?" Quill asked just as it struck. The wagon seemed to spin, moving from a slow, uneasy movement to a wild rush of vertigo. A bitter spasm of bile filled the Dolltender's mouth, and she vaguely heard Denarra moan on the floor beside her cot as the entire world seemed to collapse into thunderous madness. Horses screamed, the wagon-drivers shouted, Quill sobbed, and above everything roared the piercing shriek of the spirits on the Threshold of the Everland, torn and twisted in the Melding-made barrier between the worlds. She couldn't breathe—the very air itself bore down on her like a load of stone.

The chaos seemed to last for an agonizing age, but it eventually passed, as thoroughly as if she'd simply opened her eyes and wished everything back to normal. An easy calm descended over the wagon, and the air grew cool and light again. Quill fought to sit up, weak and trembling from the sudden shift, and turned to the Strangeling, who remained lying on the floor.

"How many times have you gone through that?" The Dolltender's voice cracked, and her mouth had a bitter, earthy taste, as if she'd been chewing on one of her leather-soled boots.

Denarra shrugged wearily and pushed herself into a seated position. "I've crossed the boundary more times than I can count, but I've never felt anything as awful as this. Something terrible is happening. It was worse than the time I drank a whole tray of Ramavarian flame-brandies. Let me tell you, darling, I thought I was sick *then*; my housekeeper told me that I apparently ran through the city wearing a soup tureen on my head and a gravy boat on my…oh, well," she stammered, blushing slightly. "Those trivial little details aren't all that important right now. At least that time the vomit was all mine."

Quill looked at the wagon's floor in sudden shame. "Oh, Denarra, I'm so sorry. I didn't know…"

The Strangeling waved away her concern and smiled. "Nothing to worry about. Sister suns know I've cleaned up worse messes in my life. Besides, why do you think I wore this uninspiring old gown? It's not like I have any intention of giving up my wardrobe and joining the Bashonak penitents on pilgrimage, you know. Say what you want to about the overthrown Immortals, those ancient spirits had far more appreciation for fine fashion and beautiful things than the pinch-faced Dreyd and their pleasure-hating followers. Come now, let's get you cleaned up." She pulled a covered jar of water from a bin against the wall and poured some of its contents into a large clay bowl. "And while we're at it, maybe you could share your little secret with me."

"What are you talking about?" Quill's face hardened in suspicion.

The Wielder laughed as she dipped a cloth into the water. "Darling, if there's one thing I've learned in my many travels, it's this: *everyone* has a secret. Myself, I've got more secrets than I know what to do with, although admittedly most of them belong to other people, and my discretion has been rather richly rewarded. So when I see a wide-eyed she-Tetawa traveling alone and prepared for a long journey in Man-infested hills far from any settlement that could be considered even remotely civilized, I know there's got to be something more going on in her thoughts than an afternoon stroll."

Denarra shrugged at Quill's reticence. "But of course you know that I wouldn't *dream* of imposing on you. You're more than welcome to keep your secret to yourself if you'd like, but I'm a pretty good judge of these sorts of things, and I think this might be something you could use a little bit of help with. There's no shame in asking for help; I do it all the time. It's why I'm here right now, in fact; a little financial miscommunication with a fellow secret-keeper back in Chalimor, Illirius Pym, which he'll no doubt have reconsidered by the time we get back there. It's not at all unlike the time I got into a bit of trouble in this unpleasant little town in the Allied Wilderlands called Swampy Creek. An unfortunate misunderstanding involving a rather handsome and remarkably well-endowed spice merchant, his utterly unsympathetic wife—who was, I might add, both surprisingly agile and utterly impervious to reason—as well as a three-legged mule with an aversion to freshwater pearls. You see, I'd been inadvertently stranded there after taking the wrong turn at Edge-of-the-Woods~"

"I'm going to Chalimor. I'm going to ask the Reachwarden to stop the Expulsion."

The Strangeling stopped, one eyebrow raised in disbelief. "You're going to do *what*?"

Quill took the rag from Denarra and rinsed it in the bowl of clean water before handing it back. "I'm going to talk to the Reachwarden in Chalimor and tell him how Vald cheated to get the Oath signed. Tobhi told me all about it. I've heard good things of the Reachwarden, and I know he'll help if he could only hear the truth from one of us. So I'm going to talk to him."

Denarra shook her head. "You sweet, silly little thing! You clearly don't have any idea what you're doing. You don't know where you're going, and you don't even know how to speak the Reach-tongue. I'd be willing to wager my snake-skin corset that you've never been this far away from home in your life. How do you expect to get an audience with the most powerful Man in the Reach, let alone get him to risk a war for a bunch of Folk whom most Humans would be happy to get rid of?"

"Simple," the Tetawa said. "You'll help me."

"Me?"

Quill nodded, studying the bracelet thoughtfully. "You're right: I don't know what I'm doing. All I know is that I've got to do something. I couldn't just sit at home and wait while our world fell apart. But I didn't think it through too much, and if you hadn't saved me, I'd be in some slave pen or worse right now." She held up her wrist. "Without this, I probably wouldn't last long in these lands. It didn't even enter my mind to worry about iron. You're right about me. I'm silly, and naïve, and small, and I don't know the first thing about Men or their world. What I do know terrifies me. But there aren't many Folk who could travel the Reach for as long as you have and still live to tell the tale. You've got more wisdom, experience, and courage than almost anyone I know, Denarra, and I need your help." She smiled. "Besides, you did tell me to ask for help. So I'm asking: will you help me save our people?"

The Strangeling gazed at the Tetawa in open-mouthed surprise, the dripping rag held limply in her hand. Suddenly she burst out laughing. "And here I thought that *I* was the crafty one! Well, I'm heading to Chalimor anyway to clear up that little matter with Pym, so it's not as though it's out of my way. All right–I'll help you, but only on one condition."

"What's that?"

"We've just got to do something about your hair. You can't very well meet the Reachwarden looking like an ill-tempered porcupine. Well, not with that complexion, anyway." Denarra planted her hands firmly on her hips and surveyed Quill with a critical eye. She sighed. "It's a good thing we've got a few weeks left before we get to Chalimor."

"The weeping reaches even here," Unahi said. Biggiabba moved down the grotto steps to sit beside her friend. The waterfall still roared, and the air still flashed heavy with dawn-brightened mist, but all of Sheynadwiin was in mourning, and even the gateway to the Eternity Tree was no sanctuary.

Biggiabba said nothing. They were an odd pair–the hulking Gvaerg-matron with the age-weathered face and eyes as dark as deep-mountain pools, and the bent she-Kyn with the faded tattoos whose black hair had long ago turned to braided silver–but they understood one another well.

The world had changed much in the years since the bloodsong called them to be Wielders, and not for the better. The Awakening had been a joyous occasion among both Kyn and Gvaergs in the old days, before the Shields came to power among the Kyn, before Men haunted the shadows. Biggiabba's Awakening happened late, much like Tarsa's, but in those days she'd had a community to embrace her and ease the unguided bloodsong toward calmer channels. After her own Awakening and long before her exile from Red Cedar Town, Unahi learned at the feet of a trio of great elders, including Mashamatti, her grandfather, who lived in his own Branch-hold near Thistlewood and took in his strange, frightened granddaughter, sharing the stories of the ancient days of the People and the Eld Green.

And then there were the Gatherings, when Wielders from all the Folk came together to share their wisdom, to dance moon-wise around the fire and sing, to mourn the dead and celebrate the newly Awakened, and to share news of their world and the lands of Men beyond. It was at Biggiabba's first Gathering that the awkward she-Gvaerg and the shy she-Kyn first met at the edge of a feast-fire. They'd been fast friends ever since. Biggiabba had wept with Unahi when the Shield of Red Cedar Town exiled the she-Kyn Wielder from her home, separating her from the sisters and that young niece who would one day come to her own Awakening; Unahi in turn nursed her friend through the scourge that mottled her grey skin and killed her only child, a fat-faced he-Gvaerg named Ore-Runner. They'd gathered medicinals in the mountains together, planted trees and healed wounded animals, driven poachers and other invaders from their homelands, and often just sat beside the other's hearth-fire in silence, content simply to smoke a fragrant pipe and gaze into the fire with a friend close at hand. And often lately, they shared the visions of Unahi's dream-world travels, where she caught glimpses of Tarsa's difficult journey and the dangers that threatened them all.

Because they had shared so many times like these, Biggiabba could tell what was going through Unahi's mind without need of words, but she wanted to hear something besides the sobs that echoed through the red-rock walls of Sheynadwiin.

"She'll be here, you old worrier. Nothing will keep her away. Blackwick told us that his merchants dropped them close to Tobhi's old home-ground. You've seen for yourself, and she's still strong. It hasn't even been a fortnight yet. They'll be fine. She'll be here soon."

Unahi looked up and smiled. "I know. We're connected more than she understands; it's one reason I gave her the staff, to keep track of her through our dreams, to share something of the journey with her. She's strong and stubborn, just like her mother. Those roots run deeply in this family. But I still can't help but worry. She's had to understand so much, with so little time." Her voice weakened. "I wish I might have spared her some of it. I wish I'd have had more time to give her everything she's going to need in the days ahead. With so much lost.... Maybe I should have stopped her. So much depends on her, and on the rest of these young ones."

Biggiabba nodded sympathetically. "It's awful lonesome, sometimes, thinking that we might be the only ones left."

"Do you think they're ready?" The she-Kyn stared off into the water.

"They'll have to be. You've done all you could, grey-eyes, so all you can do is hope for the best and trust them. There's no stopping this storm now. We just have to pray that the seeds we planted will have roots deep enough to endure."

It was a small fire, just large enough to give off much-needed heat but not so large that it would attract unwanted attention. They'd already had a few close calls with Humans this day and didn't relish another, especially when they were all so weary and worried. Men were everywhere in the Everland, even this far into the interior. Things had accelerated far beyond anything they'd expected.

This stretch of the woods was littered with piles of mossy granite boulders that jutted through the leafy canopy like green icebergs. Tobhi had found a defensible spot for them to camp for the night at the fern-covered base of one of the outcroppings, beside a small creek, and he took first watch at the top of the rocks while the others tended to the fire and themselves.

Tarsa removed her travel-worn boots, hissing as her blistered toes stretched free in the cool evening air, and leaned back with a groan. She was more exhausted than she'd ever been in her life. It would have been almost beyond endurance if so much didn't depend on their haste. They'd come so far in such a short time, and they were still so far from Sheynadwiin—so far from the Tree that called to her day and night, pulling her forward with increasing insistence. Tarsa didn't know what was coming in the days ahead, but the ice-cold knot in her stomach gave her more hesitation than hope.

A hiss of pain caught her attention, and she saw Daladir trying to pull his own boots off, without success. His face was thin and drawn, but he stubbornly kept at the lacings.

"Your feet are swollen, Ambassador," Tarsa said, pulling herself to his side. "If you get those boots off, you'll never get them on again."

He shook his head. "It doesn't matter. I've got to bathe them. They burn like fire."

"Then let me help." Tarsa took her wyrwood dagger and cut through the side of the first boot, almost to the sole, and helped the he-Kyn squeeze his foot out of it. Tarsa winced at the sight and smell; it was no wonder he was in so much pain, as some of the blistered flesh had gone bad, and infection had set in. She leaned with him to the bank and helped him remove the second boot, then gave him support as he draped his misshapen feet into the creek. With a smile, Tarsa joined him, nearly laughing as the cold water rushed over her flesh and eased the ache of the journey.

They sat there for a long time. When they could no longer feel their feet from the cold, Tarsa helped Daladir limp to the fire and began to softly massage the feeling back into the flesh, drawing on the *wyr* as she did so, trying to knit the damaged skin and drive out the festering sickness that had set in. Daladir never said a word. He didn't even flinch as her fingers probed his tender feet, but he watched her intently, his gaze bright in the firelight.

At last Tarsa nodded and released his feet, her face drawn but victorious. "I haven't tried much healing before, certainly not like this, but I think it worked. It's different from drawing out poison; you have to knit the flesh back together, not just remove something that doesn't belong. You'll still hurt, but if we cleanse your feet every day, you should be able to walk without much difficulty."

She leaned back, but Daladir caught her hand tenderly. "Thank you, Tarsa."

The she-Kyn looked at him now, blue eyes locked on green. His touch was

Old Friends

inviting, and her body responded with an almost-forgotten hunger. Her breath caught in her chest. There was something familiar in his gaze, something that she'd seen not long before.

But Jitani's deep eyes were like golden flame in her memory, and they'd burned there since she'd left Sheynadwiin. Pulling away from the he-Kyn, Tarsa retreated, suddenly shaken, to the far side of the campfire. When she finally slept, deep in the night, her dreams were of eyes, green and gold, in the darkness.

CHAPTER 12

HIDE AND SEEK

Thane's search turned up nothing for the first few days, even though he thoroughly scoured the woods and remaining slaving trains in the area. It was as if the little Brownie witch had been swallowed into the very earth itself. When at last luck came to his aid, it was unbidden but very welcome.

He sat on a rough wooden bench in the ruins of the Brownie village, waiting for the blacksmith. His horse had lost a shoe during the previous day's explorations. Being a practical Man, Thane thought it best to take care of the beast rather than push it further into the forest and risk injury, so they'd returned to the village, and the smith now attended the mare, though not with the care Thane would have preferred. He looked around. Now named Chestnut Grove in honour of the massive old trees that darkened the landscape for miles around, it hadn't taken long for Men to turn this ruined Brownie settlement into the bustling beginning of a Human outpost, complete with makeshift smithy, trading tents, and rum merchants. The trees were now being felled at a tremendous rate for lumber and to make space for cropland. Soon there wouldn't be any more chestnuts anywhere near the place, and the name would be just an empty symbol. A few ragged homesteaders and their families were preparing to move further into the Unhuman territories, ready to claim lands by any force necessary.

Irritation gnawed at Thane's thoughts as he watched more and more Men enter the town from the west. The stink of smoke, horse dung, and Human waste increased with every new traveler, and the road had been churned into slimy mud by the recent storms and hundreds of strange feet passing through Chestnut Grove toward anticipated riches to the east. The numbers could only increase. He remembered the last time he traveled through the town, shortly before he'd first discovered the dark-eyed doll-maker, when the town belonged fully to the Brownie-folk. So different from now. Their little round cabins, though rough and unobtrusive, had been cared for with pride; the path to the river had been well-maintained; privies were deep and kept clean, and the outbuildings free of rubbish. The hundreds of small, almost tame animals that lived amongst the Brownies were now long gone, having fled with their Fey friends or died under blade, bolt, and musket-shot.

His single eye scanned the remaining buildings. The wooden statues that had once adorned the town were gone now, either sold as curiosities or destroyed for kindling. Although the Dreydcaste generally condemned statuary as objects of witch-inspired superstition, Thane regretted the destruction of the Brownies' animal idols. The Man-high blocks of wood were carved to resemble various beasts and stood proudly in front of the larger structures. Some had been strikingly lifelike, while others were given a mere hint of resemblance to recognizable creatures. Either way, the artistry of those idols had been exquisite. Thane had an eye for fine craftsmanship, but there was no longer anything to admire here; now those statues, too, were gone.

He sighed and stood. It was likely going to be a while before the smith was done, as there was only one forge in the town and many people were clamouring for his help. Thane decided to examine the rest of the town to familiarize himself with the other changes in the new Chestnut Grove.

He was sipping from an unwashed mug in the rum trader's tent when the first Men arrived with news of the attack in the rocky country to the south. Thane listened as one Man stepped up to the trader and began telling the story of a powerful witch and her monstrous warriors who'd called down lightning from the sky on his friends. Thane could smell Fey sorcery on the Man, even through the stink of sweat and sour-mash. It was a familiar scent, one he knew as well as the scars on his own flesh, even though he hadn't smelled it in years.

Things were finally looking more promising.

Thane turned back to his drink and waited. A crowd gathered around to hear the details of the story, and the Seeker was among them, listening past the Man's self-serving lies and the mists of drunkenness for details that might prove useful. Eventually the assembled Men and Women shifted toward the other survivors of the attack. Thane kept his attention focused on the first Man, as the sorcery-taint was strongest on him. When the drunkard lurched off behind the trading tent to find a bush for release, Thane followed noiselessly.

He slid behind the Man and waited for him to squat with his stained breeches bunched around his ankles. Knife in his left hand, Thane swept his right arm around the Man's throat, cutting off his air and jerking him into the underbrush and away from any accidental observation. His prisoner flailed wildly for a moment, but stopped instantly when Thane nicked a bit of flesh off the end of the Man's nose.

«Keep struggling, and I'll peel that little wrinkly nub you prize so much,» the Seeker whispered into the Man's ear, waving the knife downward. «Cooperate with me and this might be the only blood I draw.» The threat worked. The Man's knees quivered, but he didn't cry out when Thane dropped him to the rocky ground. «Now, enough lies. Tell me everything about your encounter with the witch. I want every drunken detail.»

The Man's voice cracked. «It's like I said before. Me and my mates was bringin' a load of them Brownies to the market when we was attacked by this witch, one of them snake-heads from up north. She was terrible--gold skin, purple robes, and them eyes…like green fire. It was supposed to be such an easy job. It was supposed to be so quick. Just in and out. And now I see them eyes and hear that laugh all the time. And the smell of the lightnin', and roasted skin….»

«I don't care,» Thane growled. «You said there were others. Describe them.»

«They wasn't too easy to see. It was rainin' hard, and there was fire everywhere, and screamin'. Their wagons appeared out of nowhere. Lightning started flashing around us, and then the arrows came. Cobbert went down first. He'd chased that Brownie up the hill on his horse, and it was about then that….»

«Stop.» The Seeker leaned in swiftly. «What Brownie was he chasing?»

The Man's eyes bulged. «I don't know! I never seen her before! All of a sudden this Brownie runs out from under this rock, like a rabbit from hounds. Cobbert sees her first and yells at us to stop, and he then he kicks his horse toward her. He's almost got her when this lightning comes down and....» His voice trailed off. «I ran after that. We all did. The witch suddenly showed up, laughing and calling down fire all over us. We lost a lot of good Men that day, I'll tell you.»

«And what of the Brownie? Can you describe her? How do you know it was a female?»

«I saw enough of her to know that, if you know what I mean. Her hair was all pulled back on her head, light-coloured, I think. That's all I remember. I don't know if she was still alive or not. I got out of there as soon as I could.»

Thane leaned back on his heels. It could be the little doll-maker; her hair was the colour of sun-dried sand, so that feature fit. Then again, it could be any one of a thousand Brownies in the world. He had a good idea of who the Unhuman witch was–the lingering Fey-Craft on the Man was distinctive and unmistakable–but the description of the Brownie was too vague to be certain. Still, it was better than anything else he had to go on, and it was consistent with everything else he knew about the Fey: witches were drawn to one another, like flies to filth.

«Where was this, and how many days past?»

«Two days ago, in the hill-country south of here. We followed the main pass.»

Thane lifted the Man into the air again and shook him like a half-drowned kitten. «I'll feed you your own liver if I find out that you've lied to me. Now, clean yourself up–you're fouling this place with your stink.» He tossed his prisoner into the thorny underbrush and returned to the smith's yard, where he found his freshly-shod horse waiting.

After examining the work and paying a brass-penny less because of the poor quality, Thane spurred his horse southward, leaving Chestnut Grove behind in the distant dust.

«The first...messengers have arrived, Authority,» Vorgha whispered from the outer edge of the door.

Vald looked up from his desk, his brows knitted in annoyance. The Dreydmaster rarely tolerated interruptions during his studies, as this time was increasingly sacrosanct. Although he'd ordered his attendant to notify him as soon as these particular visitors returned, the timing was rather poor. He was in the middle of a vexing translation from an ancient Rinj prophecy scroll to the Reach-script of his workbook, and the older Eromar text was veiled in a deceptively simple Crafting that required intense concentration to maintain the intelligibility of the symbols. There were far too few opportunities for research lately: the voices of the Dreyd were becoming ever more insistent as the days passed, and even solitude brought little freedom to fully unravel their enigmatic messages; the unexpected repairs on Gorthac Hall were an unwelcome distraction, as was the sudden disappearance of the Spear-breaker and her associates. And earlier today the emissaries from the Reachwarden in Chalimor arrived demanding explanations for the unorthodox and possibly illegal circumstances surrounding the signing of the Oath. Meddlers and incompetents. At least the intruders of this night were wanted.

«Dreydmaster?» Vorgha said, louder this time. With a deep sigh, Vald shut the dusty book with a snap of his hand and stood to sweep his silver-buttoned coat from the back of the chair. This evening's visitors were certainly welcome, but they weren't patient, so the deeper nuances of the Dreyd mysteries would have to wait. Vorgha led the way from the room, and Vald carried his own oil-lamp. There were things in this subterranean chamber that loved neither light nor heat, and in his absence an unguarded flame might well cause mischief.

They traveled together through the roughly-hewn tunnel that curled like a dark serpent through the underbelly of Gorthac Hall. Few Human feet had willingly wandered through this dark passage since its creation in the time of the first Prefect of Eromar. Of course, in those days the rooms were saved more for illicit liaisons that often ended in the bubbling screams of Women and the occasional Man, but times had changed. Vald had ceased to enjoy such mundane carnal pursuits; the Dreyd offered so much more satisfaction than flesh could provide. Yellow bones stained red and brown with the wet mineral moisture of the tunnel still sat amidst crumbling rags in most of the rooms along the corridor, but Vald needed few chambers for his studies, so he generally left the rest undisturbed. On occasion, when particularly displeased, Vald would order a bound and blindfolded transgressor brought to one of these long-abandoned alcoves, and then go about his business while the perpetrator awoke in the company of the long-decaying dead. Those who managed to survive the shock and numbing cold were occasionally released and nearly always shattered by the experience. And those fools never caused him further difficulty.

It was the ones who escaped who annoyed him. But they were few, and rarer still were those who managed to evade his grasp for good. Years might pass away, the world might change, bodies might age and familiarity fade, but vengeance was enduring, and the Dreydmaster's reach was long. Some, like the incompetent Binder, Merrimyn, weren't worth much pursuit at all; one Seeker was enough to take care of the problem.

Others, like the Fey conjuror who called herself Spear-breaker, were a different matter entirely.

The entrance to the under-tunnel stood behind the great wall tapestry in Vald's bedchamber; Vorgha, Vald, a handful of trusted mercenaries, and the fugitive Merrimyn were the only Men now living who knew of its existence. The nosy Unhuman spy Daladir was another, but he'd be dealt with in good time, too.

They stepped from the darkness. Vorgha set their oil lamps on the bed-table and quickly wiped dust and debris from the tunnel off the Dreydmaster's jacket. Stepping toward a plain wooden box on the table, he returned with a small brush that he used to fluff out Vald's muttonchops and bristling eyebrows. Such ministrations enhanced the Dreydmaster's leonine appearance, as did the high collar on the jacket. The effort was likely wasted tonight, but Vald insisted upon being fully presentable, especially with guests such as the Not-Ravens. One could never be too careful during these delicate times.

His toilet complete, Vald sent his attendant on an errand and walked alone to the garden corridor, where he released the sanctified ash and hissed the necessary words to pass the Craft-bound guardians unhindered. The doors opened, and Vald grimaced slightly at the raucous, cackling laughter and rancid stench of sulphur and rotting flesh that rolled through the ragged brown plants in the enclosure.

The Crafted gate hovered over the dry fountain, its iridescent surface shimmering like oil on water. Vald's eyes lingered on the dozens of knee-high, sniggering Not-Ravens that crouched with gleaming talons on the withered branches of the garden's long-dead fruit trees. Like stillborn infants brought back to life against their will, they bobbed back and forth, warily watching him approach through glistening black eye holes.

«What news do you bring me?» he asked, and then caught himself, realizing that the Not-Ravens likely did not speak the languages of Men. He repeated the question, this time in the common speech of the Fey. His mouth struggled over the words with obvious distaste.

As one voice, the creatures hissed in chorus, "We have found the ones you seek, oh Man, yes, we have found them all, short and tall, and She with the shining eyes and skin green as swamp-moss, yes~she walks proudly, yes. Unbroken still." Trails of black slime dripped from their mouths as they cawed and giggled.

The Dreydmaster nodded. "Where are they?"

Again the creatures chanted in unison. "Among the trees, in the deep, dark trees, where the beasts and the shadows reign, where their shining eyes seek dark wings and feathers, oh Man. They wander toward the weeping city, still many days away, but moving ever closer, oh yes. Soon, too soon they will find the city where tears flow warm like rabbit's blood. Still they walk untouched, oh Man, and still we watch them, never failing in our duty, as promised to you, oh Man. Watch them still we shall, yes, as you promised. We are faithful to our duty."

"You have done only part of what I asked. There are others I told you to watch."

The Not-Ravens nodded and clucked to one another. "Yes, yes, yes. None escape us, none walk unnoticed. All is well, oh Man. All is well. Their feet carry them quickly, but our wings, yes, yes, they carry us faster, and the night hides us well. None walk unnoticed. Faithful we are, now and always." Their movements ceased, and their heads leaned forward menacingly. "Now, faithful you must be, yes. We hunger. Your promise you must keep."

The Not-Ravens giggled harshly to themselves. Small green points of light flared to life in their eye-holes, and they grew more agitated on the crackling branches, flapping their ragged black wings and sending rolling waves of foulness through the garden. Vald nodded curtly and snapped his fingers. A chime echoed deep in the inner hall. Vorgha appeared at the open doorway after a few moments, his pale features set in an expression of bland docility.

«Vorgha, I must discharge a debt to these visitors. Is all in order?»

«It is, Authority. I will call the guards.»

The attendant returned quickly, and with him were two grim-faced Men, their black jackets soiled with mud and the blood of the chained figure who knelt limply on the ground between them. Vald looked on without emotion.

The Wielder-witch had left too soon, paid too little attention when she'd examined her poisoned comrades. Not all were dead when she left.

Young Athweid glared up with her one remaining eye, fear and hatred burning like a guttering flame across her mangled face. The iron chains sizzled into her wrists, blistering the flesh, but it was hard to tell where the freshly-burned scars ended and those of the last days began. Her oak-leaf ears were gone along with her dark azure hair–nothing but blackened stumps remained of either–but Vald had kept her silky sensory stalks intact and tightly bound. She might have cursed him then, but her tongue and teeth had long since been torn away under the skilful ministrations of the

Dreydcaste Purifiers. She hadn't known much about Tarsa and the others, but by the end of the interrogation had surrendered that sparse information as well as minor details about Sheynadwiin and the Sevenfold Council. Even she had been surprised at how much she knew, when given the proper incentive.

And now, once again, she was going to prove useful.

Vald turned to the other Men and nodded. Vorgha led them away, and the Dreydmaster was alone with the pain-ravaged she-Kyn and the eager Not-Ravens who crowded around his legs. Vald stared at her for a long while, unperturbed by her hatred.

«What a sad, wasted creature,» he whispered as he stroked her trembling cheek. «To think that the salvation of this world depends on such as you.» His hands moved quickly, and the bindings on Athweid's stalks fell free. Her bloody mouth gaped impossibly wide with the sudden, hissing rush of agony. He turned away, and the Not-Ravens surged forward, a giggling flood of bright teeth and dark feathers.

Vald re-entered the hallway only after the guttural shrieks stopped; he wanted to ensure payment in full. The door shut behind him, and he returned alone to the long, dark tunnel that led to his library.

There would be no further interruptions this night.

Mother Baraboo's tea wasn't very good; it was thick and a bit gritty, with only a little honeyed sweetness to please the tongue. Quill didn't mind too much, though, as she'd grown quite fond of the gentle old Woman and her strange associates. The Dolltender was willing to suffer the tea to sit around the wagons. She enjoyed watching their interactions with one another, and listening to the heavy rhythm of their alien speech.

Since Denarra spent most of her own nights with doe-eyed Kinnit, Quill's visits with Mother Baraboo had become a nightly tradition, but her days generally involved chatting with the Strangeling and learning more about the Human lands around them. They were in the arid southern reaches of Eromar now, nearing the great Windy River that separated the Dreydmaster's domain from Béashaad, the province of the Reachwarden and the city of Chalimor. This world was so very different from the fragrant hills and verdant forests of the Everland. The scrubby brush and trees were short and hugged the dun-coloured earth, as wild winds howled unchallenged in these rocky hills. It all felt less tangible, somehow, as though this world of Men had been drained of some of the vitality of the Folk Threshold.

The caravan now traveled on the Old Windle Road, an ancient track that had once cut across the Reach before the Melding. That catastrophe had placed a great sea in the middle of the highway, so it had long ago ceased to be useful for westward travel, replaced by the more serviceable Great Way Road to the south. The Windle Road was still used by those on the eastern side of the Riven Sea, heading east to Chalimor, and although highwaymen and other bandits were known to menace travelers on this grassy track, the Repertory was large enough to make all but the most ambitious robbers reconsider an attack. And with the Strangeling Wielder in tow, even those rogues didn't stay long.

All these things Quill had learned from Denarra, who embraced her role as teacher with great enthusiasm, though with no particular narrative structure or order, sharing mixed bits of geographical history, cultural lore, and social customs of the Human provinces with her young friend during the daylight hours. Then, at night, after Denarra left for Kinnit's athletic embrace, Quill would hide her dolls beneath the quilts and pillows on her cot and wander over to the bonfire in front of Mother Baraboo's massive wagon, where she'd sip her bitter tea while the members of the Repertory laughed, sang, and danced together into the early-morning hours. Occasionally Denarra and Kinnit would join the revelry, but they rarely stayed for long, preferring instead their own private celebrations in his wagon on the edge of the camp.

Quill sat on a cushion beside Mother Baraboo's massive bench every night. She still didn't understand much of their language, but from this unobtrusive seat she'd quickly learned something about their personalities from the way they interacted with one another. These Humans were much louder and more abrupt than most Folk she knew, and they tended to be rather physical and familiar with one another in ways that the Tetawa found unnerving, especially since they were so large. Still, they smiled and laughed when they were happy, just like the Tetawi, and they were always kind to her.

Of all the Human members of the Repertory, Mother Baraboo and Klaus were Quill's favourites. The old Woman cooed and fussed over the Tetawa like a mother pigeon. She kept a wooden box of small candies in her wagon, and every night she handed a few to Quill to enjoy. Mother Baraboo often chattered away in the Reach-tongue, which Quill still didn't understand, but the Woman didn't expect a reply; she just seemed to be happy to have someone new to talk to.

Klaus, on the other hand, never said a word, to Quill or to anyone else, but he never objected when she helped to clean the wild game he brought to the fire each night, and he always put aside cuts of the choicest meat for the Tetawa before returning to his unpainted wagon. His silence comforted her. Denarra was lovely, and Quill adored her, but the Strangeling's exuberance was sometimes overwhelming, so the hours alone in the wagon were something of a relief. Similarly, a loving hour of Mother Baraboo's endless giggles, sweeping hugs, and incessant cheek-pinches often left the Tetawa feeling much like a youngling's over-loved play toy, and she came to relish her quiet moments with Klaus. The thick-browed and long-limbed Human never intruded on her thoughts. After Quill had made clear her willingness to help, he'd return from each hunting trip with a small deer or a handful of prairie-quail and rabbits and hand her a stone-bladed knife. She'd sit beside him near the fire and dress the meat for cooking. Once finished, she might grab her walking stick and follow him as he checked the horses one last time for the night, or wander back to help at the cooking pots while the others danced or played lively songs on their fiddles and horns. Klaus spent little time among the crowd, but he always nodded appreciatively to Quill as he retired for the evening.

The other Humans were friendly enough, but they generally kept to themselves, so the Tetawa had little real contact with them. Lartorsha danced wildly to the music, her narrow arms thrashing back and forth, until just before dawn, when the gallant Colonel Bedzo would wearily lead her back to her wagon. Adelaide of the Veil never joined the evening gatherings, although she would occasionally slip through the shadows to the campfire to fill a wooden bowl with ember-cooked meat and bread, and slip just as carefully back into the darkness. Other performers came to the fire to join the fun, but their revelries rarely brought them close to Mother Baraboo or the young Dolltender beside her.

Quill had been with the caravan for ten days when the newest visitors arrived at the evening fire. For two nights Klaus hadn't returned from the hunt until after the Dolltender went to bed, so there'd been little for her to do but sit around until drowsiness claimed her. Denarra visited with her by the fire more often now, generally without Kinnit, but on this night she'd been gone too, and her young Human plaything sat dejectedly on a log at the opposite end of the fire. A sudden commotion caught Quill's attention. Stepping out of the darkness was the giant Klaus, two forms tucked gently under in his arms. One was a skinny young Human with unkempt brown hair, pale skin, and green eyes. His blue cotton shirt was torn in places, and dried blood darkened the fabric, but he seemed otherwise healthy enough. He held a large cloth bundle in his left arm and clutched it tightly to his chest. The second figure, however, filled Quill with joy, for it was a Tetawa, a *fahr* whose dark hair was chopped in rough bangs across his forehead. His dirty, blood-spattered clothing was unusual and rather old-fashioned~a wide-brimmed, pointed hat that hung from a cord around his neck, white fluted collar, ornate blue jacket with silver buttons and lace sticking out the sleeves, and buckled shoes at the end of his soiled white hose~but he was one of her own people, and he brightened at the sight of Quill after Klaus set him down at the fire's edge.

"Praise to the Old Ones, I'm among friends," he laughed in the trade tongue, clasping her hand and shaking it vigorously.

She pulled back, a bit overwhelmed by the enthusiasm of his greeting, but responded with a smile of her own. "Welcome, cousin! I was beginning to feel awfully small around all these Humans! What happened?"

He frowned. "A brutal attack…couldn't tell what it was. If not for the timely intervention of your large friend there, we might have been torn apart like the others." He bowed and swept his travel-bent hat in greeting. "You're a welcome sight in this wild land. The name's Jago Chaak."

"I'm Quill Meadowgood, of Spider Clan in Spindletop Hollow."

The Dolltender started to speak again, but the young Human suddenly collapsed, and Mother Baraboo pulled her massive frame forward to tend to his suddenly bleeding wounds. As though summoned from the darkness, Denarra appeared, her recently-tinted hair and emerald-green dress dishevelled, her face troubled.

After a brief consultation with Mother Baraboo, who handed the Strangeling a small clay jar and clean linen strips, Denarra led Klaus back to her wagon, where he laid the youth in her bed as she undressed him and began binding his wounds. Quill and Jago followed along, but at the door Klaus stopped the Fahr and pointed to Colonel Bedzo's nearby wagon, which was to be the Tetawa's resting-place for the night. He then motioned to Quill to join Denarra.

Before leaving, Jago moved in and whispered to the *firra*, "There's something wrong in all of this. Something terrible attacked us tonight–it seemed to become something different each time we fought it. The boy's been strange ever since; he's not himself. He's changed, too." Casting a fearful glance back at the wagon, Jago skittered back to the campfire.

Quill looked up at Klaus, who'd remained beside the door, a grim, silent sentry, then trudged hesitantly up the stairs and into the wagon. All the windows were shuttered against the outside darkness, and a flickering oil-lamp glowed over the pale face of the young Man in the bed, who moaned softly in pain. Denarra motioned to the Tetawa. "Hurry, Quill, and shut the door!"

"What's wrong?" She closed the door and dropped the bar across it before walking over to Denarra's bed.

"Something dreadful." The Strangeling finished wrapping the last of the bandages across the Man's head. "I didn't want to worry you, but Klaus saw a prowler on the edge of the camp. It was a couple of nights ago, when you were with him near the horses. He only caught a quick glimpse, but it was enough to know that you were being watched."

The Tetawa's mouth went dry. "What...what did it look like?"

Denarra's eyes were warm with sympathy. "Well, I've never seen it, but it certainly sounds familiar. You know the description, darling, because it was you who told it to me. Tall, pale, yellow eyes–a rather unfriendly acquaintance of yours. It knows you're here."

Quill's legs buckled, and she sagged to her knees on the wagon floor. Denarra sighed. "As soon as he told me what he'd seen, Klaus and I decided to keep a watch out for you. We followed the creature's trail the past two nights, but every time we closed in on it, the track just seemed to vanish. Klaus is a splendid tracker, and he lost all sign of the creature; the tracks got all mixed up with others, a raccoon, a dog, a youngling. And, to be perfectly honest, I have more than a little experience in hunting down unsavoury types, and even my own skills didn't help us out too much. For such a big creature it's surprisingly cunning."

"What happened tonight?" The Dolltender's voice quivered.

"Well, we hadn't been gone for too terribly long when we heard some screams away to the north. It was a small merchant train, though not a very reputable one, from what little remained to see. One of those shady vagabond trains that picks up every troubled, desperate wanderer with a sad story, no questions asked." She stopped and considered Quill for a moment, then went on. "We got there as soon as we could, but we were too late to stop the worst of it. Whatever this creature is, it didn't worry about leaving a mess. Just ghastly." The Wielder shuddered. "There were only two survivors when we got there. The creature was nowhere to be found."

Quill looked up in alarm. "So it's still out there?"

"I'm afraid so. We didn't have time to keep looking, especially since this poor boy was so badly hurt. We figured it was best to get him and the Tetawa back to the caravan before going out again. But we'll keep an eye on you, I promise. Whatever this creature is, it won't get past us again."

"*Mishko*," the Tetawa whispered.

"There's a bit more," Denarra said, casting a worried glance at the bed. The young Man shuddered, feverish and unconscious.

"I'm not sure I'm ready to hear anything else." Quill was dizzy. The safe comfort of the past days had vanished with the grim news, and she suddenly felt as alone and vulnerable as when she'd crouched in the rain under the standing stone in the Downlands, hoping to escape the eyes of the slavers.

The Strangeling held up the Human's left forearm to reveal a three-tined black star tattooed on the flesh. A thin chain stretched from an iron cuff on his wrists to the locked binding on a small purple book on the floor, which had been hidden in the bundle in his arms. The tome was ribbed with a dull grey metal, and its pulsing toxicity made Quill thankful for the iron-ward Denarra had given her. "This isn't just some trader's brat out to make some money with a band of mercantile vagrants. I don't know what he was doing with them, but he can't be here by accident. If I've learned anything in my travels over the years, it's this one single bit of wisdom: there's no such thing as coincidence."

"Why not? Who is he?" Quill's eyes were riveted on the book shackled to the young Man's arm. The purple fabric shimmered strangely in the soft glow of the lamp.

"He's a Binder from Gorthac Hall, Quill. He bears the mark of Dreydmaster Vald."

CHAPTER 13

THE SPIRIT WORLD

The Everland night possessed a beauty that was unmatched in the lands of Men. In daylight, the sister suns warmed the world: Goldmantle, the elder sister, was the largest and most beautiful, her hue that of gilded bronze; Bright-Eye, the younger, was smaller, and she burned white-hot. They traveled across the sky-vault together, Bright-Eye's heat tempered behind Goldmantle's ample sphere, both looking down upon the Thresholds of the long-shattered Eld Green, ever-faithful sentinels over their fragmented kindred.

It was the night, however, that truly revealed the Eld Green's beauty. The Greatmoon, Pearl-in-Darkness, loomed large in the heavens. Even in the daytime the Greatmoon was an impressive sight, although only a milky shadow of his luminous radiance in the night. He was more mercurial than his sisters, more mysterious and remote; his mottled face changed shape and temper throughout the month and year. But Pearl-in-Darkness brought comfort, too, of a sort, for he'd survived the Melding intact, even while his two brothers were shattered to become the silver, sparkling rings that circled the Greatmoon and spread far across the sky-vault.

Men feared their own sky. Tobhi couldn't really blame them, as their own moon was a small, feeble guardian in comparison to the magnificence of Pearl-in-Darkness. The evening stars in the Reach were distant and aloof, not the shining, beckoning spirits of the Everland night. The single sun of the world of Men, too, seemed strangely lonely, although its white heat was similar to that of Bright-Eye. The Tetawa hadn't realized the unhappiness of that sky was until he'd spent so many nights under it. Now that he was in the Everland again, he could hardly remember the strangeness of that time, and he was glad of it.

Tobhi looked over at his sleeping companions. They'd been so strange lately, all fire and frost, sometimes laughing together, at other times falling into grim and awkward silences. Tarsa lay curled within the moss-covered roots of a great wyrwood tree, her moon-touched face partially hidden by her tangled brown hair. Daladir lay closer to the fire-pit, his face turned away from the dull flames. The Leafspeaker didn't have to see their faces to know the pain and fatigue etched there. Tarsa never complained, but Tobhi knew that her cracked ribs had been slow in healing, and it was sheer stubborn will that kept her moving so far and fast each day. Daladir, too, was wounded. Most of the ambassador's life had been spent in Sheynadwiin, where he'd learned the arts of writing, music, and diplomacy, but his knowledge of the wilds was limited to day-trips into the woods around the city—hardly sufficient preparation for this gruelling march.

Yet the trip was wearing on Tobhi, too. He missed Smudge quite a bit these days. The ill-tempered riding deer was a nasty biter, but he'd also saved the Tetawa a lot of travelling aches over the last few years, so on the whole it seemed a reasonable balance. He wondered where the little stag was. He hadn't seen him for weeks, not since trusting him to the care of one of his cousins after arriving in Sheynadwiin. Smudge was probably ensconced in some well-stocked stable in Sheynadwiin, where he was getting fat and lazy and annoying the other animals.

Tobhi sighed. Such reminiscences didn't do much to ease his own aching muscles. Although the Kyn were only a couple of feet taller than the brown-skinned lore-keeper, they had a wider stride, and he occasionally found it difficult to keep up with Tarsa's increasingly unyielding pace. Still, even though his feet were swollen and blistered each night, he was probably the least exhausted of them all, as his solid frame and journeying life had given him strength, patience, and calluses enough to travel without significant hardship. Being back in the Everland helped, too.

He was strong enough, in fact, to let their turns at watch pass, and to allow them to catch up on a bit of sleep. The days ahead weren't going to be any easier than those of the past, but he was certain that Tarsa would need to be stronger than any of them, and that wouldn't happen if she kept pushing herself so mercilessly. They were all desperate to get to Sheynadwiin, but the Wielder was particularly agitated, becoming more so with every passing day. Something drove her forward, and Tobhi wasn't sure that it was a good thing. They had to stand beside their People during this terrible time, and warn them of Vald's murderous hospitality and the full measure of Neranda's betrayal. Daladir knew about Vald's arsenal and militia capacity; his months as a careful observer in Gorthac Hall had seen some success in this subversive regard, if not so much in overt diplomacy. But they were still three days, maybe four, from the grotto city. Sudden, savage storms and the increasing presence of Humans had already delayed their arrival by at least a day, and there was no telling what difficulties still stood between them and Sheynadwiin.

The Tetawa looked at the Kyn again, this time more closely. Neither Tarsa nor Daladir stirred; their exhaustion would keep them from waking too soon. Tobhi had another reason to let them sleep. An unpleasant feeling had been gnawing at his stomach since their arrival in the Eldarvian Woods, and it grew stronger as they neared Dardath Vale. Something awful was waiting for them. He had to know what it was.

Tobhi reached into his badger-faced satchel and drew out the red cloth bundle, which he untied and opened to reveal the lore-leaves to the moonlight. He'd chosen their campsite deliberately, for it was one of the few places in this dense forest that had a clear view of the night sky. The radiance of Pearl-in-Darkness would be helpful for what he wanted to do.

As he'd done so many times in his young life, since his pepa had first showed him how to read the stories woven into the movements of the leaves, Tobhi settled his mind into the right thoughts, pushing away the hot ache in his feet, the awkward bite of a sharp tree root in his thigh, the exhaustion that weighed down on his eyes. It took a little while, but when the shift took place, he settled easily into the familiar change in his senses. His hearing and sight went distant and dull, but he could now smell the deep and earthy spice of lush vegetation and rich soil around him, and his tingling fingers almost burned with renewed awareness. The strains of the journey vanished as his full attention focused on the ridges and smooth webbing of each leaf.

He followed their spreading veins, stark against the nearly-transparent membrane in the moonlight, and traveled across their mottled texture, sometimes rough, sometimes soft and cool as river rock.

Ordinarily, this would be where he drew on the stories embedded in the leaves and their dancing patterns to understand the wisdom of the past and present. This time, however, he was moving toward divination, which was something he generally disliked. Too many things could go wrong; the future was always mixed up with emotions, fears, passions, and expectations. In spite of these dangers, he didn't have much choice. The world had grown so much more dangerous, and he needed something to hold on to, something to prepare him for the darkness at the end of this road. It was hard to clear the mind of all that mess to get to the single question that most concerned him: *What's gonna happen to us when we get to Sheynadwiin?*

He fanned the leaves gently through his fingers to mix them up, but his brows knitted in sudden worry, and he stopped. Two of the leaves were broken. He thought back, remembering the brief attempt at reading he'd tried with Tarsa in Eromar, the night of their arrival at Gorthac Hall. Frowning, he pulled the leaves out of the pile and felt them more closely: *Ehk-shewi* and *Ghwai-shewi*–the fawn and the doe. Both leaves broken, both now useless, their part in the story missing. Whatever wisdom they could bring to his speaking was lost for the moment. He'd have to craft two replacement leaves, and he had neither the time nor strength to do so now, as those forming prayers required fasting and days of concentrated attention.

He'd just have to make do without them.

Suddenly, he heard his father's voice. *There's seventy-seven leaves here, cub–no more, no less. There's ages of wisdom tied up in 'em, too. All the stories of the Folk are wrapped up somehow into them lore-leaves, so you got to give 'em honour and respect. Don't be thinkin' ye can change the stories just 'cause ye don't like what ye'r hearin'. And don't be puttin' some aside thinkin' ye can fool yeself in learnin' the story. They's all necessary, even if ye en't sure of how they go together. Ye'r just part of the story; ye can't always see the whole story until it's passed, if even then.*

Tears sprang to Tobhi's eyes. It had been a while since he'd seen his pepa, Jekobi, or his mema, Nenyi. With all the chaos, he hadn't given much thought to them. He'd always just assumed that they were like the mountains, the Moon~they would always be there.

A sudden chill crept over him. Even the Greatmoon vanished in the world of Men.

His hands trembled over the leaves in his leathery hands. Should he continue? *It en't like I'm tryin' to hide the story,* he thought. *If anythin', I'm tryin' to find out the truth of it. Mebbe them leaves don't matter none to this particular tellin'. It en't like we got much choice, anyhow. It's best to walk into the shadows with a dim lantern than with none at all.*

His pepa's words were wise, certainly, but this situation was different. There wasn't time to follow every detail of the tradition. Besides, it was only two leaves, and he hardly saw what significance they had for the current question. Too much was at stake to give in to fear. He had the gift of leaf-speaking~it would be irresponsible to avoid using it in such a time of need.

Although uncertainty still clutched at his chest, Tobhi slid his fingers through the stack of leaves, feeling each for the warm edge that called to its place in the story. When he'd pulled twenty-five free, he started lifting them to the air, following a pattern that opened up before his extended fingers as his mind returned to stillness. One leaf here; the next above it; the next to the far left of the first; the next beneath that one, and so on, until each leaf was in place. Again he pushed his thoughts toward his question, and this time he didn't hesitate.

The pattern glimmered for a moment in the moonlight, and then the leaves began to spin their story, moving back and forth, above and below, spinning faster and faster. Tobhi watched carefully. His eyes grew wide.

Clash of kindred. The Wielder in war. Blood in the water. The Tree falls. Death rides soft wings.

Trembling, Tobhi closed his thoughts to the question. He'd seen enough. The leaves stopped and slowly drifted to the ground, and the Tetawa joined them, his body trembling as the reading became clear.

Tarsa was marching to her death.

"What are we going to do?" Quill asked the next morning, disheartened. They'd spent a restless and uncharacteristically silent night caring for the young Binder, and dread had gradually settled over the Tetawa's heart. She wondered if she would ever feel safe again.

Denarra sighed and looked down at her hands. "We're just going to have to prepare for the worst. At least we have each other in terrible times like these." She held up her fingers and examined her painted nails from different angles in the light. "The periwinkle is going to be last month's colour in Chalimor, but there's simply no getting around it. We're just going to have to grieve and go on bravely, chin up, a song on our lips and in our hearts, and hope that not too many people notice our woeful lack of…."

"I meant, what are we going to do about *him*?" Quill motioned irritably toward the Binder.

"Oh, of course, darling, of course." Denarra stood and shrugged. "Well, I'm not exactly sure what the end result is going to be, but I don't think he's much of a danger to us right now. He's lost a lot of blood, so he's not too likely to wake up strong enough to cause us much mischief, for a little while, anyway. He slept pretty soundly last night. Besides, I've added a few 'special' features to this wagon to protect us from any unfriendly guests, and they didn't make a fuss when we brought him in, so I'd wager that he's not too much of a threat to us."

"But you said he's a Binder. Aren't they the witch-Men who trap spirits inside their books?" The Tetawa shuddered as she looked at the strange purple tome lying atop the quilt, but she averted her eyes quickly, as it seemed to respond to her attention, and its sudden awareness sent a sickening ripple through the wagon.

Looking back at the bed, Denarra nodded, her eyes dark. "Yes. That book is part of him, wrapped by dark powers into the very weave of his Human soul. It grows with him as he becomes older and ever more powerful. The oldest Binders have massive tomes that groups of slaves often carry, as they're much too heavy for the Binder to bear by himself. But they're not the worst of the Dreyd-pledged. The Binders are the middle rank of the order. The Seekers hunt us down and bring us to the Binders, who use their witchery to force our spirits into their ancient snaring-books. But it's the Reavers who are the worst, Quill. They're the ones who take the powers collected by the Binders and craft them into terrible conjurations. Vald is said to be a Reaver of incredible power. And I doubt that he'd let a Binder wander free, especially during this awful time. Something's not right here."

A thin, strained voice whispered, "You're right. I'm not what you think."

The she-Kyn and Tetawa turned to see the young Human struggling to sit up. His face was a sickly grey, and a nasty green-and-blue bruise discoloured his right cheek, but his eyes were bright.

Stepping in front of Quill, Denarra planted her hands on her hips and glared in annoyance. "An eavesdropper as well as a Binder~you're a cheeky little vagabond, aren't you? You're *supposed* to be unconscious." She folded her arms. "It's only fair to warn you that I've taken on a few Binders and Seekers in my time, so you'd better not try any tricks. I know a thing or two about your kind."

He smiled slightly and slid back into the blankets. "Nothing to fear~I just wanted to let you know that I'm not going to hurt you."

Denarra snorted. "You'd be wiser to be more worried about your own hide, my ragged pup; we can take care of ourselves."

Quill stepped out and peeked at the Binder, curiosity and suspicion mingled in her eyes. "He's not using the Reach-speech." She moved forward slightly. "Who are you? What are you doing here?"

The young Human's smile disappeared. "I'm just a pilgrim heading eastward."

"I've never seen a true pilgrim with such a lovely snaring-book shacked to his wrist, or one wearing such fine silks. They may be tattered from travel, but they're undeniably of less-than-modest origin. You'll have to do better than that." Denarra laughed, but there was a hard edge to the sound. "Besides, I saved your scrawny skin, so the least you can do is tell me on whose behalf it was that I ruined my favourite green riding dress."

For a moment the Binder looked as if he might resist, but his wounds and exhaustion were too much. He crumpled back into the bed. "Merrimyn Hurlbuck."

"Very well–did you see what attacked you, young Hurlbuck? What are you doing all the way here? You're quite a long distance from Eromar City."

His face flushed. "My reasons for being here are my own. I told you that I'm not going to hurt you, and I meant it." He turned away, his face toward the wagon's walls.

Denarra swept haughtily toward the door. "I'm bored now, Quill–it's time for supper, anyway. We'll let him sit here and pout by in grim solitude. Maybe later he'll be a bit more talkative. I just pray that whatever it is that attacked him isn't still creeping around the camp. After all, my wagon is outside the main circle of the caravan. We probably wouldn't even know he was being massacred until it was too late. Fortunately, however, we now know his name for the lonely gravestone; I hear it's the way Humans prefer to be memorialized after death…for those who are actually missed, that is."

She looked over her shoulder, but Merrimyn remained with his back to the she-Folk, unresponsive except for a slight defensive shrug of his shoulders. As she followed Quill out of the wagon, Denarra called back, "Let us know if you change your mind, Merrimyn Hurlbuck. A good hot meal among friends is a rare thing these days, but we can't have you in the circle if we can't trust you." She shut the door softly behind her.

Jago Chaak was waiting for Quill at the mid-morning campfire. Mother Baraboo embraced Denarra and began regaling her with a breathless story in the Reach-tongue, so Quill was somewhat relieved to have someone to talk with. Ordinarily she'd have been forced to simply look around, a docile and smiling mute.

Jago patted the log beside him. "Where have you been? I was up with the dawn waiting to see you."

The Dolltender picked up a small clay bowl and ladled stew into it, then grabbed a chunk of thick grain bread. "We were talking with the Human you came in with."

"Really?" The *fahr's* eyes grew fearful. "What did he say?"

Sitting down, Quill began to eat. "Not much, although he does speak Folk-tongue," she said between bites. "He's not very talkative. I don't think he trusts us much."

"Doesn't trust *you*?" Jago laughed. "It seems like it's the wrong way around, doesn't it?"

"Maybe." She went back to her meal. She didn't want to talk about the Binder anymore. She just wanted to eat.

Sensing a shift in her mood, Jago blushed. "I'm sorry~I shouldn't be so direct. We've only just met. Please, forgive me. It's been so long since I've been around other Tetawi, so it's easy to forget myself."

Quill smiled gratefully and returned to her meal. They sat quietly. Finally, bored and a little bit ashamed, the Dolltender said, "We didn't get much of a chance to talk last night. Who's your family? Why are you all the way out here?"

Jago grinned, grateful for the return to conversation. "I'm a toymaker. My father also made toys, so I learned the craft from him. We lived in a small village near the Tuskwood, far to the west. I set out on the road after he died, and I've been traveling ever since. The brigands destroyed my wagon, or I'd show you my dolls."

Her eyes shining with interest, Quill put down her bowl. "Your what?"

"Dolls. They're my specialty."

The *firra* clapped her hands together joyfully. "I make dolls, too! Apple-head husk dolls." It was the first time she'd ever met another dollmaker. She wondered if he could speak to his dolls, although she rather doubted it, as he referred to them as playthings.

"Now this is a rare pleasure! My own dolls are painted wood~nothing quite so soft and expressive as apples. I'd be most interested in seeing how you make yours." Jago's enthusiasm nearly matched her own. His bright gaze was so intense that Quill turned away, flushing scarlet. Only one other *fahr* had ever been able to make her blush like this, and he was far away on his own dangerous path.

Something caught her eye beyond the fire. Merrimyn stood in one of Denarra's dressing robes at the edge of the firelight, his shackled arm and snaring-book wrapped tightly in a magenta quilt from the Strangeling's bed. He smiled wanly at the Dolltender and approached. "I hope you don't care if I've changed my mind."

"You'd better talk to Denarra. She wants to know a little more about you before you get too comfortable."

The Human looked a bit hurt at Quill's curt tone, but he moved in the Strangeling's direction. The Tetawa's eyes followed him. He was young, perhaps no more than twenty summers, if her limited experience with Humans could be a reliable measure. It was clear, though, that his youth hadn't spared him a hard life. His eyes darted nervously back and forth, watching every movement. His shoulders were hunched slightly, as though anticipating danger from any of the people around him. Last night's attack wasn't the first or only time he'd been hurt; the fading bruises around his neck and shoulders gave testament to a much longer familiarity with pain.

They were too far away to hear, but whatever Merrimyn said to Denarra seemed effective, because she flashed her most charming smile and led the young Binder back to the fire, where Mother Baraboo gave him a hug and a bowl of stew. He sat beside the massive Woman and was soon lost in conversation with her.

"'There's no such thing as coincidence,'" Quill whispered, recalling Denarra's observation as she studied the Binder. "I'm not sure I like what that means for us now." She turned to Jago, but Merrimyn's appearance had ended the conversation. The toymaker was gone.

Proclamation

Declared by His Esteemed Martial Authority,
The Governing Prefect,
Lojar Vald,
Dreydmaster and Pledged Defender of the Sovereign State of Eromar,
Independent Affiliate of the Reach Confederacy.
Dated the Third day of Sunmark,
one thousand and eight years
since the Ascension of the Revered Dreyd.

Be it here Declared to all Lawful Citizens of the Sovereign State of Eromar, and to all Lawful Citizens of the Reach Confederacy, that the Insolent, Self-Styled leaders of the Unhumans of the Territory formerly known as THE EVERLAND have been Cast Aside by their Right-Thinking Kindred who seek Peace with Men.

Be it here Declared to all Lawful Citizens of the Sovereign State of Eromar, and to all Lawful Citizens of the Reach Confederacy, that the Prefect and his Governing Council have Long Asserted the Sovereign Rights of Eromar to the Territory formerly known as THE EVERLAND, a Land that Rightfully Belongs under the Authority and Domination of Eromar. The Sovereign Rights of Eromar, and indeed of the Reach Confederacy, can no longer Countenance the Flouting of Law and Order in the Reach by Self-Proclaimed non-Human nations. The Grotesques of the Territory formerly known as THE EVERLAND have too long Threatened the Common Safety, Challenged the established Authority, and Defied the Will of the People of Eromar and the Reach Confederacy by Proclaiming an Independence that is not recognized by Law, by Civilized Tradition, or by Sound Judgment.

Be it here Declared to all Lawful Citizens of the Sovereign State of Eromar, and to all Lawful Citizens of the Reach Confederacy, that the Wiser, Braver Leaders of the Territory formerly known as THE EVERLAND have Now been Convinced of the Folly of Resisting the Magnanimity of the Prefect and Council of Eromar, and They have Affixed their Signatures to the Right Lawful Oath of Westward Sanctuary, which Exchanges the Wilderness of the former EVERLAND for Cultivable Lands in the Eastern Expanse of Duruk, which has been Procured for the Benefit of the Unhumans of the Territory formerly known as THE EVERLAND by the Sovereign State of Eromar.

Be it here Declared to all Lawful Citizens of the Sovereign State of Eromar, and to all Lawful Citizens of the Reach Confederacy, that the Unhumans of the former EVERLAND are now Legally Bound to Surrender their Claims to their Former Territory, which is Now under the Sovereign Dominion of Eromar, and to Repair in Reasonable Haste to their New Homes in Duruk. Those Creatures who Refuse to Acknowledge the Legitimacy of the Oath of Western Sanctuary are henceforth Declared to be Outlaw Lawbreakers and Trespassers, and thus Beyond the Protection of Eromar and the Reach Confederacy. Those Unhumans who Obey the Lawful Authority of Eromar are Hereby granted Safe Passage to those Territories reserved for their Use in Duruk.

Be it here Declared to all Lawful Citizens of the Sovereign State of Eromar, and to all Lawful Citizens of the Reach Confederacy, that the Territory formerly known as THE EVERLAND is now under the Sovereign Dominion of Eromar, and thus Under the Authority of the Articles of the Reach-Pact. All Lawful Citizens of Eromar and the Reach Confederacy are Hereby Given Notice that the Territory formerly known as THE EVERLAND is open for Settlement and Lawful Cultivation to those who acknowledge the Authority of the Sovereign State of Eromar and its Prefect and Governing Council through Actions and Oath. The Laws, Customs, and Demands of Eromar are Henceforth the Supreme Authority of the Territory formerly known as THE EVERLAND.

Be it here Declared to all Lawful Citizens of the Sovereign State of Eromar, and to all Lawful Citizens of the Reach Confederacy, that Settlement and Cultivation under the Above Terms is open in Measured Parcels under the Following Guidelines: Unmarried Men may Claim no more than Five Hundred parceled Acres without a Writ of Property from a Designated Land Claims Minister; Married Men without Children may Claim no more than 1,000 Parcels without same Writ; Married Men with Children may Claim no more than 2,500 Parcels without same Writ. Parcels will be Forfeit if less than Half of the Claimed Parcelage is Left in its Present Uncultivated State, but will be Verified by the Land Claims Minister if said Cultivation is Undertaken with Due Diligence.

Be it here Declared to all Lawful Citizens of the Sovereign State of Eromar, and to all Lawful Citizens of the Reach Confederacy, that Settlement is to Begin Immediately, and Will Continue until all Parcels have Been Allotted. All Laws,

Customs, and Demands of Eromar will Prevail in Deliberations and Conflicts resulting from Settlement. Any Unhumans of the Territory formerly known as THE EVERLAND who Resist Settlement are henceforth declared Outlaws beyond the Protection of Law. All Lawful Citizens of the Sovereign State of Eromar are hereby Absolved of Penalty in Defending their Persons and their Claimed Property against such Insurgents. All Unhumans who Refuse to Repair to their New Lawful Territories will be Removed by the Martial Representatives of Eromar and Transported to those Territories, with all Due Care taken for their Swift, Merciful, and Permanent Re-establishment.

This Proclamation is Hereby Authorized by Lojar Vald, Dreydmaster and Governing Prefect, and Witnessed by the Governing Council of the Sovereign State of Eromar. Their Seals are thus Affixed Hereto on the Third day of Sunmark, Year of Ascension 1,008.

CHAPTER 14

DARKENINGS

At first Jitani thought that Sinovian had been injured, or worse; she hadn't seen him resting so quietly in months. He sat on the upper wall of the first great gates to Sheynadwiin, his chin in his hands, as the sister suns rose upward toward the sky. Jitani stood on the far end of the wall. The gates themselves were older than living memory. Drawn from the red granite and living heartwood of two colossal wyrwood trees on either side of the roadway, so carefully and cunningly carved with intricate leaf and vine lacework, some believed that the magnificent gates had been formed by the ancient Makers themselves. The gates had once stood wide open, welcoming all to the great city of peace. But that was before the betrayal of the Oathsworn and the subsequent assassination of most of those who'd signed Vald's treaty. Now the gates were shut against both the world beyond and the growing shadow within. It was an unhappy reminder of grim times.

Shaking her head, green hair heavy in the moist morning air, Jitani pulled herself along the narrow ledge to her brother's perch. His stalks twitched, but he ignored her as he stared off to the east. She sat down beside him and followed his gaze.

"Not much smoke this morning," she said. "The Redthorns are keeping the fires in check."

The warrior nodded. "So far. But it's getting harder each day."

"Will we be able to hold the city?"

Sinovian didn't respond for a while. When he did speak, his voice was gentle. "Our people are brave and strong, but the days of war and blooding are long past for most of them. I don't know. Perhaps. If we can keep the gates from being breached, we should be able to resist. We have enough food for a few months. Beyond that, I can't tell."

They sat together in silence. After a long time, Sinovian placed his hand on her knee. All was forgiven. It had always been their way, ever since they were hot-tempered younglings sparring with homemade spears and hatchets, neither one giving ground or expecting mercy. They might rage against each other, they might battle and fuss and quarrel and sulk, but they always sat down at the end and let comfortable silence speak their forgiveness for them.

Even so, Jitani had wanted to explain to Sinovian why she'd given her seat on the diplomatic mission to the young Wielder. It wasn't just passion, although the mercenary couldn't deny that motivation–she'd wanted to know the tender touch of the tattooed she-Kyn from their very first meeting, and the feeling had merely intensified with the realization that Tarsa shared the attraction. Just being in the Wielder's presence made Jitani's remaining sensory stalks quiver.

It had been a very long time since she had known such desire. Since the brutal wounding of her younger days, when two of the stalks had been cut off in an ambush, her ability to feel the world and its sensations had diminished, sometimes so much that she wondered if she'd lost the ability to feel anything at all beyond hot anger and pain. Tarsa's sudden arrival in Sheynadwiin was a welcome reminder that she could still have such hunger, though the Wielder's subsequent departure to Eromar had complicated matters considerably.

Jitani had wanted to share these reasons with her brother, along with the more relevant one: Tarsa was better suited to the task of helping the diplomats in Eromar. Although Jitani had travelled throughout the lands of Men and understood their words and ways, the Redthorn Wielder walked with a kind of protective innocence that had long been a stranger to the golden-eyed adventurer. Jitani had seen far too much of the Reach and its ways; the poisons she would have encountered in Eromar City might well have driven her past the point of endurance.

To survive the coming days, Jitani knew that she'd need to hold on to whatever hope still remained in her heart, and she knew too well that

Eromar would have extinguished that flickering spark. It kept her sane. It gave strength to her sword arm and fear to her enemies. It enabled her to sit on the great gates of Sheynadwiin and contemplate the peace city's precarious future without hurling herself headfirst off the walls and into blessed oblivion.

There was so much that she wanted to say to Sinovian, but silence was familiar, and it carried far less risk of misunderstanding. She didn't want to open up another argument, or worry her brother, who was charged with planning the city's defence. They would talk another day, when there was less to burden them both.

Jitani scanned the horizon, knowing that Tarsa wouldn't be there, but hoping to see her anyway. Hope. Such a small, fragile thing, but so very powerful. It was what made these dark days bearable.

The dolls were agitated again.

Quill had tried to give them their daily ration of tobacco and cedar, with a bit of corn-mush added as a treat, but they remained clustered together on the bed, their dark eyes boring into her as she tidied the wagon on her scheduled day of chores. For two days now the dolls had refused their meals, preferring instead to sulk. Green Kishka was the most unpleasant about it, with Cornsilk and Mulchworm mostly feigning disinterest.

Quill's tending wasn't going too well these days. She'd tried a couple of different times to sit down, clear her mind, and engage the dolls in conversation, but even before she fully relaxed into the chant, a nagging disquiet would rise up and scatter her thoughts. There was little time for such concentrated ceremonies these days, with all the necessary duties that kept the caravan functioning smoothly, and the addition of Merrimyn to Denarra's wagon cut sharply into the private time she might otherwise have had to speak with the dolls.

But there was something else that made communication that much more difficult. The dolls were afraid. The Skeeger had followed them from Spindletop. They kept trying to speak with her, but the shadow in Quill's mind held them back, so now they stared at her in frustration and fear, pushing hard against that barrier. Sometimes at night Quill would glance out the window and catch the flash of yellow eyes shining in the darkness. Even in daytime she could feel the hot track of those eyes on her neck.

There were few times these days when she didn't feel utterly exposed to the world.

Others, too, felt the strain, and stories had already started to spread. With the exception of Mother Baraboo, Klaus, and Merrimyn, all the Humans avoided the Dolltender entirely. A few fights had broken out among the performers in the troupe, causing even the gregarious Mother Baraboo to get angry. She waded into each conflict, her massive bulk listing precariously, and boxed every ear she could reach, sending all aggrieved parties to opposite sides of the camp until their tempers cooled. Klaus rarely came around anymore, preferring instead to scout around the camp both day and night and keep their elusive stalker at bay. His grim face had become drawn from exhaustion, yet he maintained his unyielding vigil. Merrimyn helped around the camp, but he said little to anyone but Denarra and Mother Baraboo, preferring instead to take afternoon rides with the Strangeling or, when Denarra was otherwise occupied, to sit and brood on the steps of the wagon. On occasion, Quill would look up to see the Man's brown eyes regarding her with a strange, distanced gaze. This didn't ease her discomfort.

Jago had become increasingly clingy and followed Quill everywhere; the Dolltender had never met a more skittish Tetawa in her life. He refused to go anywhere near Merrimyn and had even taken a clear dislike to Denarra and the others. The only person he seemed to regard with any good will was Quill, and that growing bond held little appeal for the Dolltender.

Of everyone in the caravan, only Denarra seemed relatively unfazed by the tangible tension. She'd broken off her dalliance with Kinnit, preferring instead to remain with Quill and Merrimyn at night, regaling them with various tales from her wild adventures and travels throughout the Reach. Quill half suspected that the Strangeling was making up most of the outlandish stories, but as she was in need of distraction, and as Denarra was impossible to dislike, the Tetawa had come to look forward to the evening storytelling session. Even Merrimyn seemed less burdened by whatever memories and griefs had followed him here. He might not have been any less of an enigma to them than before, but he was quickly becoming something of a friendly acquaintance~and perhaps even more than that with Denarra. They'd been spending a great deal of time together lately, especially in the afternoons, when they'd disappear together for hours at a time while Quill sat under Klaus's watchful eye.

The hilly country was becoming more domesticated, with small towns and homesteads scattered throughout the gentling land. Their early evening shows had more of an audience, and twice now they'd been able to stop beside one of the villages and entertain a larger crowd. Although the hills were generally rocky and often rugged, the lower country seemed to grow more fertile as they moved eastward, and massive fields of wheat, corn, and other grains spread out around the road. Quill had never seen anything like these before, as Tetawi crops tended to be small and tightly nestled among their orchards, with all sorts of plants growing in the same soil. These Human farmers seemed to prefer segregated crops that couldn't nourish one another. It hardly seemed a sensible way of cultivating food, but she wasn't a farmer, and this land was so very different from her own, so she just left it as yet another strange mystery of Human behaviour.

Chalimor was still well over a week away, and then the truly difficult part of the journey would begin. Quill shuddered. What then? She'd planned to go right up to the Reachwarden and argue her case, but that was before she'd realized just how enormous her task was. The Reachwarden was the single most powerful Man in the Reach, the elected representative of what was clearly a massive and expanding population. Why would he listen to a single little Tetawa? Would he even be able to understand her? Denarra was here now, but would she follow to the end of this journey? What if the

Reachwarden refused Quill's plea? Would she ever be able to get back home?

Would she even have a home to go back to?

A loud rapping on the wagon's door broke through Quill's reverie. It was Jago's characteristic knock: five rapid taps, followed by two more. She breathed a deep sigh and swept a scarf over the dolls to hide them from prying eyes.

As Jago consistently refused to enter the wagon, Quill opened the top half and let it swing outward. The *fahr* stood on the stairs and smiled.

"What is it, Jago?" Quill asked, not even trying to keep the irritation from her voice.

He smile wavered. "Well…I was just wondering if you might enjoy a late-afternoon walk. It's a lovely day."

Indeed, the weather was quite fine. They'd been in this site for a couple of days, a small, spring-fed hollow, just off the main track of the Old Windle Road. It was a good site to refill their supplies, as it was nestled in the hills just north of the small town of Widley's Pike. Their first day in the hollow had been marked by unyielding rain, but dawn had brought sunshine and a cool crispness to the air. The perfume of midsummer flowers wafted through the wagons along with the sounds of music rising up from among the wagons. It was a day to treasure.

Jago shifted uncomfortably. Quill blushed, suddenly realizing that she'd ignored his request as she stood lost in her thoughts. For a moment she considered returning to the wagon and finishing her chores, but the sudden urge to run through wildflowers and get away from all the stress and strain of the caravan took hold of her. Besides, Denarra and Merrimyn had been gone most of the day themselves, probably enjoying a ride to the market at Widley's Pike. There was still plenty of daylight remaining; she could get back in time to finish cleaning up.

"Of course I'll go, Jago," she smiled as she untied her apron and threw it on her cot. "It's far too lovely an afternoon to waste it inside." She followed the *fahr* outside, taking special care to shut the door firmly behind her.

Jago's mood brightened considerably as they walked away, and his own infectious eagerness took hold of her. They raced each other through the wagons, laughingly dodging the tall people as they rushed toward the wooded hills.

In the shadows of the trees, a large figure watched as the two giggling Tetawi slipped out of the safety of the caravan and moved closer to the forest. There was no need for pursuit…not yet. They would arrive in the trees soon enough. He didn't want to surprise his quarry too soon.

The hunt was almost over.

Tarsa crashed through the underbrush, her heart in her throat, as the next blast of the musket exploded behind her. The Men were everywhere. Tobhi and Daladir rolled together into the ravine. The Tetawa's breath was slow; the wide cut on his forehead bothered him more than Tarsa had first thought. Daladir's glance met hers as he pulled Tobhi to his feet.

They could hear voices behind them–the Men weren't going to give up too quickly on this pursuit. Taking a deep breath, Tarsa pulled her sensory stalks free of their soiled linen wrappings and slipped her hands into the rich black soil at her feet. As her six digits wove through the roots and around worms and beetles, the *wyr* flowed through her, and she chanted out to the spirits in the trees around them, to those of the deep earth beneath them, to those of the thin stream that soaked through her travel leathers. Even the air responded to her need. A thick cloud of mist rolled down the ravine and swallowed the Folk in its chill embrace. They could hear the Men shouting out in sudden fear, their voices muffled and distant.

A crashing burst echoed through the trees, followed by a sound like branches thrashing in a mighty storm. A deep, rolling groan moved through the earth. Daladir threw his hands over his ears as the sharp, snapping crash of moving stones pierced the forest. The ground trembled again, and the noise repeated again, closer now. Sweat streamed down Daladir's face. The fog obscured his vision, but he could hear enough to know that the Men had forgotten all about their quarry~they were fighting for their own lives now. Screams and shouts of pain bounced strangely off the mist-shrouded trees for what seemed an endless time. At last the cries faded, and all the he-Kyn could hear was the soft, easy whisper of leaves as they settled back to rest.

Tarsa looked at the ambassador, her eyes heavy with exhaustion. "The mist will move ahead of us for a little while, at least until we get near the city," she whispered. "I don't think we'll have any more trouble today~we're almost there, and Sheynadwiin is well-defended from outside attacks." She sighed deeply and re-wrapped her stalks. "These Men will think twice before coming any closer to the city."

Daladir nodded. "These ones, yes, but you can't stop them all."

The Wielder turned away from the he-Kyn and moved down the ravine.

Tobhi's wound had rattled him a bit and left him with a biting headache, but he was soon able to walk on his own, and they started off again. They moved more slowly now. Even with the mist to guard their movements from unfriendly eyes, all three were weak, wounded, and hungry, and although Sheynadwiin was relatively close, they were more in danger now than they'd been since coming back.

Men had never penetrated so far into the Everland, not even during the Battle of Five Axes, when a small battalion of Mannish troops foolishly entered The Wild to the north to protect Human prospectors from Gvaerg and Tetawa attacks. The short, definitive battle that followed left no doubt that the Folk were the sole inheritors of the Everland, and the memory remained strong, even three hundred years later. But now Men roamed freely through the forests and mountains, becoming bolder and more brutal as they drove birds, Beasts, and the other Everland peoples from their ancient homes and deeper into the domain's hidden heart.

Daladir watched Tarsa closely. Tobhi had confided the results of his leaf-speaking to the he-Kyn, with the hope that together they could protect the young, wilful Wielder from harm. Now they both moved carefully, hoping to challenge whatever evil waited in her future.

Tarsa didn't seem to notice, or even to care; her need to reach Sheynadwiin consumed her. As the Redthorn Wielder came closer to the city, she finally understood what had been driving her for so long. The Tree called to her. She had no choice but to answer.

As they moved out of the ravine and back toward Sheynadwiin, Daladir noticed that the ground was torn up in places. There were scattered weapons and fragments of clothing, yet no blood or bodies remained behind to mark the devastation.

"Did the earth take them?" he asked, his voice low in the thick murk.

Tarsa turned. "They aren't dead."

"But all those noises, those screams~it sounded like a slaughter."

The Wielder smiled grimly. "That's what I hoped they'd think, too. Some fog, a few moving trees and shifting stones, and they scattered like sparrows in a storm."

Daladir looked puzzled. "Why didn't you kill them?"

"I thought about it," Tarsa said, moving forward again. "And I really wanted them to die. But their bones don't belong on our land. This soil holds and nourishes our people, not theirs."

She stopped and looked at Tobhi, whose own face was thoughtful. "I've thought a lot about this since the last time I fought Men in the Everland. Back then I responded with hate~I hated those Men for digging up our graves and defiling our lands. And I unleashed a terrible abomination upon them." She shook her head. "I wanted them to hurt as much as I did, as much as all our people have been hurting. But I don't hate them anymore, not after seeing so much pain and hunger when we were in Eromar. Those empty-eyed children…all the hope in their lives has been destroyed by the Dreydmaste'rs unending hunger. He's used his people's fear and need against them. I don't want to be like him. Even the Men lost in the *wyr*-storm at Gorthac Hall weren't wholly to blame."

Tarsa's voice wavered for a moment. "That's what Unahi has been trying to teach me. I'm finally coming to understand what she said. It's not enough to be a warrior if your heart is burdened by hate. I can still fight those who mean us harm, and I can still be filled with pain and rage; I'll still kill if I have to. But I'm not going to corrupt everything I love with the poison that has so tormented Eromar. Hate isn't our way. It won't be my way any longer."

They stood silently together in thought. Suddenly, the fog closed in around them again, thick and clammy. The sound of muffled voices briefly echoed through the trees, only to be swallowed once more by the thick vapour. Fear returned. It was impossible to know if these voices belonged to Men or to one of the occasional Kyn patrols in the area, but the travellers weren't interested in finding out. Hearts pounding, they waited for a while longer until the voices faded, and moved again toward Sheynadwiin.

CHAPTER 15

FROM SHADOW AND SMOKE

One of Quill's favourite songs as a cub had been a sweet tune about an adventurous young wildflower who sought freedom and adventure in the wide world beyond sheltered garden walls. As she and Jago picked a thick bouquet of sunflowers, daisies, and strange, cup-shaped purple bulbs with brilliant golden streaks through the petals, her thoughts drifted back to the song, and to the longing she'd once felt to be free from the predictable life of Spindletop.

She'd long ago forgotten that dream, yet now she was here, part of a traveling performance troupe, living with a flamboyant Strangeling Wielder and a Dreyd spirit-Binder, wandering up a flower-strewn hillside with an eccentric Tetawa toymaker. Never in her most ambitious dreams would she have imagined such a life, but it wasn't such a bad one, even considering the creature that stalked the night searching for her. In the golden sunshine of the late afternoon, all danger seemed so distant. The only reality was here and now, among the fragrant flowers and whispering grasses. She couldn't remember when she'd felt so fully alive.

No, that wasn't exactly true. There was one other time, one that returned to her every night, one that brought both pain and pleasure with its memory. *Etobhi.* Her heart ached with sudden longing. *Where are you, beloved? Have you reached your destination safely? Will you be waiting for me in our little cabin in Spindletop when I return? Will either of us....*

She sniffled softly, and Jago looked up from the grass where he was sprawled fanning himself with his blue hat. "Everything okay?"

"Yes." Quill returned to picking flowers, but the pleasure was gone, and a great loneliness took its place. Now all she wanted was to be back in the wagon, where she could cry with the dolls, away from the open, eager eyes of this young *fahr*. "I'm just not feeling too good anymore. I probably shouldn't have come."

Jago's face fell. "Well, we ought to head back, anyway; it's getting late," he said, his voice soft, and Quill looked up at the hill with a start. She hadn't realized how far away from the caravan they'd wandered. The sun was still above the horizon, but it was descending swiftly.

Wrapping the flowers together with a small ribbon from her pocket, Quill followed the toymaker down the hillside. Jago's shoulders were hunched, and he walked ahead of her with a wounded air. He fancied her; his every movement made that abundantly clear. For a moment the Dolltender thought about explaining everything to him, to let him know that he had nothing to do with her mood, but it was just too much effort. Besides, it wasn't as though she'd ever given him any reason to believe that she had intentions toward him; if anything, she'd become increasingly impatient with his presence over the past few days.

Jago stopped and looked off into the distance. Quill followed his gaze to the top of the hill. Her skin went cold with fear. In the blinding light of the failing sun, a large shadow moved down the hillside toward them. She couldn't make out any features, but it was enough to send familiar terror surging through her.

"Whatever it is," the toymaker said, "it's awfully tall, and it's coming here." He pointed to the line of thick trees to their right. "We'll never make it to the caravan~maybe we can lose it in the trees." He grabbed Quill's hand and they ran together toward the woods. She could hear something cry out in the distance behind her, but the noise was swallowed by the pounding drum of her heart as they rushed down the hill and into the green timber.

The smell of dry pine washed over them. They wove back and forth through the trees, feet slipping across the thick blanket of evergreen needles on the forest floor. Jago led the way, moving up the hill and down again, back and forth, until all signs of their pursuers and all direction were lost. The light of the approaching sunset streamed through the forest canopy, but the golden shafts of light did little to brighten the trees; the gathering gloom seemed deeper, more malevolent.

Her legs weak, Quill collapsed to the ground. Jago's pale face was now flushed. He looked like a tawny bullfrog, cheeks bulging with each deep breath. They lay on the ground and tried to catch their breath.

"What…do we do…now?" Quill gasped. Her lungs ached. She wasn't sure if she'd be able to stand, but her mind screamed for her to move. Their pursuers weren't gone yet.

"I don't know," Jago began, and then he let loose a wordless cry. A shadow loomed up from behind Quill. She turned to see a massive figure emerge from the enveloping twilight.

Jago's cry became a piercing scream. The shadow dove forward. It grabbed Quill by the arm and flung her to the side, where she rolled headfirst into the trunk of an bristly pine. A strangled howl tore through the trees, but the Dolltender didn't hear it. Her body bruised and battered, her mind stunned by the fall, Quill fell into merciful darkness.

Behind her, after a brief struggle on a thick bed of crushed pine cones and broken needles, the feast began.

Garyn stood on a rocky outcropping overlooking the city and valley beyond. The forest burned throughout Dardath Vale, the flames lifting high and bright even through the thick smoke that surrounded the city. Men burned the wyrwood trees as a warning, and a promise of more to come. The influence of the Eternity Tree kept the smoke from choking Sheynadwiin, but the rest of the Vale lay wrapped in the ashy fume. Right now a wide assembly of Kyn, Tetawi, and Gvaergs fought to control a few of the blazes that had started in the city, while others had taken up arms and prepared for the first wave of invaders.

Guerrilla warfare had kept the first groups of Men from coming too close to the city and other Everland settlements, but as the numbers of invaders grew, harassment and delaying tactics became less successful, and many towns and settlements now lay abandoned as the Folk and Beasts fled into the more inhospitable reaches of the mountains, forests, and deep swamps. Though small bands of warriors still struck at the edge of the advancing horde, there was little hope that they could fight off an entire army of Men, especially Men armed with the murderous mechanical weaponry of Eromar. These killers knew no honour in war, no restraint or balance. They came to kill, to destroy, and to steal~nothing less. Garyn had hoped that the emissaries he'd dispatched to Chalimor after Tarsa and Tobhi went to Eromar would arrive with a timely reprieve, but there was little hope of that now; any Kyn traveler returning to Sheynadwiin would be dead or captured long before reaching the gates of the city. Besides, the Reachwarden in Chalimor had little support from the Assembly of States to interfere with what Eromar claimed was an entirely domestic matter. No Man had the courage to risk civil war for the Folk, no matter how just the cause.

Now it was a simple choice: fight, or surrender. And surrender wasn't a choice at all. They'd prepared for any eventuality, and though they'd fight to keep the invaders from the city, the elders, she-Folk who weren't warriors, and younglings were preparing to flee into the vast cavern system of the Gvaergs, who would hide and protect them. Garyn had also ordered that all the most important artefacts of the city be taken to the caves, so wagons full of medicine sashes, codices chronicling the histories and ceremonies of the Folk, rare stone carvings and wyrwood statuary, flutes, baskets, rugs, and other precious articles joined the refugees beneath the earth. If the city fell, Redthorns and other warriors would fade into the forest and strike from the shadows. Yet if the city fell, so would everything, including....

Garyn shuddered. No. He had to believe that it wouldn't come to that.

He turned and moved down the trail, back toward the Gallery of Song, to speak to the Wielders. Of all his many counsellors, Garyn trusted their guidance the most. It took a little while to get down the cliff face, as the path was narrow and steep, and his bad leg made such movement treacherous. Although his beloved Averyn had protested against the vigil on the cliff, zhe didn't intervene; instead, zhe waited patiently for the Governor at the base of the trail. They walked together in silence, hand in hand, and tried to drive from their thoughts the screams and shouts that filled the air around them.

Only a few Wielders remained at the Gallery of Song, most having gone throughout the city to assist the warriors and wounded as best they could. The Oakfolk elder Grugg and the elder she-Kyn Unahi sat on one of the many benches carved into the lower exterior of the Gallery, sharing a small pipe between them. A heavy weariness washed over Garyn as he looked at them. Those two had spent the better part of the day extinguishing fires; the exhausting toll of their Wielding etched their faces like the creases on weathered bark. Yet here they were, at the Governor's request, ready to advise him again in this desperate time.

Unahi nodded as Garyn and Averyn approached. "Any sign?"

"None." Garyn shook his head in resignation. "We can expect no help from Chalimor. None of the raptor scouts have seen sign of aid. I'm afraid we're on our own."

"What of the northern Gvaergs? Are they not concerned with Sheynadwiin's fate?" Grugg's deep, woody voice rose up from the ground, where he had lowered himself to dig his roots into the moist earth. "Do they not know of our need?"

"They know," Averyn acknowledged, "but they're under siege themselves. This was no random movement–it was a carefully planned invasion. Eagle and sparrow-hawk messengers have arrived throughout the day to tell us of battles going on south, in the Tangletop Forest, between Men and the allied Tetawi and Kyn towns. To the north, in the Wyrmwall Mountains, the Gvaergs are being driven back by Men with massive thunderburst cannons. Even the swamp-dwarfs of Blackfly Fen are under attack, and the swamp is aflame. We were prepared for the troops of Eromar, but not for the waves of squatters and land-robbers that surged ahead of them. They've had a great deal of help from within, and much of the terrain that we'd expected to slow their advance has been mapped and bypassed by the earlier invaders...and by some of the Human merchants we'd once trusted as friends and allies. Vald's fist is closing over the entire Everland, not just Sheynadwiin."

Shakar

Unahi frowned and drew deeply on her pipe. "True, but the Tree is *here*. Vald is going to strike us the hardest, because we offer the most powerful resistance, both in fact and symbol. As long as the Eternity Tree stands, the Folk will be able to withstand the rise of Men."

A thunderous roar split the air, and the earth at their feet exploded apart, sending them all sprawling. As the noise and smoke subsided, Garyn lay on the ground, struggling to catch his breath. Averyn moaned softly behind the Governor; Unahi wheezed loudly on the other side of the bench and tried to rise. Garyn couldn't sense Grugg's presence.

Through the dust and smoke a slender figure emerged. Her shimmering white robes fluttered on the rising wind in sinuous rhythm with her copper tresses and unbound sensory stalks. In one shapely hand she held a long, silver-hafted axe; in the other, she held the shredded flag of Sheynadwiin–a golden tree on a green field, surrounded by seven leaves representing the Branches of the Kyn Nation.

"If it is the Tree that holds back the tide, then perhaps we should attend to that problem," the newcomer said as she casually dropped the flag before Garyn's horrified eyes. A group of armed Shields followed her, bearing between them a still-smoking cannon.

He stared at the remnants of the flag. "Neranda," he whispered, "what have you done?"

"No, dear uncle–I no longer answer to that name. Have you not heard? My loving people have given me a new name to treasure, a new name that honours the lifetime of sacrifices I have made for them, a new name to reflect the unending toil, pain, and misery I have experienced at the hands of people so blinded by shadows that they cannot see the light they so desperately need." She looked toward the waterfall and lifted the axe to her shoulder, red scars bright on her pale blue face. "Remember my new name, dearest uncle, for it will echo throughout history when I finish what the Purging too long delayed.

"I am Shakar."

CHAPTER 16

PLAYING GAMES

The pain was excruciating, but Quill fought to open her eyes. If she was going to die, at least it would be with a fight~she'd come too far and seen too much to just surrender to her fate with her eyes shut.

She groaned softly and rolled over. It was still light; she couldn't have been unconscious for too long. A sudden wave of nausea struck her, testing her new-found resolve as she tried to keep the bile from rising. The raging ache in her head remained, but the sickness wasn't as crippling as she'd feared, so she took a deep breath, pulled herself up on trembling knees, and looked around.

Just up the hill from her, beneath the trees, lay a long form, its face obscured by Jago, who sat kneeling with his back to the Dolltender. His shoulders shook.

Her knees still weak, Quill leaned against a tree and slowly stood, using the tree for support. She didn't try to walk; she wasn't sure she'd even be able to stay on her feet. At least the threat was over.

"Are you hurt?" she whispered hoarsely.

Jago, still shaking, didn't respond.

Taking another deep breath, Quill pushed herself forward and was surprised to find that her legs, though shaky, held her weight. With infinite care, she moved up the slope, until she was close enough to see past Jago to the body on the ground.

Her heart froze.

It was Klaus.

"He's been watching all this time. I should have expected that it would be him," Jago said, his voice thick. Quill's legs began to quiver again. The toymaker wasn't crying. He was *laughing.*

"What's happening here, Jago?"

"All these days, all these nights, they've been watching me~all of them, the sneaking spies." Jago turned, and Quill let out a strangled shriek. The skin on his face was tight and translucent across a skull that seemed to grow longer and more bestial as she watched in horrified fascination. His watery eyes shimmered yellow in the deepening dusk. But it was the jagged teeth and long, serpentine tongue that riveted the Dolltender's gaze, for they were coated thick and crimson with the steaming blood from Klaus's savaged chest.

And as she watched, Jago's body changed. His arms and legs grew long and mottled, splitting through the Tetawa-sized clothes with ease. Thick, ropy muscles rippled under the writhing skin, and glistening ooze bubbled up on the grey flesh. His hair seemed to be drawn back into the massive head, and long, craggy claws erupted on pale hands where once four small brown digits had held Quill's own. It happened so quickly, and the Dolltender's mouth went dry as the nightmarish figure stood tall before her.

The creature smiled, his bloody teeth shining with a light of their own. "Now, don't you worry about old Klaus here." His voice was thin and wet, spattering past his ravaged lips. "He was brave to the end. He even put up a bit of a fight…until I chewed his heart out."

The Dolltender stumbled backward against the old pine. "The Skeeger. It's you. You've been hunting me all this time."

Jago slid toward her with eel-like grace. "Such a smart little dolly." Talons slashed across Quill's face, sending her tumbling down the slope with a scream.

"I was once of Magpie Clan, one of the few changelings in the flock. I used to fly for days, unrestrained, unhindered." He loped down the hill and landed beside her again, an eager leer on his face. She held a hand against her cheek to stanch the heavy flow of blood. Her head spun. He was toying with her, drawing out the moment as long as possible.

"They didn't like my games, couldn't understand them. They punished me. They threw me from the Clan, and they took away my wings forever." His face twisted and he snapped his yellowed teeth in fury. "They never understood how delicious fear could be–not until they felt it themselves. They took away my Clan-shape, but they couldn't take my Shifting-skill. So I made them play lots of games, and I won every time, until they bored me."

Quill struggled to her feet again. His taunts were meant to scare her, to make his feast that much sweeter. But he'd misjudged the Dolltender. Blood dripped down her face, and the fear in her eyes was now mingled with cold rage.

"That's why you killed poor Bryn, and all the others~they were just *toys* to you."

"Just toys." He stopped and stood tall, and his face went slack and cold. "They thought they were stopping me by stealing my wings, but I didn't need them." He skittered forward on all fours, his body suddenly that of a familiar pale raccoon with yellow eyes, and Quill stumbled back.

He giggled and moved forward slowly, returning to his monstrous Man-shaped form. "I didn't need them at all. I just went down, deep inside and changed *myself*. And it's so much more fun now. They used to be afraid when I'd sneak into their rooms and wrap a rope around their necks before having my fun." Grinning, Jago twisted his hands across an invisible rope and make a cracking noise deep in his throat. "But then~ah! When I became *this*, their terror lasted even longer, even after death. And it was…so beautiful."

Jago lowered his head, and his eyes flashed orange in the deepening darkness. "But one night, as I was about to have some real fun with a handful of little playthings I lured all alone to a forest, a mean and selfish maggot with her nasty little dollies spoiled all my fun. They took my toys away from me." He looked up at her. The smile was gone. "They never asked if they could play; they never even said 'thank you.' They just took my toys and left me all alone."

He moved forward, slowly, menacingly. "But I don't like that sort of game. I play by the rules, and I'm going to teach you how to play, too."

Jago slashed out again, but this time Quill was ready, and she dropped to the ground as his claws ripped into the thick bark of the old pine. Jago howled and pulled his hand away. A bloody nail remained embedded in the tree.

"Cheater! You're a cheater! That's *not* the way you play the game!"

The creature lunged again. Quill rolled down the slope, hands scrambling at the ground as she fell, and stumbled to her feet as Jago launched himself into the air and landed on all fours beside her. He caught her this time, and she cried out as his hands tore at her upper chest.

Leaning down, his breath hot and rank in the Dolltender's ear, Jago hissed, "I'll show you what happens to cheaters. It's a long, slow lesson." The blistered purple length of his squirming tongue slid wetly between his glimmering teeth.

Quill went limp. Jago leaned in, giggling triumphantly, but it was a mistake. On her fall down the wooded hillside, the *firra* had pulled a small, sharp branch from the ground and held it at her side. Now the creature was close, and she was ready. Quill's hand snapped forward and drove the sharpened point of the stick into his left eye, sending yellow slime spurting across her hands and face. Jago threw himself backward with a piercing howl and rolled his face into the dirt, trying desperately to drive away the blazing agony.

Leaping to her feet, the Dolltender looked around. The area was thick with dead wood, so she pulled a stout, lichen-rimmed branch from the mulch and swung it with all her strength at Jago's head as he looked up again. The branch caught him full in the mouth. He dropped shrieking to the ground. Teeth, blood, and a chunk of his ravaged tongue lay on the forest floor.

Quill bellowed inarticulately as she swung the branch again. Jago sprang out of the way, and the momentum of the aborted blow set the Dolltender off-balance to tumble hard to the ground. The creature, now insane with rage and pain, threw himself at her again.

But Jago never landed. The night erupted in a flash of mauve fire, and he flew through the air, crashing into a stand of young pines. Fragments of sap-coated wood rained down on the shape-shifter's writhing body, but it wasn't the pain of the tree branch that pierced his right thigh or the maddening agony in his shattered face that drew his wordless wails now.

A familiar voice echoed eerily through the woods. "Let's play a different game, shall we, darling? I like this one much better than that nasty fun you seem to enjoy so much. I call this game 'let's-send-this-beastly-degenerate-back-to-the-Darkening-pit-where-he-belongs.'" Denarra stepped out of the pines, emerald eyes blazing, and lifted her right hand in the air, where a ball of blinding purple fire flared to life. "But I should warn you—I play to win." She flung the fireball with a deft twist of her wrist, and it caught Jago full in the chest.

"Now, Merrimyn!" she cried out, and the flushed-faced Binder emerged from the darkness to stand beside her with his snaring-book held high. Jago flailed and shrieked, twisting maniacally to free himself from the crackling flames that raged across his body, but he was helpless to resist their combined efforts.

Denarra raised both hands into the air and drew Jago through the air toward her. Filaments of blue lightning now streaked from all directions among the dark trees to wrap around the struggling creature. Merrimyn chanted, his voice strange and resonant, the words unlike anything spoken by mortal Men. The air itself sizzled and hummed. His voice seemed to suck the very life from the green wood around them. Denarra shuddered. The lightning dimmed slightly, and it seemed for a moment that she might collapse, not from the strain of her own Wielding but the nearness of Merrimyn's binding. She gritted her teeth. Sweat beaded on her brow, and her hair slipped free of its braided coil, but the Strangeling ignored the distractions and maintained her pose, her hands still holding the screaming Skeeger high from afar.

At last, Denarra straightened and grinned. The moment of danger passed, and more lightning streamed out of the forest to wrap ever tighter around Jago's flailing body, lifting him high above the duo. The Binder held his snaring-book open and thrust it forward toward the thrashing figure. There was a sudden flare of white light. A screeching wail of torment ripped through the night. All went dark. There was a heavy thump, and Jago's Tetawi-formed body fell lifeless to the earth, its spirit lodged firmly within the depths of the snaring-tome. Silence joined the darkness, settling heavily on the hillside.

"Denarra?" Quill's trembling voice called out.

"I'm here, Quill. We both are." The Strangeling suddenly appeared at the Dolltender's side, her body wreathed by a soft blue glow to light her way. She was followed closely by Merrimyn, who held his shackled book tightly to his chest and trembled with the mingled ecstasy and revulsion he always experienced when Crafting.

"Jago…is he…?"

"Yes, darling, he's gone. He's not going to hurt you again." She dabbed a kerchief at Quill's bloody cheek and held the shaking Dolltender tightly.

"How did you know we were here?"

Denarra's eyes were soft. "We saw you two in the meadow. We were riding as fast as we could. I even called out to you."

"That was you? The sun was in my eyes. I…I couldn't see."

"Well, we were just fortunate that Klaus was keeping watch over you both from the forest."

Quill began to cry, her voice lost in her sobs. "Jago…k-killed him. I didn't know."

"Shhhh. Of course you didn't. Klaus was a good and loyal friend; he wouldn't have thought twice about protecting you, even with his life. He died honourably. We'll give him a good burial."

«No, you won't. We have a long journey ahead of us, and we'll be starting now.» Denarra looked up to see a cloaked Man standing in the clearing, his face obscured by a beaten, broad-brimmed hat. He stepped over Jago's torn and twisted body, and looked up, his single blue eye shining in the eerie light.

«Disappointing. I'd expected you to be a bit more difficult to track down this time. Your penchant for unsubtle pyrotechnics isn't the only thing that hasn't changed, Denarra; you and your friends seem to make a habit of blinding your enemies.» He kicked Jago's cooling remains. «Fortunately, some of us have ended up a bit better off than this wretched creature.»

"Vergis Thane," Denarra whispered, her face suddenly pale. "Wouldn't you know that he'd upstage my fabulous entrance." She sighed and stood up, wiping the dust from her hands. "Well, darlings, I hate to be the bearer of unhappy news, but we're in real trouble now."

CHAPTER 17

THE DOE AND THE FAWN

Sheynadwiin was in chaos. The gates of the city still held against the invading Men, but the battle within was between the Folk themselves. The Shields were locked in battle with the Wielders at the waterfall. Fire, ice, crackling storm, living stone, walking tree, club, cudgel, axe, and dagger met one another, and blood fell hot and steaming into the pool.

Biggiabba drew rocks down from the cliff above and sent them spinning into the Shields and their followers, but one of the Shields pulled a small iron globe from his robes and threw it at the Gvaerg, where it exploded into hundreds of small, piercing splinters that buried themselves deep in her flesh. Her concentration broken, the rain of stones ceased, and the Shields rushed forward, their axes raised to cut down the ancient Gvaerg.

But then Jitani was at the Wielder's side. A he-Kyn Shield swung his axe at her head, but he was a scholar, not a fighter, and his aim was careless and far too slow. Jitani caught the blade with the edge of her wyrwood sword, using the momentum to twist her body inwards and send the weapon flying. In the reverse movement, she brought her sword back down in a wide arc and cut through the stunned Shield, dropping him dead to the ground.

Jitani wasn't alone in coming to Biggiabba's defence. She was joined by her brother, whose own hatchet dripped scarlet. There was no more powerful Redthorn warrior in Sheynadwiin than Sinovian Al'daar, and his raging war-cry reminded everyone of the reason. He moved with the deadly grace of a cougar, his scarred body marked with fresh battle-paint and cuts, and those few Shields who tried to rush him lay sightless on the blood-stained earth.

Still, there were many Celestials, and even together Sinovian and Jitani knew that they couldn't hold them all back. The roar of cannon-fire echoed loudly through the city, followed by a chorus of screams near the gates. Civil war within, and invasion without. The great peace city of the Kyn Nation was falling.

The Redthorn lifted his hatchet and began his death song.

"You might want to wait on that," Tarsa called out as she rushed past him into the crowd of Celestials. She was a green-skinned whirlwind, her staff piercing armour and flesh with *wyr*-shaped spikes. The Redthorn Wielder was followed by her Tetawa friend and his sharp, darting hatchet, and a dark-haired he-Kyn who bore the spear of a fallen Redthorn and wielded it against the Celestials with desperate fury. A raging wind erupted around them, wrapping the Shields' own long robes around their legs like winding sheets, dragging them to the ground, where Tobhi struck at their weapon hands. Sinovian, Jitani, and the newcomers fell upon the Celestials like a thunderstorm, pushing them backward and away from the sacred pool. The sudden ferocity of the defence broke the invaders' spirit, and they scattered in panic.

Catching their breath for a moment, Tarsa and Jitani turned to each other and shared a small, secret smile. It was fleeting, but long enough for Daladir to catch the exchange. Its meaning was unmistakable.

"Hurry," Biggiabba called out weakly. "There are more inside—they're trying to hew the Tree!"

Tarsa nodded and sprinted to the cave behind the falls. Tobhi, Jitani, and Sinovian followed closely behind. Daladir trailed them, his face dark with sudden grief.

They had thought it would be difficult to get into the city, but Tarsa had called upon the *wyr* of the earth to guide them swiftly and safely inside. The soil had parted and roots unravelled themselves, opening a newly-formed tunnel beneath their feet. When the ground closed over their heads again, Tobhi and Daladir had watched in amazement as a passage spun open through the earth ahead.

That strange cavern oozing with mud, roots, and worms was nothing like the tunnel they were in now, which led to the Eternity Tree. This passage radiated the weight of hallowed age, yet there was no time for either of the he-Folk to admire the lichen-covered markings on the wall, or the glowing blue water that rushed down the centre of the tunnel into the pool beyond. Already they could hear the clash of arms in the chamber ahead, and Tarsa was running desperately toward the glowing light.

The young Wielder reached the standing stones at the bridge and stopped in dismay. The small, brown-skinned guardian was dead, his head cut apart by a single brutal blow. The shattered remnants of dozens of masks lay scattered across the ground, and hundreds of comets streaked in bloody trails across the shimmering sky above. Tarsa looked ahead to see a furious battle taking place at the edge of the gleaming lake. A handful of Wielders held the shore against twenty or more Shields, but their defences were weakening, and the invaders gained more ground with each clash of arms. Wielding was impossible in the presence of the Tree, as its own power overwhelmed any attempt to call upon the *wyr*, so the guardians depended on their ancient skills with arms and war-craft. In the front ranks stood Unahi, her silver hair flowing free behind her, a bloody war-club in her hands. It had been many years since she'd last fought an enemy with a weapon, but she'd never forgotten how to do it. What age had slowed, wisdom had honed to deadly precision.

Tarsa rushed across the bridge, heedless of the danger, and threw herself into the rear ranks of the attackers, her spiked staff smashing skulls and slashing bodies with abandon. Unlike the Shields at the waterfall, these Celestials didn't move away. They were steadfast in their purpose and had trained well for such an eventuality. They closed in against her, meeting each blow with their own. Soon her own warm blood streamed to the dark soil, mingling with that of her enemies.

Tobhi reached the bridge and watched Tarsa and the others cut a swath through the Celestials. His eyes moved upward, and he froze. One Shield stood slightly apart from the others, her copper hair falling soft and long behind her, an axe with a glimmering shaft in her hands. She moved forward with grim certainty, toward a bent, silver-haired figure who'd been pushed backward into the water but who still fought on, fiercely undeterred.

No! his mind screamed. *Not her!*

But he knew now that he'd been terribly wrong. *Clash of kindred.* He'd been so sure that he knew whose death the lore-leaves predicted. *The Wielder in War.* The two broken leaves; there should have been twenty-seven leaves in the reading, not twenty-five. *Blood in the water.* It wasn't Tarsa at all.

The Tree falls.

It was the doe who would die, not the fawn.

Death rides soft wings.

It was Unahi.

Daladir and Jitani rushed into the melee to aid Tarsa, but Tobhi ran around the swarming mass of Shields and Wielders in raging combat and threw himself into the lake. He lunged forward, splashing desperately, but fell back as a great tremor tore through the waves.

There was too much death and destruction in this sacred place. It was breaking the balance, sending catastrophic ripples through the fabric of the Everland. The Tree was in pain. Tobhi would never reach the old she-Kyn in time.

Unahi fought on, her stout club holding its own against the iron blade of a Shield's sword. She never saw the copper-haired Lawmaker at her back.

Tobhi called out to Tarsa, who turned to see Neranda raise the axe high.

The Redthorn Wielder struck out furiously, screaming to Unahi, who'd been pushed nearly to the trunk of the Tree, still unaware of the danger behind her.

Neranda looked up, her violet eyes shining with tears, and then, with a choking sob, she brought the silver axe down, splitting Unahi's skull, driving the elder she-Kyn's body forward, where it was impaled on the iron blade of the Celestial who faced her. Their bloody task finished, the Shields pushed Unahi's broken form into the water and stepped back to the shore.

There was a crack, and a thunderous groan rose up from the very heart of the Eld Green, as though all of Creation was being torn apart from with in. The stars rained down above the horrified spectators, the moons and planets faded into endless shadow, and the pool became a raging cauldron of blood. The light of the lake faded, and darkness took its place.

The Eternity Tree fell. From the lightless depths flew thousands of white-faced owls, as quiet as despair.

And in their silent wake came Death.

The Fall

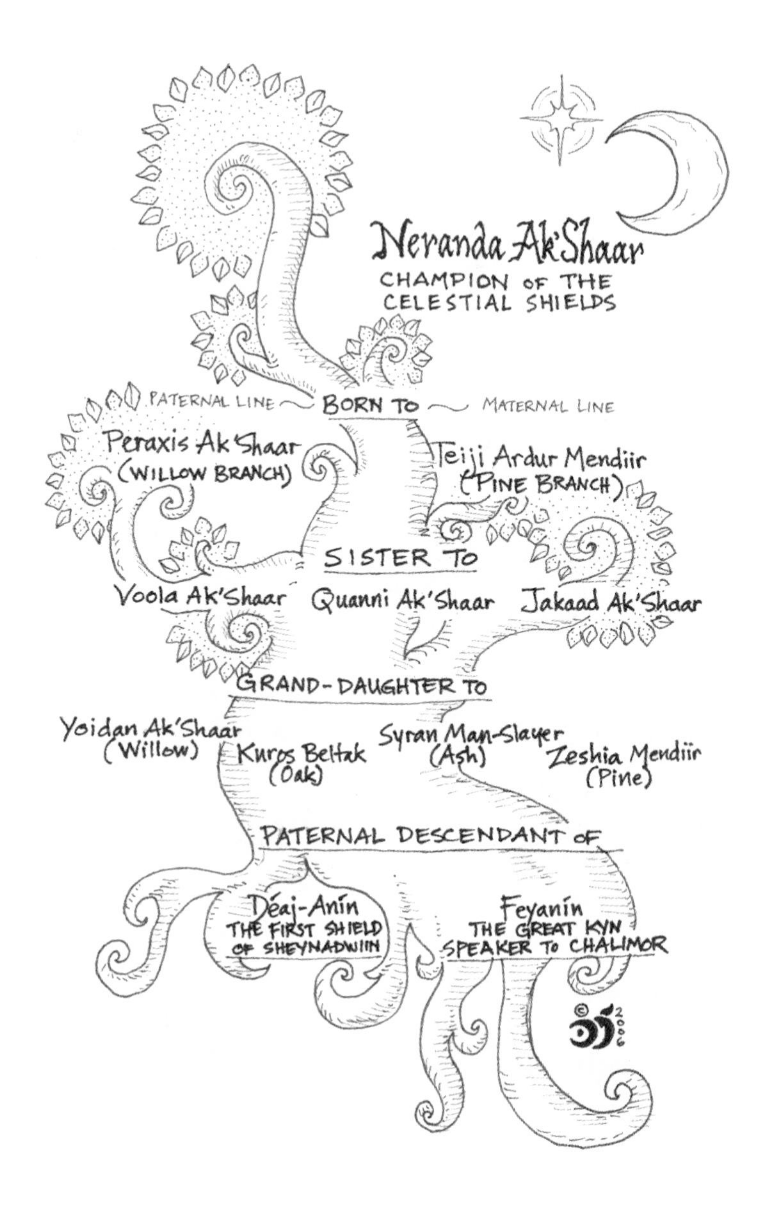
Neranda Ak'Shaar
CHAMPION OF THE CELESTIAL SHIELDS
PATERNAL LINE
BORN TO
MATERNAL LINE
Peraxis Ak'Shaar
(WILLOW BRANCH)
Teiji Ardur Mendiir
(PINE BRANCH)
SISTER TO
Voola Ak'Shaar
Quanni Ak'Shaar
Jakaad Ak'Shaar
GRAND-DAUGHTER TO
Yoidan Ak'Shaar
(Willow)
Kuros Beltak
(Oak)
Syran Man-Slayer
(Ash)
Zeshia Mendiir
(Pine)
PATERNAL DESCENDANT OF
Déaj-Anín
THE FIRST SHIELD OF SHEYNADWIIN
Feyanín
THE GREAT KYN SPEAKER TO CHALIMOR
© 2006

NAMES AND OTHER STORIES

A

- ADELAIDE (OF THE VEIL). Mysterious singer and member of Bremen and Crowe's Medicine Show and Repertory of Thespian Delights.
- AIRSHIPS. The primary military and mercantile transportation craft of the Ubbetuk Nation. These galleons draw elemental energies from the air for lift, causing dramatic atmospheric disruptions and great lightning storms that can be seen for many miles. Called Dragons by Humans; the preferred colloquial Ubbetuk name is Stormbringers.
- ALCHAEMY. The twin Human sciences of physical change, both bodily healing and elemental transmutation.
- THE ALLIED WILDERLANDS. A southern province of the Reach. It is a loose confederation of independent townships inhabited by rugged and self-reliant Humans who often trade with and marry among the Folk.
- THE ANCESTRALS. The first of the Kyn to emerge from the Upper Place to the Eld Green; the primeval ancestors and progenitors of the Kyn Nation.
- ANDAAKA. A southwestern province of the Reach best known as the home of Bashonak, the heart of Dreyd-worship in the Republic.
- ATHWEID. Young Celestial she-Kyn diplomat to Eromar.
- AVERYN. Zhe-Kyn healer; consort and advisor to Garyn Mendiir.
- AVIALLE. The River-Mother; a spirit-being of the Eld Green.
- AWAKENING. The first emergence of *wyr*-powers in the life of a young Wielder, generally around the time of puberty. It is often a physically traumatic experience; if a Wielder is unguided in the transformation, the uncontrolled *wyr* can lead to madness and/or death.

B

- BASHONAK. The capital city of the Dreydcaste in the Reach. It is a massive stone fortress at the edge of the Tuskwood in Andaaka, known as much for its rigidly authoritarian creeds as for the skilled military training of its adherents.
- BATTLE OF DOWNED TIMBER. The last battle of a war between the allied forces of the Everland and Eromar against brigands from the Lawless. Lojar

Vald was a young man at Downed Timber, and his life was saved by a he-Kyn warrior, Damodhed, who later expressed regret for not letting a Lawless fighter kill the future Dreydmaster.

- BATTLE OF FIVE AXES. The last great battle between Humans and the Folk, where Human prospectors and their military protectors were driven from the Everland by a confederation of Folk warriors.
- BÉASHAAD. The capital province of the Reach, located on the eastern edge of the continent. Its inland region is a temperate mix of hills, farmlands, and wide prairies, while its coastal waters teem with marine life. The great metropolis of Chalimor is built on the eastern shores of Béashaad.
- BEAST-TRIBES. The various communities of animals, birds, and Beasts who call the Everland home. Each group has its own chosen leaders, and those leaders often meet in council.
- BETTHIA. Long-suffering wife of Lojar Vald.
- BIGGIABBA. Gvaerg Matron and Wielder.
- BINDER. The second rank among the Dreydcaste. They draw the essence of spirits caught by Seekers into their snaring-tomes for use by Reavers.
- BIRCHBARK HOLLOW. A rugged valley in the Everland, at the eastern edge of the Meshiwiik Forest; home of the Brown Lodge and the Igwimish Mound, the central council house and ceremonial ground of the western Tetawi.
- BIRD. A young Moth Clan he-Tetawa of Spindletop.
- BLACKFLY FEN. A dense and fetid swamp at the southern tip of the Everland, inhabited by furtive swamp-dwarfs known as Powries.
- BLACKWICK. The aged Chancellor of the Ubbetuk Swarm.
- BRANCH. One of the seven clans of the Kyn. Each Branch is named for an ancestral tree-spirit and is known for its gifts in particular spheres of Kyn life: Willow, trade and diplomacy; Oak, leadership and philosophy; Ash, healing; Thorn, defence; Cedar, lore and the arts; Apple, horticulture; and Pine, mysticism and dream-guidance.
- BREMEN AND CROWE'S MEDICINE SHOW AND REPERTORY OF THESPIAN DELIGHTS. Travelling performance company and refuge for outcasts and eccentrics.
- BRIGHT EYE. The smaller of the sister suns of the Everland.
- BROWNIES. A pejorative but widespread Human term for Tetawi.

C

- THE CANOPY VEIL. The barrier between the Eld Green and the mortal world of Humanity.
- CARINNE. Binder and Dreydcaste administrator in the south Eromar city of Chimiak.
- THE CELESTIAL PATH. The philosophical principles of Luran-worship, descended from Dreyd teachings brought by the Proselytors who accompanied the first Human traders into the Everland. The Path is characterized by a denial of the flesh and an emphasis on the power of the purified mind, a commitment to hierarchy and obedience, a rejection of the *wyr* and the relational values of the Way of Deep Green, and an embrace of the individualistic and commercial values of Humanity.
- CELESTIALS. Kyn followers of the Celestial Path.
- CHALIMOR. The capital city of the Reach of Men, named for its location between the white shores of Chal Bay and the rugged slopes of Mount Imor; political, artistic, and cultural centre of Humanity; home to the great Hall of Kings, the Reachwarden, and the Sovereign Republic Court.
- CHANGELING. A Tetawa with the ability to shape-shift into the form of her Clan animal. The shape-changing Tetawi witches~Skeegers~are related to Changelings but without the calming Clan influence.
- CHANTING SASH. A woven or braided belt, generally of wyrweave or sturdy linen, into which a Wielder sews or beads some of her more powerful prayers, stories, and medicinal formulas. The sash serves as a calming memory aid to help balance the Wielder's mind and emotions as she does her work.
- CHESTNUT GROVE. The Human name for the former community of Spindletop.
- CLAN. The primary social and political foundation of Tetawi life, with each being matrilineal in authority and descent. All Clans are named for an animal, which is deeply honoured by all members of that Clan. The most powerful are the Four Mother Clans: Raccoon, Spider, Kingfisher, and Trout.
- CLOUD-GALLEON. See AIRSHIP.
- COLONEL BEDZO. Blade-swallower, orator, and member of Bremen and Crowe's Medicine Show and Repertory of Thespian Delights.
- CORNSILK. Apple-headed spirit doll of Quill Meadowgood.
- CRAFTING. The Human use of occult ritual and elemental alchaemy to shape

the fabric of reality.

D

- DALADIR TRE'SHEIN. Ash Branch he-Kyn diplomat for the Everland; stationed for some time in Eromar City.
- DAMODHED. Uncle of Reiil Cethwir and noted warrior of the Battle of Downed Timber.
- DARDATH VALE. The ancient valley home of the Kyn city of Sheynadwiin in the heart of the Kraagen Mountains.
- DARKENING. A pocket of Decay within the mortal world.
- THE DEEP GREEN. The ancient ceremonial and kinship traditions of the Eld Green; maintained by the Wielders. Also known as the Old Ways.
- DEERMEN. Deer-headed Ferals of the Kraagen Mountains.
- DENARRA SYRENE. Eccentric Strangeling Wielder and adventurer.
- DOLLTENDER. A Tetawa *wyr*-worker who draws on hand-made dolls ~ usually with dried-apple heads and corn-cob bodies ~ for spiritual guidance.
- DOWNLANDS. A more neutral name for the Barrow Hills of the southern Everland.
- DRAGON. The Human name given to a mechanized Ubbetuk airship.
- THE DREYD. An order of now-immortal Human priests and sorcerers who overthrew the old Immortals of Men and assumed their place, thus causing the cataclysmic Melding.
- THE DREYDCASTE. The rigidly authoritarian and Human-supremacist followers of the Dreyd. Their holy city and seat of power is Bashonak.
- DREYDMASTER. A leader of the Dreydcaste. There are generally no more than three Dreydmasters in the world at any single time, though the Dreydmaster of Bashonak is widely regarded to be the authoritative voice among them.
- DREYD-PLEDGED. Followers of the Dreyd and their teachings.
- DROHODU. "Grandfather of the Mosses." Spirit-being; green-skinned consort to Zhaia and father of the Kyn.
- DURUK. The westernmost province of the Reach, characterized by broken and blasted lands at its eastern border, wind-swept prairies in the centre, and stormy coasts in the west. Its largest settlement ~ aside from the tent-cities of the Jaaga-Folk ~ is the notorious Harudin Holt.

E

- THE EDGEWOOD. A dense pine and scrub oak forest to the south of the Everland and within the territories of the Spindetop Hollow Tetawi.
- THE ELD GREEN. The lush, ancient world of the Folk before the arrival of Men.
- THE ELDARVIAN WOODS. The largest forest in the Everland. Deep and shadow-filled, this dense woodland is the home of the largest population of wyrwood trees in the Reach and is thus vigorously protected by the Folk.
- EROMAR. A heavily industrialized and militaristic province that abuts the Everland on the north, east, and south. Eromar is the primary political antagonist of the Folk of the Everland.
- EROMAR CITY. The capital city of Eromar, built on a bluff overlooking the Orm River. It is the location of Gorthac Hall, the home of the Dreydmaster Lojar Vald.
- THE ETERNITY TREE. The physical manifestation of Zhaia, the first mother of the Kyn, the source of the *wyr* in the Everland, and the living covenant between the Folk and the land.
- EVERLIGHTS. Perpetual Wielder-shaped balls of soft-glowing *wyr*-fire.
- THE EXPULSION. The Eromar-led campaign to drive the Folk from the Everland.

F

- FAHR. In the Tetawi tongue, the word for a male.
- FEAR-TAKES-THE-FIRE. A he-Kyn ambassador to Eromar who dies under mysterious circumstances.
- FERALS. Folk whose bodies resemble a union of Humans and Beasts, such as the birdlike Harpies, the antlered and hoofed Deermen, and the sly and furred Fox-Folk.
- FEY-FOLK. A slightly pejorative term among Humans for the Folk. "Fey" designates mystery or strangeness at best, evil otherness at worst.
- FEY-WITCH. The common Dreyd term for Wielders and other *wyr*-workers.
- FIRRA. In the Tetawi tongue, the word for a female.
- FIRSTKYN. Town chieftains among the Kyn before the separate towns were unified.
- THE FOLK. The collective term for those peoples and nations originating from the Eld Green, including the Kyn, Tetawi, Gvaergs, Ferals, Beast-tribes,

Wyrnach, Ubbetuk, and the Jaagas, among others. While such an encapsulating term acknowledges the shared post-Melding history of such peoples, it can also erase their significant cultural, geographic, ceremonial, and physical distinctiveness.

G

- THE GALLERY HOUSE. The home of the Kyn Governor in Sheynadwiin; located at the back of the Gallery of Song.
- THE GALLERY OF SONG. The central gathering chamber of the Kyn Assembly of Law and the Sevenfold Council.
- GARYN MENDIIR. Pine Branch he-Kyn Governor of the Kyn Nation and Speaker of the Sevenfold Council.
- THE GATHERING. The ancient council-meet of the autonomous Kyn towns before unification. Replaced by the Assembly of Law.
- GISHKI. Spider Clan she-Tetawa of Spindletop and cousin of Quill Meadowgood.
- THE GOBLIN CHANCELLOR. See BLACKWICK.
- GOBLINS. The common term used by Humans for the Ubbetuk; often perceived by Ubbetuk as an insult, as it associates them with a mythological race of idiotic monsters common in Human folktales before the Melding.
- GOLDMANTLE. Largest of the sister suns of the Everland.
- GORTHAC HALL. The sprawling, many-gabled estate of Lojar Vald in Eromar City.
- GOVERNOR. The political leader of the unified Kyn Nation.
- GRANNY TURTLE (JENNA). Spirit-being and creator of the first Tetawi people.
- THE GREAT ASCENSION. The Human name for the Melding; refers to the rise of the Dreyd over the Old Immortals of Men.
- THE GREATMOON. See PEARL-IN-DARKNESS.
- THE GREAT WAY ROAD. Major east-west travel and trade route through the Reach of Men.
- GREEN KISHKA. Apple-headed spirit doll of Quill Meadowgood.
- GREENWALKER. An adherent of the Way of Deep Green.
- GRUGG. An elder Wielder of the Oak-Folk.
- THE GVAERG NATION. One of the Seven Sister Folk nations, the Gvaergs are rough-featured, hairless giants who live in vast cave cities beneath the earth.

Their link to the *wyr* is through earth-borne spirits. Gvaerg society is rigidly divided into proud and pious Houses under the ancestral authority of aged patriarchs. The suns are deadly, as their light turns he-Gvaergs to dead stone, but wyrweave wrappings can defend against that fate.

- GWEGGI. Ubbetuk carriage driver and amateur poet.

H

- HAK'AAD. Celestial he-Kyn diplomat to Eromar and son of Imweshi.
- HARUDIN HOLT. The western-most city of the Reach, second in size and influence only to Chalimor. It is a tiered and sprawling city built on the lime stone cliffs of the storm-shattered Reaving Coast, and is best known as a haven for pirates, mercenaries, criminals, and fortune-hunters. Though it is managed in the name of the Lord Mayor, the Three Guilds are the true power of Harudin Holt.
- THE HEARTWOOD. The *wyr* essence of the Eternity Tree.
- THE HIGH HALL. The seat of political and spiritual Dreyd authority in grim Bashonak.
- 'HOLD. See THRESHOLD.
- HUMANS. The collective term for those peoples and nations originating from the lands beyond the Eld Green, including such diverse populations as the theocratic Dreyd of Andaaka, the fiercely independent miners and foresters of the Allied Wilderlands, the republican aristocrats of Béashaad, and the defiant tribespeople and merchants of Sarvannadad. While such an encapsulating term acknowledges the shared post-Melding history of such peoples, it can also erase their significant cultural, political, and physical differences.

I

- ILLIRIUS PYM. Well-connected merchant of questionable virtue in Chalimor.
- IMWESHI. Celestial she-Kyn diplomat to Eromar and mother of Hak'aad.
- IRON. Deadly poison to all Folk but Ubbetuk and Gvaergs. This virulent quality is well known to many Humans, and they use it to their advantage against many of the Folk, particularly the Kyn.
- IRON-WARD. Amulets created by the Gvaergs for their Folk kith to protect the latter from the toxic effects of iron.

J

- THE JAAGA-FOLK. One of the Folk peoples, descended from the Strangeling unions of Kyn and Humans. Though not one of the Seven Sister nations, the Jaagas consider themselves and are generally considered by other Folk to be kith of the Seven Sisters. They are a musical, largely nomadic, patrilineal people who inhabit the northwestern wilds of the Everland, as well as the sweeping grasslands of the Reach province of Duruk.
- JAGO CHAAK. Strange Tetawa toymaker.
- JEKOBI. Raven Clan he-Tetawa of Birchbark Hollow, Leafspeaker, and father of Tobhi Burrows.
- JENNA. See GRANNY TURTLE.
- JITANI AL'DAAR. She-Kyn warrior and mercenary; sister of Sinovian.
- JYNNI THISTLEDOWN. Badger Clan she-Tetawa of Birchbark Hollow, healer, and maternal aunt of Tobhi Burrows.

K

- KAANTOR. The Human Blood King of Karkur and treacherous instigator of the Melding.
- KEI'SHAAD MENDIIR. Pine Branch she-Kyn of Thornholt Town and mother of Garyn Mendiir.
- KELL BRENNARD. Former Reachwarden; currently First Magistrate on the Sovereign Republic Court. During his term as third Reachwarden, Brennard advocated the incorporation of the Everland, its people, and its resources into the larger sovereignty of the Reach of Men.
- KINNIT. Acrobat and occasional lover of Denarra Syrene; member of Bremen and Crowe's Medicine Show and Repertory of Thespian Delights.
- KITH. Family, relations. Depending on context, the term refers to either immediate, extended, or distant relationship through blood or adoption.
- KITICHI. In Tetawi tradition, the trickster Squirrel spirit.
- KLAUS. Groom, hunter, and caretaker of Bremen and Crowe's Medicine Show and Repertory of Thespian Delights.
- THE KRAAGEN MOUNTAINS. A massive mountain range bisecting the Everland from north to south.
- THE KYN NATION. The most numerous and widely-dispersed of the Seven Sister nations. The *wyr* of the Kyn is drawn from the green growing world and

elemental forces of nature, although an increasing number of Kyn follow the Celestial Path and ways separated from the *wyr*. Kyn have a heightened sensitivity to the spirits of nature through their serpentine sensory stalks. Their matrilineal branches are descended from the seven sacred trees of the Everland. Sheynadwiin, the great peace city of the Everland, is their political and cultural capital.

L

- LARTORSHA. Ecstatic dancer and member of Bremen and Crowe's Medicine Show and Repertory of Thespian Delights.
- THE LAWLESS. The rugged, snow-swept region at the margin of the Reachwarden's influence. It is without a central government, although there are numerous small settlements scattered throughout the area that maintain their own laws and order. While home to many brigands, outlaws, and petty despots, it is also home to many fiercely independent people~Folk, Human, and Beast~who settle their own grievances and avoid conflict unless it is forced upon them.
- LEAFSPEAKER. A Tetawi *wyr*-worker who interprets the patterns of *wyr*-shaped leaves to communicate with the Spirit World and to preserve stories and teachings. The leaf-reading skills are the Tetawi expression of Kyn teachings, thus highlighting some of the co-operative links between the two peoples.
- LOJAR VALD. "The Iron Fist." Prefect of the state of Eromar and ambitious Dreydmaster.
- LORE-LEAVES. *Wyr*-working tools used by Tetawi Leafspeakers.
- THE LOWER PLACE. One of the three primary worlds of existence in the Eld Green and, to a lesser extent, the Melded world. It is a realm of chaos and shadow, though not evil.
- LUBIK. Trout Clan elder *fahr*; pepa of Medalla and Gishki, uncle of Quill Meadowgood.
- LURAN. Moon-maiden. The Celestial manifestation of the Human Dreyd entity Meynanine; revealer of the Celestial Path to the Kyn Shields. For most Folk, the Greatmoon of the Everland, Pearl-in-Darkness, is male; the virginal female representation is drawn from Human cosmology.

M

- THE MAKERS. Ancient predecessors of the Wielders who first learned to harness the *wyr* currents of the Eld Green. Though powerful, the Makers became selfish and tyrannical, and they were overthrown by the Folk; those who survived taught their Wielding descendants to be humble, and to use their powers in service to the People. The Shields drew upon the old memories of the rebellion against the Makers in their instigation of the Purging.
- MEDALLA. Spider Clan she-Tetawa of Spindletop and cousin of Quill Meadowgood.
- MEDICINALS. The herbs, roots, plants, bones, insect stingers, animal glands, and diverse other pharmacopoeia used by the Folk for healing.
- THE MELDING. The catastrophic union of the Eld Green and the mortal world of Humanity a thousand years past.
- MEMA. "Mother" in the Tetawi tongue.
- MERRIMYN HURLBUCK. Young Human Binder and fugitive from Eromar City.
- METHIEUL. Youngest daughter of Lojar Vald.
- MOLLI ROSE. Tetawa Clanmother, Spirit-talker, and leader of the confederated Tetawi settlements of the Everland.
- MOTHER BARABOO. Rotund leader of Bremen and Crowe's Medicine Show and Repertory of Thespian Delights.
- MOUNDHOUSE. Stout Tetawi cabin with sharp eaves, cedar-tiled arched roof, interior and exterior carved support posts, and deep-set hearth. Moundhouses generally surround a ceremonial mound at the centre of the settlement.
- MULCHWORM. Apple-headed spirit doll of Quill Meadowgood.
- MUNGO. Rabbit Clan he-Tetawa and father of Quill Meadowgood.

N

- NAMSHÉKÉ. "Storm-in-Her-Eyes." The youngling name of Tarsa'deshae.
- NENYI. Badger Clan she-Tetawa of Birchbark Hollow and mema of Tobhi Burrows.
- NIGHTWASP. Ubbetuk mechanical summoning insect.
- NERANDA AK'SHAAR. "Violet Eyes, Daughter of the House of Shaar." Celestial she-Kyn of Pine Branch. Legislator and Shield.
- NOT-RAVEN. A malevolent ghost and flesh-eating spy of the Human world.

O

- OAK-FOLK. A small and furtive people of the Everland. They are spirit-bonded to ancient trees and spend their lives tending their home groves. Though shy, Oak-Folk can be fierce opponents when treated with disrespect.
- THE OATH OF WESTERN SANCTUARY. The name given by Lojar Vald to the writ of expulsion presented to the Everland Folk.
- OATHSWORN. Pejorative term given to the Kyn conspirators who signed the Oath of Western Sanctuary in defiance of the legitimate Folk leaders of the Sevenfold Council.
- OINARA. "Strange New World." The Human name for the Melded world, derived from a word in the now-defunct dialect of Pei-tai-Pesh.
- THE OLD IMMORTALS (OF MEN). The gods of Humanity who were over thrown by the Dreyd during the catastrophic Melding. Though displaced, it is rumoured that the Old Immortals did not die and have long plotted their return to ascendancy.
- THE OLD WAYS. The teachings and traditions of the Eld Green that were pre-dominant among the Kyn before the rise of the Shields.
- THE OLD WINDLE ROAD. An ancient travel route that bisected the Reach of Men before the Melding. After the Melding, it was replaced by the Great Way Road.
- ORE-RUNNER. Biggiabba's deceased son.

P

- PEACE-CITY. A site of sanctuary, where violence and physical conflict are for bidden, and where all given refuge. The Kyn capital of Sheynadwiin is the oldest peace-city in the Everland.
- PEARL-IN-DARKNESS. The Greatmoon of the Everland. He is sole survivor of a trio of celestial night-spirits of the Eld Green; his brothers were shattered in the Melding, but their broken bodies remain in the form of a sparkling silver ring that surrounds the world in both night and day. Pearl-in-Darkness emerges from his grief to show his face to the Everland every thirty days; for most of that time, he is in various stages of mourning for his lost brothers.
- PEPA. "Father" in the Tetawi tongue.
- PEREDIR. The mortal world of Men before the Melding.

- POX. A blistering, feverish illness that originated in Human lands and has caused successive waves of death among the Folk, especially the Kyn. Death from the pox is slow and excruciating.
- PRADU STYKE. He-Kyn Celestial captain and opportunist.
- THE PURGING. The decimation of the Wielders by fear-maddened Kyn during the last great pox epidemic. Up to two-thirds of Wielders were killed during the three-year campaign of terror, during which time the Shields rose to power.
- PURIFIERS. Dreydcaste interrogators and defenders of orthodoxy.

Q

- QUALLA'AM KAER. The fifth and current Human Reachwarden.
- QUILL MEADOWGOOD. Tetawa of Spider Clan. Dolltender and *wyr*-worker.

R

- RAMYD THALSSON. Human merchant and father of Garyn Mendiir.
- THE REACH (OF MEN). Also known as the Reach Republic. The primary political and economic power in the Melded world, dominated by Humans and their ambitions.
- REACH-TONGUE. The common Mannish tongue in the Reach.
- REACHWARDEN. The elected leader of the Reach Republic, chosen for a five-year term by a majority of parliamentary representatives.
- REAVER. The highest rank among the Dreydcaste. Reavers use alchaemical formulae and crafting to control the spirits captured by Binders.
- THE REALIGNMENT. According to Celestial doctrine, the final cleansing of the Melded world of all corruption and impurity. Only rigid adherence to the ways of the Celestial Path will provide safety during this tumultuous future event.
- RED CEDAR TOWN. A Kyn town in the southern Everland; youngling home of Tarsa'deshae.
- REDTHORN WARRIOR. Greenwalking warriors dedicated to the Old Ways and the vigorous defence of the Folk.
- REIIL CETHWIR. He-Kyn diplomat to Eromar.

S

- SADISH. Only surviving son of Lojar Vald.

- SEEKER. The lower rank of the Dreydcaste. Seekers wander through the Reach in search of Folk Wielders and Human witches, whom they bring to Dreydholds for the use of Binders and Reavers.
- SENSORY STALKS. Fleshy head-tendrils that give the Kyn a deeper sensitivity to the elemental and emotional world around them. He-Kyn have one on each temple; she-Kyn have two on each side; zhe-Kyn generally have three, with two on one side, one on the other.
- SETTLEMENTS. Tetawi community sites.
- THE SEVENFOLD COUNCIL. A political assembly of Folk leaders, called only at times of great importance to all the Folk.
- THE SEVEN SISTER NATIONS. The Kyn, Tetawi, Gvaergs, Ubbetuk, Wyrnach, Ferals, and Beast-tribes, representing most of the Everland Folk.
- SHAKAR. "Traitor" in the old Kyn tongue.
- SHEDA. Eldest daughter of Lojar Vald.
- SHEYNADWIIN. The ancient peace-city and capital of the Kyn Nation, nestled at the heart of Dardath Vale among the Kraagen Mountains.
- SHIELD. The spiritual, political, and economic leaders of the Celestial Path.
- SHOBBOK. The Winter Witch; a spirit-being of the Eld Green.
- SHUDWAGGA. High-ranking member of the Consulting Council of the Ubbetuk Swarm.
- SINOVIAN AL'DAAR. He-Kyn Redthorn warrior and resistance fighter; brother of Jitani Al'Daar.
- THE SISTER SUNS. The two celestial spirits of the daytime: Goldmantle, the bronze elder sister, is calmer and larger than Bright-Eyes, who burns white-hot with the fires of youth.
- SKEEGER. Cannibalistic Tetawi changeling.
- SMUDGE. Ill-tempered mule deer mount of Tobhi Burrows.
- SNAKE-HEAD. An insulting term used to refer to the Kyn. It refers to their thick, vaguely serpentine sensory stalks.
- SPINDLETOP. A small Tetawi settlement in the Terrapin Hills of the southern Everland.
- SPIRIT-WEAVER. Human term for Wielders.
- THE SPIRIT WORLD. The hidden realm of elemental beings, the dead, and spirits of the Green world.
- STONESKIN. A fierce carnivorous creature with an unquenchable appetite. Named for the layer of protective stones embedded in its flesh.

- STORM-BORN TWINS (SKYFIRE AND THUNDER). In shared Folk tradition, two powerful and much-respected transformer spirits of the ancient times.
- STORMBRINGER. The preferred Ubbetuk term for their airships, named for the storms that surround each airship when in flight.
- STORM DRAKE. A massive winged and lightning-spitting serpent that inhabits the upper sky.
- STORY LEAVES. See LORE-LEAVES.
- STRANGELING. A descendant of a he-Kyn/female Human union. If born into a Branch, the descendant is understood as a Kyn; if born out of a Branch (that is, if the youngling's father is non-Kyn), the descendant is generally defined as a Strangeling. The Jaagas are a distinct people born of Strangeling unions and humans.
- THE SWARM. The collective Ubbetuk Nation.

T

- TANGLETOP FOREST. A dense wood at the southeastern edge of the Everland.
- TARSA'DESHAE. "The Spear, She Breaks It," "She-Breaks-the-Spear," or "Spear-breaker." She-Kyn of Cedar Branch. Redthorn Warrior and Wielder. Niece of Unahi.
- THE TERRAPIN HILLS. The rocky hill country around Spindletop at the eastern rim of the Edgewood.
- THE TETAWI NATION. One of the Seven Sister nations, the Tetawi are an honest and forthright people, short and brown-skinned. Their social and political lives are centered in their matrilineal Clans, each of which is descended from a spirit animal of the Eld Green. They make their homes in squat moundhouses, generally in rough hill country or in forested areas. Their connection to the *wyr* is through empathy with the Beast-folk; due to this, Tetawi are the greatest healers amongst the Folk.
- THISTLEWOOD. A small pine forest in the southeastern Everland.
- THORNHOLT. The second-largest Kyn city in the Everland, located in the southern Eldarvian Woods.
- THRESHOLD. A pocket of the Eld Green that survived the Melding. The Everland is the largest 'Hold in the Reach.
- TOBHI (ETOBHI) BURROWS. Tetawa of Badger Clan. Leafspeaker, scribe, and lore-keeper.

- TOWNS. Kyn community sites.
- TRADE TONGUE. The shared economic and political language of the Folk.
- TREE-BORN. See KYN NATION.

U

- UNAHI SAM'SHEYDA. Cedar Branch elder she-Kyn Wielder of Thistlewood. Aunt of Tarsa'deshae.
- UNHUMANS. The pejorative term used by Humans for the Folk.
- THE UPPER PLACE. One of the three primary worlds of existence in the Eld Green and, to a lesser extent, the Melded world. It is a realm of order and light, though not necessarily good.

V

- THE VEIL. See THE CANOPY VEIL.
- VERGIS THANE. Unassuming one-eyed Seeker of the Dreydcaste.
- VORGHA. Trusted attendant of Lojar Vald.

W

- THE WAY OF DEEP GREEN. See THE DEEP GREEN.
- WELTSPORE. Toxic hallucinogenic fungus sometimes used in assassinations.
- WHITECAPS. Members of the Ruling Council of the Ubbetuk Swarm.
- WIELDER. Greenwalkers and *wyr*-workers of the Kyn.
- WILD ONE. A pejorative Celestial term for a Greenwalker.
- WITCHERY. The use of *wyr* or other medicine skills toward selfish and generally destructive aims.
- THE WYR. The life source of the Everland, formed from the living voices and embodied memories of the ancestors, the spirits of the Eld Green, and the life-spark of the Folk themselves. It is the elemental life-song of creation, drawing on and giving sustenance to all remnants of the Eld Green, strengthened by attentive care and weakened by neglect. Its embodied manifestation is the Eternity Tree.
- WYRNACH. The eldest of the Seven Sister Nations, the Wyrnach are also known as the "Spider-Folk" for their eight limbs and multiple eyes. They are a rare and reclusive people, standing well over eight feet high, and are well

known among the Folk for their *wyr*-fed powers of divination.

- WYRWOOD. A type of tree that grows only in 'Holds, the wyrwood is a vital resource to the Folk. Its leaves and naturally-shed outer bark, when stripped and pounded into flexible fibres, can be used for durable wyrweave fabric, clothing, and armour; its red roots and fallen branches can be shaped by Wielders into both armour and weapons, as can its rarely-accessed heartwood; and its golden sap is both nourishing and medicinal. The tree roots of living wyrwood draw poisons out of the surrounding soil, thus purifying both earth and water. Its lofty canopy provides housing for many Folk, as do the massive trunks of the more ancient trees. In many ways, the wyrwood tree provides the daily link between the Folk and the *wyr*-currents of their homeland.
- WYR-WARD. A device of Human Crafting that addles the mind and blocks the access of Wielders to the *wyr*, thus leaving them vulnerable and confused.
- WYR-WORKER. Those Folk gifted with the strength and talent to draw upon and guide the *wyr* toward particular aims or goals.
- WYRWEAVE. Fabric made of the inner fibres of the wyrwood tree.

Z

- ZHAIA. Tree-Mother. The ancient spirit of the green world from whom the seven Kyn Branches are descended.
- ZHE-KYN. A third gender among the Kyn that shares some of the qualities of both the she-Kyn and he-Kyn. Zhe-Kyn are border crossers between genders, and they often excel at healing, which requires sensitivity to the different challenges of the often distinct male and female social worlds.

BOOK THREE
AN EARLY LOOK AT

DREYD

Book Three

Coming Fall 2007
from Kegedonce Press
www.kegedonce.com

The Eternity Tree has fallen, and with it falls Sheynadwiin. The forces of Eromar ravage the Everland, and the skies are filled with the smoke and ash of burning forests. Those Folk who do not escape into the far mountains and hidden valleys are driven into the broken westlands of Humanity, where Dreydmaster Vald reveals the full vision of his grand ambition, one that will annihilate even the memory of the Kyn and their kind.

Yet not all the Folk walk down the Darkening Road. As the Redthorn Wielder, Tarsa'deshae, and her group of freedom fighters travel west to free their people, a young Tetawa Dolltender and her Strangeling comrade head to the East, to plead their case to the Reachwarden in great Chalimor, the shining capital of the Reach of Men. Unexpected allies stand at their side, even as deadly enemies rise up to surround them.

Surrender is not an option, for the Folk stand at the edge of oblivion. Never since the Melding have they faced such danger. Will their roots hold fast, or will they be cast adrift into the storm?

Can they find a safe middle path on this way of thorn and thunder?

CHAPTER 1
EXCERPT

When Tobhi opened his grit-rimed eyes, it was still daylight, although the solitary sun moved swiftly toward an orange dusk. Waves of heat still radiated off the rolling grasslands. His only companions were a couple of mean-eyed buzzards who glared at him, as if annoyed at his rudeness for not being dead. He shared their confusion, if not their motivation. For a moment he wondered if he actually might have passed beyond the mortal world, but the burning thirst in his cracked and dusty mouth was evidence enough of life–if the old stories were true, as they so often were, the dead certainly wouldn't be thirsty. His hair was tangled and matted with dried blood; he couldn't remember the last time he'd washed it.

Tobhi waited for a long time to move, but when there was no doubt that he wasn't dead, and that the buzzards weren't likely to go away on their own, he painstakingly pulled himself up, and promptly collapsed again. After a few more false starts, he finally made it to his knees and remained there, unsteady but determined. Looking toward the west, he saw the wide stretch of dusty road and beaten grass that moved far into the horizon, but he didn't see any of the uprooted Folk or the Men who drove them forward. Except for a few bodies lying at irregular intervals down the rough path in the distance, he was the only living Folk in sight.

A sudden chill went up his spine. He might be alone at present, but the Human scavengers who followed behind the exiles would be along shortly–the pickings were good these days, and the Men were well-armed with iron and other poisons. If not for Vald's soldiers and their unknown reasons for protecting their wards from further attack, these two-legged parasites would have decimated the Folk long ago. A single crippled Tetawa would pose no problem to them, especially one weakened by thirst, hunger, and heartbreak.

Still, death by oblivion was one thing. Allowing himself to be murdered was another thing entirely. Tobhi looked to the east and groaned. He could see them now, a line of figures in the far distance, moving fast. They would reach him by sunset.

He tried to stand, hoping to hobble into the tall grass and find a hiding place, but the pain in his injured leg was too much, and he collapsed again with a groan. His knee wouldn't possibly hold his weight.

He scanned the ground for options. The grass beside the road was matted down for a long distance, but a couple of wide depressions beneath the broken vegetation caught his attention. An idea suddenly took hold of his thoughts. He might not be able to hide above the ground, but escape might be possible below it. He didn't know much about this land, but there was one thing he could recognize, even in this alien place: he knew the look of badger territory. He was, after all, born to the Badger Clan, and the spirit of Buborru the Keeper, wisdom-bearer of the Tetawi Clans, was in the Burrows blood.

Taking a deep breath, Tobhi pulled himself forward on his elbows, ignoring the pain as sharp stones tore into his still-tender flesh. It took longer than he expected to get to the dip in the grass. By the time he reached it the daylight had turned crimson, stretching like a bloody stain across the prairie. The Men would see him soon, and then there would be no opportunity for escape.

He dug into the grass and pulled thick wads free of the hole, spreading dry brown soil across his fingers. It was as he'd hoped—an old badger sett, long abandoned, if the musty scent was any indication. All Tetawi could feel the presence of their Clan-beast and close kith, and there was no such feeling here. For a moment he felt woefully alone, until he realized that, had a badger been in the hole, he might have had to send it fleeing into the very danger he was trying to avoid.

Still, he realized with growing desperation, it would be good to have a badger's help, as the hole was too small—he couldn't fit. His wide brown hands dug frantically at the dirt, which crumbled in his fingers and collapsed into the tunnel, filling it further with each movement he made. The heat and drought had damaged the soil and weakened the den walls. Even if it had been large enough, the burrow might well have fallen in as he tried to dig into it.

Such knowledge didn't stop his digging. It was still his best choice, his only real hope. He was much too big for the hole, but if he could just open enough to drag part of his body into it and then pull the broken grass back over his exposed body, the fading light might be enough to hide him. He had to try. Frustration burned his eyes as the dirt flew. His hands moved faster and faster, digging deeper and deeper as soil fell again.

The soft crunch of boots on dry grass nearby brought an end to the Leafspeaker's efforts. He stopped digging and remained head-first in the hole, breathing heavily, tensing for the attack. If he was going to die, he'd do it with some measure of dignity. Badger Clan was proud and defiant–he was too weak to put up much of a fight, but he'd at least draw blood before dying.

His teeth bared, Tobhi spun around with a snarl.

The Way of Thorn & Thunder continues…

Daniel Heath Justice is a citizen of the Cherokee Nation and a permanent resident of Canada. He was raised in the small mining town of Victor, Colorado, and currently teaches Aboriginal literatures at the University of Toronto. He is also the author of the novel *Kynship: The Way of Thorn and Thunder, Book 1* and the forthcoming conclusion of the trilogy, *Dreyd* (all volumes published by Kegedonce Press), and a nonfiction study of Cherokee literature, *Our Fire Survives the Storm: A Cherokee Literary History* (University of Minnesota Press), as well as numerous essays about Indigenous literary studies.

For more information on Daniel's creative and scholarly work, go to www.danielheathjustice.com.

Other Titles From

Kegedonce Press

w'daub awae, speaking true.

Kynship

The Way of Thorn & Thunder

Book One

By Daniel Heath Justice

ISBN: 09731396-6-8 (paper)
ISBN 13: 978-0-9731396-6-2

Steepy Mountain

love poetry

By Joanne Arnott

ISBN 0-9731396-3-3 (paper)
ISBN 13: 978-0-9731396-3-1

The Glass Lodge

By John McDonald

ISBN 0-9731396-4-1 (paper)
ISBN 13: 978-0-9731396-4-8

Seven Deer Dancing

By Rolland Nadjiwon

ISBN 0-9731396-8-4 (paper)
ISBN 13: 978-0-9731396-8-6

my heart is a stray bullet

By Kateri Akiwenzie-Damm

ISBN 0-9697120-9-X (paper)
ISBN 13: 978-0-969-7120-9-1

Angel Wing Splash Pattern

By Richard Van Camp

ISBN 0-9731396-0-9 (paper)
ISBN 13: 978-0-9731396-0-0

Honour Earth Mother

Mino-audjaudauh Mizzu-kummik-Quae

By Basil Johnston

ISBN 0-9731396-1-7 (paper)
ISBN 13: 978-0-9731396-1-7

skins

Contemporary Indigenous Writing

Edited by Kateri Akiwenzie-Damm & Josie Douglas

ISBN 0-9697120-6-5 (paper)
ISBN 13: 978-0-9697120-6-0

Without Reservation

Indigenous Erotica

Edited by Kateri Akiwenzie-Damm

ISBN 0-9731396-2-5 (paper)
ISBN 13: 978-0-9731936-2-4

Spirit Horses

By Al Hunter
Featuring artwork by Leo Yerxa

IISBN 0-9697120-8-1 (paper)
ISBN 13: 978-0-9697120-8-4

Go to
www.kegedonce.com
for more information